A Chilling Discovery . . .

Meg took another order from one of the new customers and clipped it above the kitchen hatch. She hesitated and turned back, rising on her tiptoes to look for Sage. He hadn't returned. "Hey, Lucky, where'd Sage go?"

Lucky looked through the hatch. "He's still out back. I'll fill those." She headed into the kitchen and, quickly slicing bread, put the new orders together on a tray and carried them out to Meg. She checked the kitchen again. *What was taking him so long?* She waved to Janie to stay by the cash register, and headed down the corridor. Sage was squatting by the door, his back to the wall, taking deep breaths.

"Sage!" Lucky rushed to his side. "Are you sick?"

Sage shook his head. He pointed wordlessly to the back door.

"What is it?"

He rose and took Lucky's hand, leading her out the door to the Dumpster behind the building. He pointed to a mound of snow and ice. Lucky stared, unsure what she was supposed to see. A tuft of blonde hair stuck incongruously out of the snow. A chill ran through her. She was staring at a death mask—a death mask of ice. It was the face of their customer, the tall, elegant blonde woman. Dark clotted blood had frozen on the side of her head. A single jeweled earring dangling from one ear flashed in the thin winter light. The rest of her was buried under three feet of snow . . .

A Spoonful of Murder

Connie Archer

BERKLEY PRIME CRIME, NEW YORK

THE BERKLEY PUBLISHING GROUP
Published by the Penguin Group
Penguin Group (USA) Inc.
375 Hudson Street, New York, New York 10014, USA

Penguin Group (Canada), 90 Eglinton Avenue East, Suite 700, Toronto, Ontario M4P 2Y3, Canada
(a division of Pearson Penguin Canada Inc.) • Penguin Books Ltd., 80 Strand, London WC2R 0RL,
England • Penguin Group Ireland, 25 St. Stephen's Green, Dublin 2, Ireland (a division of Penguin
Books Ltd.) • Penguin Group (Australia), 250 Camberwell Road, Camberwell, Victoria 3124, Australia
(a division of Pearson Australia Group Pty. Ltd.) • Penguin Books India Pvt. Ltd., 11 Community
Centre, Panchsheel Park, New Delhi—110 017, India • Penguin Group (NZ), 67 Apollo Drive,
Rosedale, Auckland 0632, New Zealand (a division of Pearson New Zealand Ltd.) • Penguin Books
(South Africa) (Pty.) Ltd., 24 Sturdee Avenue, Rosebank, Johannesburg 2196, South Africa

Penguin Books Ltd., Registered Offices: 80 Strand, London WC2R 0RL, England

This is a work of fiction. Names, characters, places, and incidents either are the product of the author's
imagination or are used fictitiously, and any resemblance to actual persons, living or dead, business
establishments, events, or locales is entirely coincidental. The publisher does not have any control over
and does not assume any responsibility for author or third-party websites or their content.

PUBLISHER'S NOTE: The recipes contained in this book are to be followed exactly as written.
The publisher is not responsible for your specific health or allergy needs that may require medical
supervision. The publisher is not responsible for any adverse reactions to the recipes contained in
this book.

A SPOONFUL OF MURDER

A Berkley Prime Crime Book / published by arrangement with the author

PUBLISHING HISTORY
Berkley Prime Crime mass-market edition / August 2012

Copyright © 2012 by Penguin Group (USA) Inc.
Excerpt from *A Broth of Betrayal* by Connie Archer copyright © 2012 by Penguin Group (USA) Inc.
Cover illustration by Cathy Gendron.
Cover design by Diana Kolsky.
Interior text design by Kristin del Rosario.

ISBN: 978-0-425-25147-8

BERKLEY® PRIME CRIME
Berkley Prime Crime Books are published by The Berkley Publishing Group,
a division of Penguin Group (USA) Inc.,
375 Hudson Street, New York, New York 10014.
BERKLEY® PRIME CRIME and the PRIME CRIME logo are trademarks of
Penguin Group (USA) Inc.

PRINTED IN THE UNITED STATES OF AMERICA

10   9   8   7   6   5   4   3

ALWAYS LEARNING   PEARSON

To cast in order of appearance:
Jennifer, Stephanie, and Tom

Acknowledgments

With thanks and appreciation to Paige Wheeler of Folio Literary Management for her hard work, good advice, and expertise and to Emily Beth Rapoport of Berkley Prime Crime for her enthusiasm and support for the Soup Lover's Mysteries.

Thank you to Marianne Grace for her copyediting skills in making this book the best it could be; and to everyone at Berkley Prime Crime who had a hand in bringing this book to life.

Many thanks as well to the writers' group: Cheryl Brughelli, Don Fedosiuk, Paula Freedman, R. B. Lodge, and Marguerite Summers for their criticism and encouragement.

www.conniearchermysteries.com

Chapter 1

"I KNOW YOU worry about me, Mom, but you don't have to. And I know you'd love my new apartment. Elizabeth is renting it to me, for a while at least, till I figure things out."

Lucky sighed. "I know what you're going to say, but the shop is a big responsibility. And I'm really struggling—struggling with everything right now." Shivering in her down jacket, she blew on her hands to keep them warm. Lingering rays of winter light cast long shadows over the snow.

"The apartment's small, but the back windows overlook a garden. It's not in bloom now, of course, but it will be in the spring. It feels peaceful, and I think I'll be able to sleep well there. I haven't slept very much since . . . since I got the call about you and Dad."

Lucky looked down at the freshly turned earth, large, dark scars against the snow, covered now with only a light dusting. In a short time, the earth would sink, snow would cover the mounds and eventually grass would grow. Her parents would rest in peace.

"I wish I could tell you how sorry I am that I haven't been

here—that I stayed away all these years and didn't come
home after college. I wanted to do something special—live
for something other than tourist season, but I never accom-
plished very much at all. If I could do over the last few years,
I'd have come back and hugged you and Dad every single
day of your lives."

Lucky didn't know how she would ever recover from the
guilt that washed over her every day. She remembered how
hard her parents had worked and how she had rejected that
life for herself. Now she was completely alone. Alone even
at the gravesite. No one could hear the one-sided conversation she was having with her parents, the only conversation
she could have with them now. Death was so final, and there
was nothing in her life that had prepared her for the shock
of her parents' fatal car crash.

"I've brought these for you. They're just evergreens and
two roses, one for you and one for Dad." Lucky knelt and,
dividing her bouquet in two, placed the greens and a rose in
each of the containers at the headstone. She stepped back
and stood for a few more moments, remembering her mother's smile and the scent of her cologne, until she shivered
again in the icy wind, her tears already frozen on her cheeks.

BY THE TIME she reached Snowflake's main street, Lucky's
face was numb with cold. She pulled her woolen scarf up to
her nose, hoping to reach By the Spoonful, her parents' soup
shop, without running into any more old friends and
acquaintances. Everyone had been so kind, but whenever
condolences were offered, she felt as if she would burst into
sobs. She missed her parents terribly. They had always been
there for her. She had never considered the day when that
would not be true.

The streetlights had already blinked on in the darkening
evening, and lights in the shape of large snowflakes hung at
each pole all the way down Broadway. Local shops had
closed, but the windows of By the Spoonful Soup Shop were
brightly lit and fogged from the warmth inside. Lucky stood

across the street as if seeing the restaurant for the first time. The old blue and yellow neon sign her Dad had been so proud of still hung in the front window. For a moment, she imagined her parents, Martha and Louis Jamieson, would be inside. She could rush into the warmth and throw her arms around them, as she did when she was very young.

Her grandfather Jack stood at the cash register now. It was dinnertime, and the simple restaurant was filled to capacity with tourists and locals alike. The menu was a rotating variety of soups, stews and sandwiches, depending on the time of year. Hearty meat-filled soups or thick lentils for winter, lighter ones for the summer. Each soup was served with a generous hunk of crusty bakery bread or ladled into a bread bowl. Tonight's special was an original created by Sage, the Spoonful's talented chef.

Her parents had hired Sage DuBois while Lucky was at college, and his expertise kept the menu delicious and unique. His special tonight was a soup based on yams, potatoes, carrots and red peppers in a creamy broth with white pepper. Lucky had worked up an appetite walking all the way from the cemetery and looked forward to a large bowl of the new soup as soon as she could take a break.

She hadn't intended to stay away from the restaurant so long. Her grandfather was sometimes overwhelmed by the rush of customers and became confused. She couldn't imagine herself taking over the business her parents had left to her, but she also couldn't imagine the end of By the Spoonful either. Her grandfather Jack had made it clear he was only holding on, running the shop until she was ready to take over—if that was what she wanted to do. He had been very patient and hadn't pressured her, but Lucky knew he was waiting for a definite answer. She wondered how much longer she could delay.

Taking a deep breath, she crossed the street and pushed through the glass front door. A bell tinkled overhead, barely noticeable in the clatter and conversation of customers. Almost every table was full, and, as usual, Hank Northcross and Barry Sanders, two of the Spoonful's very regular regulars, sat at a corner table playing a game of Connect Four, large mugs of hot chocolate with whipped cream nearby. Hank's bellow could be heard above the din of the restaurant as he lost another round of the game. Barry, smiling and victorious, leaned back in his chair clasping his hands over his protruding belly and took a sip of hot chocolate.

Jack looked up from counting bills. "Lucky, my girl. I've been worrying about you. It's just gone three bells." Jack was a World War II veteran who had served in the Navy. Lucky had listened to sea lingo her entire life and could even tell time Navy style.

Lucky grinned in response. "I'm fine." She stepped behind the cash register and gave her grandfather a bear hug, even though he stood a good seven inches taller. She kissed him on the cheek. "I love you, Jack." She had never called her grandfather by any other name. He had always insisted that to her, his only grandchild, he was Jack. He wanted no titles. Those were for old men, and he was never going to be one of those.

Jack held her at arm's length and gave her a careful look. "Sure you're all right?"

Lucky nodded. "I am. It's just . . . every second with a loved one counts."

A sadness passed over Jack's lined face. "One of life's tougher lessons, my girl. But your parents did a great job. You'll be fine. I'm not really worried about you."

The truth was, Lucky was starting to become a little worried about Jack. She had noticed a few things since she'd returned home—moments of confusion and gaps in reality. At first, she had taken some of his remarks as jokes or flights of fancy, but later she realized he had spoken seriously. She determined to keep a much closer eye on him from now on. He was the only family she had, and she was the only one who could really watch out for him.

Lucky pushed through the swinging door and headed down the hall, hanging her coat and winter gear in the closet. She kicked off her snow boots and slipped on a pair of loafers. She pulled a fresh apron off the shelf—her mother had designed these, bright yellow with an outline of a steaming bowl of soup. On her way back to the front, she peeked into the kitchen. Sage was stirring one of the large vats, a mound of chopped vegetables piled on his work table.

"Hey, Sage. How's it going?"

He looked up and smiled, muscles bulging in his arms as he returned to chopping. "Under control, boss."

Lucky nodded. "Let me know if you need any help back here. We've got two waitresses out front tonight."

"Keep them out of my kitchen. Please!" he called out in response.

Lucky smiled. Sage was a maestro in his domain. A highly trained and creative chef, her parents were thrilled to find him. They had been able to hire him at a salary he could have doubled at one of the ski resorts. Frankly, she wasn't sure why he had stayed on as long as he had. His skills would have been welcomed anywhere. She just hoped he wasn't thinking of looking elsewhere for work now that her parents were gone.

Lucky had once suggested a recipe for a new soup and asked his opinion about adding salad choices in the summertime. She had felt a definite resistance. Nothing overt, just a stiffening of his posture, but there was something unspoken there. Perhaps he thought she was criticizing his abilities, which was far from the truth. Or maybe he didn't like having to take orders from a woman so close in age. Lucky had asked him a few times to call her by her name, but so far he avoided using it, preferring to address her as "boss." Then again, maybe he was standoffish because he wasn't sure if she would run the business as her parents had done. In all fairness to Sage, she hadn't definitely decided if she would continue on with the restaurant.

If Sage chose greener pastures, Lucky didn't know how she would ever find another chef as skilled. It wouldn't be possible to maintain the same standard of food if Sage were to leave. She brushed the worry aside. *Time will tell, time will tell.* She repeated it to herself like a mantra as she headed back to the cash register to relieve Jack.

The next few hours flew by. At eight o'clock, Lucky sent Jack home, and an hour later, the last diners had gone. Janie and Meg, two local girls who waitressed for them, had cleared the tables and were slipping on their coats. Lucky could hear Sage banging around in the back as he cleaned up his work area. She grabbed the key under the cash register to lock up, but before she reached the door, it flew open, ushering in a frosty blast of air. Sophie Colgan stepped inside, slamming the door behind her.

Lucky's heart sank. Sophie was probably the last person in town she wanted to see.

Chapter 2

FRIENDS SINCE CHILDHOOD, they had drifted apart in high school. Lucky excelled as a student, while Sophie pursued her love of athletics, particularly skiing. Sophie was now a top ski instructor at the Snowflake Resort. Tonight, she was still dressed in her ski gear.

In retrospect, the final blow to their friendship had come when Lucky made the decision to attend college in Wisconsin. During their last year of high school, Sophie became distant and cold, indulging in cutting remarks at Lucky's expense, pretending they had never been close. Lucky made several attempts to bridge the gap and rekindle the friendship, only to be rebuffed. Sophie carried a huge chip on her shoulder about being a "townie" and deeply resented Lucky's ambition to escape from their small Vermont hometown. Lucky suspected Sophie now took out her aggression on the slopes. She was momentarily confused, wondering why Sophie would come to the Spoonful at this hour. Surely she knew the restaurant would be closing.

"Well!" Sophie flashed a smile. "I heard you were back

but I could hardly believe it. What a surprise—Madison not to your liking anymore?" Lucky detected the thinly veiled sarcasm in her tone.

"It's not that . . . I . . ."

Sophie cut her off. "Sorry about your parents."

"Thanks."

"That must be tough."

Lucky didn't respond, too afraid any sympathy would bring on tears. She did her best to smile. "You look great, Sophie."

"Thanks. I stay in shape. So do you." Sophie's glance raked over Lucky's slacks and sweater. "You look well cared for." Lucky translated that to mean Sophie considered her pampered and spoiled—someone who thought herself too good for the little town of Snowflake.

She couldn't imagine Sophie had stopped in just to say hello. "Look, we're closing right . . ."

"Oh, I didn't stop in for the menu." Sophie had cultivated the habit of speaking aggressively, cutting off Lucky before she could complete her thought. Sophie looked beyond her and flashed a dazzling smile. Lucky turned to follow her gaze. Sage, dressed for the cold in his peacoat, came through the swinging door. He returned Sophie's smile and joined her.

"Oh. Sorry. Didn't know you two . . ." Lucky trailed off.

"'Night, boss," Sage said, holding the door open for Sophie.

Sophie turned and, with an impish smile directed at Lucky, waved her hand in the air. "See you around sometime." Sage shut the door behind them. Lucky moved closer to the window and watched as they walked away, Sage's arm thrown over Sophie's shoulder.

"Good night," Lucky said to an empty room. She stood for a long moment at the window, doubting whether she had made the right decision to return. Had it been the shock of her parents' death that had caused her to change course so quickly? After their funeral, she had returned to Madison and packed up her life. Now, had she burned all her bridges? There was no turning back. Was it really the right thing to do? *Time will tell,* she told herself once again. She locked the door and moved slowly around the room, turning off the lamps, all too aware of her own loneliness.

Chapter 3

"WHAT DO YOU call that color? It's so yummy, it looks like something I'd want to eat." Elizabeth leaned closer to the paint can. She had stopped by for an early morning visit to make sure Lucky was settling into her new apartment.

Lucky laughed. "Pumpkin."

"I knew it." She smiled. "That's why I liked it."

Lucky replaced the lid on the gallon can carefully, pressing it down until it was tightly sealed. She wiped her hands on a paper towel and, carrying a cup of coffee, joined Elizabeth at the kitchen table.

"Thanks for the furniture too."

"It's nothing. I keep odds and ends in storage in case one of my tenants needs something. It's become quite a collection over the years."

Elizabeth Dove, Lucky's landlady, was an old friend of her parents and had recently been elected Mayor of Snowflake, Vermont, population 953. That figure was more accurate in summer months. But in winter months, with nearby ski slopes and winter cabins, their tiny hamlet tripled its population. Elizabeth's hair, now that she was in her late fifties, had turned a glistening silvery white. She wore it in a short, youthful style and refused to color it.

Lucky hesitated. "You'd be honest with me, wouldn't you? I wouldn't want to paint the kitchen anything you wouldn't approve of."

"I'm very serious. I love it, and I'm just happy you're willing to do all this work. Saves me having to hire someone. And this room could definitely use some freshening up. I feel a little guilty having you do all this on top of everything else you have to deal with at the Spoonful."

"It's good therapy for me. With my schedule, it'll probably take me a few days to finish, but I'll get it done." Lucky was heartened by the thought of making this space her own. There was something about surrounding herself with her own warm choice of color that would make it feel that much more like a real home.

"I'll start on it tonight. When I get back."

"That reminds me." Elizabeth smiled. "I've brought you a little present."

"Oh no! You've done so much already," Lucky cried. It was true. Elizabeth was there to greet her at the train station the day she returned permanently from Madison. Elizabeth believed it was important for Lucky to see a familiar face waiting for her. She knew very well how keenly Lucky would miss her mother. Although she couldn't possibly fill that role, Elizabeth was determined to be the next best thing. It didn't matter that Lucky was all grown up now and six years out of college. Elizabeth had known her since the day she was born, and had loved her parents dearly. She had never had children of her own, so Lucky was the closest thing she would ever have to a daughter.

Elizabeth rummaged in her large shopping bag and pulled out a long rectangular box. "Open it."

Lucky smiled in response and opened the top lid. Inside she saw a fold of black flannel. "What is it?" She looked at Elizabeth questioningly.

"You'll see."

Lucky carefully pulled and wriggled the contents out of the box. The face was carved wood—a folk art piece—with a black hat and cloak and a long skirt of dried grass. She carried a broom of straw.

"She's a genuine New England kitchen witch."

Lucky laughed. "She's fabulous."

"And she'll bring you good luck."

"Thank you. I love her! I'll hang her right by the kitchen door."

"I've got to get going, but I'll give you a call in a day or so to see if you need anything. And you call me if there's anything—anything at all—you need. I have a good shoulder for crying on." She touched the top of Lucky's head and leaned down to kiss her cheek.

Lucky hugged Elizabeth at the door of the apartment and stood at the railing watching her as she descended the stairs. When the front door shut, Lucky hurried back to the kitchen to check the clock. She was running late. The restaurant would open in half an hour. Jack would already be there, warming up the large vats of soup that Sage had prepared the night before. Sage would arrive soon too. This was one of his mornings to pick up fresh breads and rolls from Bettie's Bakery. She hurried to the bedroom and stripped off her jeans. She pulled on a pair of warm slacks and a sweater, then brushed her honey blonde hair back into a ponytail, not stopping to put on lipstick or makeup.

At the front door, she tugged on her boots and slipped into her jacket and scarf, zipping up as she rushed down the stairs. The front steps of the small apartment building and the narrow sidewalk had been cleared of snow. Lucky hurried, anxious to get to the Spoonful as early as possible before opening time. She didn't notice the slick ice that had formed overnight. Before she knew what was happening, her legs flew out beneath her. She fell backward, landing on her rear and hitting her head. She slid gracelessly several feet before coming to a stop outside the front door of the Snowflake Medical Clinic, next door to her apartment building. As she lay on her back seeing stars and trying to catch her breath, the Clinic's door opened. Elias Scott was staring down at her.

"Lucky! Are you all right?" He reached out a hand to help her up.

Lucky's face turned beet red. *Of all the people. What a clod I am,* she thought. "Yes. I'm fine."

Lucky grasped his hand and, with his help, managed to get to her feet, painfully aware of her disheveled state and lack of makeup.

"Are you sure? It looked like you hit your head."

Lucky reached behind and felt the back of her head. "I think my ponytail saved me."

Elias stood there smiling. Lucky was too embarrassed to return his smile, even though he was several years older, had been her secret love from middle school all through high school. He first came to Vermont as an intern at a large hospital in a nearby town just as she was starting middle school. He spent as much time as his schedule allowed in Snowflake, often eating at By the Spoonful.

By the time she graduated from high school, he was already in practice at the Snowflake Clinic. Lucky took a good look at him. His hair was still dark, and his deep blue eyes hadn't changed. His dimples showed when he smiled. Her knees had always grown weak when he came into a room, and she forever prayed that no one would find out he was her secret crush. She would have been teased mercilessly. He was as handsome as ever. She felt, as she always had, like a gauche schoolgirl around him. He still had the same effect on her as he had had years before. Each stood there awkwardly for a moment, unsure what to say next.

Elias spoke first. "I'm very sorry about your parents. They were wonderful people. And I heard you had moved back for good. Is that true?"

"Yes. It was rather sudden. After my parents . . . well, I felt I wasn't doing anything very important in Madison."

"Where are you living now?"

"Right here," Lucky responded, pointing to the apartment building next door to the Clinic.

"You're kidding!"

"Nope. Elizabeth Dove owns it. She's renting me one of her apartments till I decide what to do about By the Spoonful."

"You're planning to keep it going, I hope?"

"I . . . I haven't decided for sure yet."

"Well, if it means anything, I hope you do. I eat there often. Great place. And speaking of eating, perhaps you'd join me for dinner some night?"

Lucky was flabbergasted. He was treating her like an adult. "Oh. Well. Yes, I'd love to. Do you mean stopping in at the Spoonful?" As soon as the words were out of her mouth, she realized her gaffe.

"Not at all. Come by my place and I'll cook for you. I bought the old white Victorian over on Hampstead Street, the one at the corner with the tall pine tree in the back."

"That's wonderful. It's a beautiful house."

"It's even more beautiful inside. And I promise to give you the grand tour. I'll stop by the restaurant soon. You pick the night. I'd love to catch up and hear all about the University and your adventures in Madison."

Lucky was too stunned to think of anything to say. She stood on the sidewalk with her mouth open as Elias waved and reentered the Clinic.

Chapter 4

TODAY'S SPECIAL WAS a vegetable broth soup with tiny meatballs, mushrooms and parsley. Several other choices were already steaming in the large pots on the stove. Lucky popped into the kitchen. Sage was wrapping rolls and breads in foil for warming later. "Is Jack here yet?"

Sage looked up. "He was out front a minute ago."

"I'll find him." Lucky walked the length of the corridor and opened the back door to the restaurant. Jack was standing in the small parking lot, looking anxiously up and down the access alley.

She called out to him. "Jack, what are you doing out here? Where's your coat?"

"Waiting for my wife. She should have been here by now. I told you that," he replied testily.

Lucky froze. Jack's wife, her grandmother, had died twenty years before. She walked closer and touched his arm gently. "Jack."

He ignored her. She tried again. "Jack, come inside. It's too cold to be out here."

"She won't be able to find me," he insisted plaintively.

"Yes. She will," Lucky lied. Her heart sank as she realized the implications. Jack was losing touch with reality. Was it Alzheimer's—the dreaded disease? Jack would have gone to the Clinic if he felt he had a problem. But then, maybe he didn't realize there was a problem.

"Come inside where it's warm. Have you had any breakfast?"

Jack looked in her eyes. He was finally back. "Lucky . . ."

"Yes, it's me."

"What . . . ?"

She took Jack gently by the arm and guided him inside to the restaurant. "Sit down right here." She pulled a chair out for him at one of the corner tables. "I'll be right back. I want you to eat something."

She rushed into the kitchen. "Sage, could you fry up a couple of eggs for Jack? I'll make him some toast."

"He okay?"

Lucky didn't feel comfortable confiding her worries to Sage. "He'll be fine." She plopped two pieces of bread into the toaster and hurried back to Jack with a cup of coffee.

"Drink this. It'll warm you up."

"Lucky, my girl, I'm fine. No need to baby me."

"I know, but I don't like to see you not eating—especially in the morning."

Another wave of guilt swept over her. Here she was dragging her feet about taking over the Spoonful, and Jack had been handling it all by himself for weeks. She was so caught up in her own concerns, she hadn't really considered he could be having serious problems.

THE RUSH OF customers kept her busy throughout the morning. She didn't have a moment to worry about Jack. She glanced over at him often as he stood at the cash register, while she manned the counter. He seemed to be doing fine in spite of her concerns.

As soon as the heaviest of the morning rush was over, the

restaurant quieted down. Most of their early customers were townspeople, and Lucky knew them all, some better than others. Hank and Barry occupied their usual table in the corner to play another game. Marjorie and Cecily—two sisters in their fifties who ran the Off Broadway ladies' clothing store—always stopped in later for brunch before heading down the street to start their day. For sisters, they were nothing alike. Cecily was petite and chatty with jet-black hair cropped in a flattering pixie cut. Marjorie, on the other hand, was reserved and rather intimidating. She had chosen to color her hair blonde and wore it in a severe bob. They lingered over their cups of tea at the counter.

"Dear, it's so good to see you again. All grown up too. Your mother would've been so happy to know you've come back." Cecily's statement was made in good conscience, but it reminded Lucky that she had missed out on those years that she could have been closer to her parents. Marjorie smiled and nodded in agreement.

Before Lucky could respond, the bell over the front door rang. A tall, very attractive blonde woman stepped inside and closed the door, cutting off the blast of cold air. She stood for a moment, looking around at the few remaining customers. At the very same moment, Sage came out of the kitchen behind the counter.

"Hey, boss, I'll need some more clean bowls before lunchtime, I . . ." He froze in place, staring at the blonde woman. Then he turned quickly, not completing his request, and retreated to the kitchen.

The noise level in the restaurant dropped, and a few people surreptitiously turned to watch the blonde as she approached the counter. Lucky could tell her outfit was very expensive. She took a stool a few seats away from the sisters.

Lucky pulled an order pad out of her pocket and approached her. "What can I get you? Coffee to start?"

"No, thanks. Just a container of tomato soup and half a grilled cheese sandwich to go, please." Her voice was a rich vibrato with a hint of smokiness, without arrogance, but with an authoritative quality—someone whose requests were granted without question.

"Coming right up." Lucky jotted down the order and placed it on the opening to the kitchen. Sage's hand grabbed the slip of paper and disappeared. Hank and Barry had stopped their game and were staring openly at the new arrival. Who was this woman who aroused such interest?

Lucky returned to her conversation with Marjorie and Cecily. "You'll have to stop by and see us when you can take a break. We have some new things in. I think you'll like them—good for the young crowd," Cecily said.

"I'd love that. I gave a lot of things away before I moved, and I could use some new clothes."

"We'll give you a discount, dear," Marjorie offered. "Stop by later if you like."

Lucky noticed the new order was ready in record time. She picked up the bag and carried it to the cash register where the blonde woman paid with a few bills pulled from a soft leather wallet. Hank and Barry had finally lost interest in the new customer and turned their attention back to their game. Jack handed the woman her change, and she left the restaurant without another word.

Lucky stacked the dishes from the counter while Marjorie and Cecily gathered up their things. Lucky leaned closer to them. "Do you know who that woman is?"

The sisters glanced at each other, their lips pursed. Marjorie finally leaned over the counter and whispered conspiratorially, "That's Patricia Honeywell. She's rented the cabin up at Bear Path Lane for the winter. She skis every day, I've heard."

"That's not all she does every day," Cecily chimed in.

Lucky looked from one to the other and waited, but no further gossip was forthcoming. It was impossible to live in a town so small and not have everyone know every iota of your business.

"And what's that?" Lucky finally prompted.

"Well, dear, let's just say she certainly has a way with men—lots of them. Every Tuesday she picks up two orders to go, but nobody knows who she's dining with."

"Maybe she has a big appetite."

Marjorie smiled wickedly. "She sure does. But it's not for food."

Chapter 5

LUCKY STRETCHED HER neck and rubbed her temples again. Numbers swam in front of her eyes. She had spent the last two hours this evening poring over the Spoonful's business records. Her Dad's method was old-fashioned and handwritten. The records were well organized, but something wasn't making sense. Enough money had been coming in from the business to pay all the expenses—rent, insurances, food licensures, taxes and salaries, but there should have been much more profit. Perhaps her parents had reinvested in the business? The interior hadn't been renovated, Lucky knew that much, but maybe they had purchased equipment she wasn't aware of.

She reached for another thick accordion file and pulled it out of the cabinet, patiently riffling through receipts for the past two years. She found no large expenditures—no new freezer units, stoves or dishwashers. The restaurant equipment wasn't the latest design, but it was practical and serviceable. The Jamiesons had no vices and certainly didn't indulge in any luxuries. They had always been hardworking, thrifty people. They counted their pennies, Lucky knew, remembering how hard they had worked to help her through college. So why didn't the numbers jibe?

She took another sip of tea from the mug on the desk and pulled a thick envelope from the back of the drawer. This was full of cash register receipts bundled by date. On the reverse side of each was a scribbled name. She groaned and leaned back in the chair. She finally understood what she was looking at. These were IOUs and they were uncollected. If these had been paid, Lucky was sure her Mom or Dad would have returned the receipts to their customers or at the very least, made a check mark over the name when a customer finally paid. Lucky flipped through the slips of paper, recognizing quite a few of the scrawled signatures—all local people and all longtime customers. Her parents had been carrying them for the last couple of years, too compassionate to demand payment, and wanting to allow them their pride. Her Mom and Dad had undoubtedly told them they could pay when things eased up.

Times had been tough in recent years, not just in Snow-flake but in other towns as well. Many had lost promising jobs when the biofuel plant in a nearby town closed down. Other small businesses had suffered a similar fate, if not closing then compelled to reduce their workforce. Some residents had lost their homes to foreclosure. Her parents had been feeding people who couldn't pay. It was the only explanation. The restaurant was filled to capacity almost every day. Even allowing for expenses and perishable food, there should have been a much greater profit.

She heaved a sigh and slumped down in the cracked leather desk chair, large enough for her Dad's frame. She had a big heart, but the Spoonful needed more of a cushion. One unforeseen plumbing emergency or equipment malfunction and they'd be underwater. Lucky cringed at the thought of pressuring customers for money owed, yet this was no way to run a business. There had to be a limit. Several people owed more than a thousand dollars. Was there a discreet way to remind them to pay their IOUs? She had no wish to embarrass anyone, but it galled her to think how her parents struggled after being so generous to others who were down on their luck. Perhaps a friendly reminder through the mail? But that would necessitate hours of going through these receipts, deciphering names and sorting out who owed how much. Perhaps the best thing would be to do nothing, but put a stop to the practice. She'd have to talk with Jack to make sure this didn't continue.

Lucky bundled up the receipts in rubber bands and returned the envelope to the file drawer. Perhaps Jack could tell her why her parents had made no effort to collect these debts. A low level of anxiety fluttered in her stomach. She hadn't had a chance to delve into her parents' personal finances, but she'd have to do so soon. The value of their house would have fallen, but surely it would still have a great deal of equity—they had bought it more than twenty years before. She'd find out soon enough when she talked to their accountant and the Realtor. Hopefully, they hadn't borrowed against their home to keep the business afloat. She leaned over, laid her forehead on her hands and closed her eyes for a moment. It all seemed overwhelming. She quelled the fear and reminded herself to take one step at a time.

Heavy footsteps reverberated down the corridor, past the office door. Then two male voices, one loud, the other quiet but insistent. The commotion brought her back to the present. She couldn't make out the words, but from the tone, an argument was taking place. One man was doing his best to keep the other quiet. It wasn't Jack—she would have recognized his voice. She pushed herself out of the chair and, opening the door quietly, stepped into the corridor. Sage was at the kitchen door with a stranger who wore a down parka that had seen better days. Realizing they were no longer alone, Sage quickly shoved a small roll of cash into the stranger's hand. The man in the ragged parka looked over his shoulder. His face was wolflike, his expression angry.

"Hi, boss," Sage responded to her curious look.

"Everything all right?"

"Oh, sure. My brother just stopped by. Remy, this is my boss, Lucky Jamieson." Remy's face instantly shifted to a disarming smile. The resemblance to Sage was striking, but this was an unkempt, rakish version of Sage. Lucky was sure they'd been arguing about money and Sage had been pressured to provide some.

"Nice to meet you, Remy."

"Likewise." When he smiled, his face lit up, the earlier anger vanishing.

Charming, Lucky thought. *Charming but completely slippery* was the phrase that occurred to her.

Lucky scooted past them and headed down the corridor to the restaurant. Jack was closing out the cash register and slipping bills into a zippered bag for deposit at the bank. Janie and Meg had their coats on and were giggling over a tube of lipstick in front of the mirror near the door. Jack looked up when he had finished counting. "I can stay and lock up if you want to head home."

"No, I'm fine, Jack. You go. You've had a long day. I just needed some time to concentrate on the books. By the way, there's something I'd like to talk to you about."

"What's that, my girl?"

Lucky looked at Jack closely. His face was pale and his shoulders were stooped. He seemed exhausted. "You know what, it's not an emergency. We can catch up tomorrow." Lucky kissed Jack on the cheek and watched him as he headed down the corridor to the coat closet. Janie and Meg were whispering heatedly between themselves. When they noticed Lucky watching them, they scooted into the corridor and stood by the kitchen door.

"Hey, Sage. Need some help?" Janie called out. Meg hung back, a slow flush creeping up her cheeks.

Sage muttered from the kitchen, "Nah, I'm fine."

Lucky closed the cash register, locked the door and turned off the lamps and neon sign. She returned to the office and stuffed the cash bag into her purse. Sage waved good night to her as he passed by her door, Janie and Meg following in his wake. As the girls walked through the door to the parking lot, following Sage, Janie gave Meg a shove in his direction.

Lucky smiled and shook her head. *Somebody has a big crush,* she thought. *But I'm hardly one to poke fun. When I see Elias, I can barely string a sentence together.*

Chapter 6

LUCKY DIPPED HER roller into the paint tray and carefully spread the last coat over the remaining wall. When she finished, she stepped back to admire her handiwork. What a difference some color made. Outside, the wind blew in short, angry gusts and ice crystals formed a thick layer of frost on the windows. But inside, the pumpkin-colored walls made it easy to forget the harsh winter. She pulled off the soggy roller and tossed it in the wastebasket, washed out the paint tray and stripped off her gloves. It was finally finished. Lucky had worked every night after coming home from the restaurant, one wall at a time. She gathered up the plastic on the floor and pulled the protective tape off the wainscoting.

When all the mess was disposed of, she collapsed in a kitchen chair, imagining her pictures and her mother's dishes and pots and pans here. If only her mother could be here to see her new place. She could picture her reaction but quickly pushed the image away. Too painful. Too fresh. She had considered moving into her parents' home, but feeling overwhelmed with the business, it seemed impossible to take over a house with all its chores, not to mention a mortgage.

Selling was the best thing to do. Maybe she'd keep some larger pieces of furniture, and her mother's delightful blue handmade pottery dishes, but the rest she could happily donate to charity. Very soon she'd have to go through their house and make those decisions, but she'd wait until she felt a bit more stable.

Lucky touched the nose of her kitchen witch for good luck and headed to the bedroom, stripping off her painting clothes. She slipped into her pajamas and climbed under the covers. Mentally, she reviewed the next day's chores as she started to drift off to sleep. The first thing was to get to the bank to deposit the cash. A jolt ran up her spine. The cash! Where was it? Dear Lord, she had left the cash bag on the desk in the office. How could she be so forgetful? She'd have to return to the Spoonful and get it. It wouldn't be safe to leave it lying in the open like that. Then she thought, *Why not leave it?* Only she, Jack and Sage had keys. It wasn't as if crime in the little town of Snowflake was a problem, but what if . . .

She groaned and rose from the bed, dressing again for the outdoors. If she hurried, she could get to the restaurant and back to her bed in half an hour. She put her jacket on over her pajamas, slipped on boots and gloves and pulled a cap over her head.

The streets were deserted. It was almost midnight, and given the freezing temperatures, most everyone was in bed. She turned the corner on Broadway and heard laughter and music from the Snowflake Pub as she passed by. Streetlights were swaying in the wind. She hunched deeper into her coat and kept going, not anxious to run into anyone while she was wearing pajamas. When she approached the Spoonful, she ducked down the narrow alley leading to the back. She unlocked the door and hurried into the office, breathing a sigh of relief when she saw the cash bag sitting on the desk. How could she be so careless? Losing this money would hurt them terribly.

Lucky stuffed the bag into her purse and locked the back door as she left. She retraced her steps, but this time as she approached the Pub she noticed two dark figures in a doorway ahead of her. Was someone lying in wait? Conscious of the large amount of cash in her purse, she hesitated and came to a halt. Perhaps she should cross the street and avoid whoever was in her way. Before she could make a decision, the shadows moved, revealing two figures. A woman's voice carried clearly in the chill night air.

"What did she mean?"

A man replied. "I have no idea! I swear."

"Then why would she say that about you?"

"I told you—she has it in for me. I told you . . ."

"Yeah—your version . . ."

The voices were familiar. They were crystal clear, even though the two figures were at the end of the block. It was Sophie and Sage. They must have come from the Pub. She couldn't imagine where else—every other business was long closed. They still hadn't seen her. She didn't want Sophie to know she had overheard her argument with Sage. Sophie would not take it well. Before she could cross to the other side of the street, the figures turned toward her, walking briskly in her direction. She had hesitated too long. If she crossed now, it would be obvious she was trying to avoid them. Sophie recognized her first. Her head cocked, as if unsure how much Lucky had heard.

"Here you are again! You seem to be everywhere these days, Lucky. Always lurking."

Sage's hand was on Sophie's shoulder. Lucky noticed that he squeezed it slightly, as if to silence her. Sophie wriggled her shoulder free from Sage's grasp. His expression was tight and closed down.

"Hello, Sophie—Sage."

"Hey, boss," Sage replied.

Sophie skirted around Lucky, dragging Sage by the hand. "See you around," she shot over her shoulder at Lucky. They continued walking toward an SUV parked at the corner. Lucky turned away and hurried back to Maple Street and her apartment, chagrined that she hadn't managed to avoid yet another confrontation with Sophie.

What were they arguing about? Who was the "she" Sophie had mentioned? What was it Sage said? *She had it in for me?* Could he have been talking about her—Lucky? No, that couldn't be. They must be talking about someone else, because Sophie had replied, *Why would she say that about you?* Lucky had certainly never spoken about Sage to Sophie.

Lucky breathed a sigh of relief when she reached the entrance to her building. Sophie's friendship had been so important to her when they were young. An only child, she had never felt able to fit in with other kids. She envied her classmates who lived in big, noisy families. It was Sophie, outgoing and brash, who befriended her and made her feel one of the crowd. Sophie's behavior now didn't surprise her at all. There was nothing new about it, but it was disheartening to be away for so many years and return to find that Sophie still harbored the same old animosity toward her. Was it so terrible that she had yearned for something different and taken a chance? She shrugged off the feeling. If Sophie couldn't let go, so be it. She had every right to be walking the streets at midnight if she felt like it—even in her pajamas. It was just that Sophie—and Sage too—could be so intimidating. She suspected neither of them liked her very much at all.

Chapter 7

LUCKY PICKED UP two soup and bread bowl orders from the kitchen hatch and placed them on the service area at the end of the counter. Janie grabbed the plates and whisked them to her waiting customers. Lucky glanced down at her hands. A few stubborn speckles of paint remained on her fingernails from the night before. She quickly washed her hands at the small sink behind the counter, scrubbing with a stiff brush until her hands were completely clean. When she turned back, Elias was seated on a stool, smiling in her direction. She hadn't seen him arrive. Her heart beat a little faster. Several days had elapsed since she had slipped on the ice in front of the Clinic. Every day since then she had wondered when she might see him again. Today he wore a dark green jacket. A soft plaid scarf hung around his neck. Lucky smiled in response and nervously pushed a stray lock of hair behind her ear. This was the second time Elias had caught her unaware, although this was a far less embarrassing situation.

Cecily, sipping tea at the counter, glanced up sharply and then craned her neck to look at Elias. Lucky was sure Cecily had picked up on her nervousness. She cursed herself for having a complexion that betrayed every emotion. She took a deep breath and approached him.

"What can I get you?"

"How 'bout a bowl of chili and half a BLT, please, miss." Elias smiled provocatively.

"Coming right up." Lucky ignored his smile and placed the order on the clip above the kitchen hatch. There were nervous flutters in her chest as she turned back to him.

"On your way to the Clinic?"

"Yes. But we might close early tonight. Have you seen the weather report? There's a bad storm blowing down from Canada. Supposed to bring high winds and three more feet of snow."

Lucky nodded in response. It didn't surprise her. Thick white clouds had turned dark gray, blotting out the sun. The wind had picked up and the snowflake lights shivered and wriggled on the lampposts. The barometer was dropping.

The bell over the door rang as Susanna Edgerton, the wife of the Snowflake Chief of Police, rushed in. Her cheeks were bright red and almost matched the scarf around her neck. She was carrying a small tote bag and quickly grabbed a stool next to Marjorie.

"Ladies." She nodded in the direction of the sisters. "My, it's really getting cold out there."

"What can I get you, Susanna?" Lucky asked.

"I'd love a bowl of that wild mushroom soup if you have any today."

"We sure do. You've been out doing errands?"

"Yes. I needed to pick up my prescription at Flagg's and a few other things, but I'm heading home after this and waiting out the storm. I just hope we don't lose power."

Lucky stuck a slip for Susanna's order on the clip, and Sage reached out and grabbed it. She picked up Elias's order and carried it to him.

The door flew open once again, and a blast of cold air hit Lucky. She shivered. It was Patricia Honeywell, the blonde who arrived almost every day. Several heads turned to stare.

Elias looked up and returned to his chili. Susanna, Marjorie and Cecily exchanged looks and fell silent.

The tall blonde woman had called her order in this time, and it was waiting on the counter. Lucky carried the heavy paper bag straight to the cash register.

"Thank you, dear," the blonde replied, and dropped a twenty-dollar bill on the counter, several dollars over and above the cost of her meal. Jack made change, but before he could hand it to her, she turned and walked out the door. Jack raised his eyebrows and shrugged, putting her change into the tip jar. Lucky returned to the counter and refilled Elias's coffee.

He looked up and smiled. "So, how's your schedule this week?"

Lucky couldn't believe her ears. Was he referring to the promised dinner? Was he really asking her to dinner in front of the biggest gossips in Snowflake? She was dumbstruck.

"Uh, well . . ." She decided that perhaps it was best to treat this lightly. "You know how busy my social life is. I'll have to check my calendar," she said, all the time wishing he had picked a more private place to speak to her. Lucky glanced quickly at Marjorie and Cecily. They were staring unabashedly.

"How about Friday? I'll pick you up here if you like."

Lucky knew without checking the mirror that she was blushing. "Oh, no need. I'll come over about seven thirty."

"Great," Elias replied, taking a last sip of coffee. "I can pick up some groceries and get cooking early. See you then."

Lucky struggled to hide the foolish grin spreading over her face. "That's so kind of you to offer to cook for me."

"*Kind?* "Kind" sounds rather boring—like something a doddering aunt might do. I certainly hope my company's more exciting than that." When Elias smiled, dimples formed on his chin. "Sorry I have to rush off. I need to get back to the Clinic. Jon's anxious to get home."

"Jon?" Lucky was momentarily confused.

"Jonathan Starkfield—my partner at the Clinic. Oh, I

forgot. You've probably never met him. When Dr. Stevens retired, Jon joined the practice. You'll have to stop over sometime and I'll introduce you. He's a family specialist as well. Great guy. Been in practice many years—lots of experience." Elias placed some bills on the counter, rose and waved as he went out the door.

Lucky felt she could breathe again. She hadn't forgotten Elias's invitation. To tell the truth, it had been on her mind since the day she had slipped on the ice. Part of her had pushed the idea away, too afraid it was something offered in the moment and not genuine at all. She half expected that when she saw him next, he would have forgotten. She mentally shook herself. *He's just being nice because you're an orphan now. He wants to make you feel at home, as if you have connections again. Keep it together. Don't let a school-girl crush put ideas in your head,* she told herself fiercely.

Lucky carried Susanna's order to her and busied herself picking up dishes and wiping down the counter, studiously avoiding the stares of the ladies. When they realized Lucky was not about to join them, they returned to their conversation. Lucky knew her dinner date with Elias was now grist for the gossip mill.

Chapter 8

ELIZABETH STOOD AT the kitchen counter, carefully wrapping the pottery dishware in stiff paper and stacking each piece in a box. Lucky was busy going through the bookcases and bureaus for personal items she intended to box and store for now.

The Jamiesons' home was a modest farmhouse, a mile out of town. No one was very sure how old the building was, but originally it had been a barn, later converted to a home. Its clapboard siding was painted deep red, and a large peaked dormer dominated the center of the structure, part of the original barn. A pine wreath still hung on the front door, its needles and pinecones frosted with ice. Martha Jamieson loved decorating for the holidays, and Lucky imagined her mother struggling to get the wreath placed just so.

"What did the Realtor say?" Elizabeth called out.

Eleanor Jensen was the only Realtor in Snowflake. She had no competition in town but was savvy about the marketplace and knew what property was worth to the last dollar. Lucky halted in her task and rose from the floor. "Haven't had a chance to talk to her yet. She's going to stop by today. I've given her a key in case I'm not here. She'll give me an idea what the market will bear right now."

Elizabeth turned to her. "Are you sure you want to do this? You might really regret selling your parents' home— your home—someday."

"I don't know what else to do. I don't have time to take care of a house, nor the money. There's a second mortgage, by the way. I suspect my parents borrowed against the house to keep the business afloat."

"They surely had life insurance policies?" Elizabeth questioned.

"I still have more papers to go through, and to answer your question, yes, they did. But it's not a lot in today's dollars. It really would be a relief for me not to be worrying about the house on top of everything else."

"I understand, dear, but let me know if you change your mind, or if a loan would help you out. I can help you. The Spoonful will do fine, I'm sure."

Lucky wasn't so sure about Elizabeth's confidence in her. She had moments when she thought that maybe the best thing would be to sell everything—the furniture, the house, the business—and pick up and start fresh somewhere else. But where? And there was Jack to consider. There was so much to do and so many things to take care of, every day felt like a long list of chores, with no end in sight.

Lucky finished with the bookshelves and moved on to the bedroom. She pulled open the top bureau drawer and took out her mother's small collection of jewelry, piece by piece—none of it valuable, but treasured because they were gifts from the people her mother loved most in the world. She had even kept the purple plastic earrings in the shape of pansies that Lucky, at age ten, had given her as a birthday gift. She came to realize as she grew older that her parents had expected their little girl to be feminine, all ruffles and frills, certainly not the tomboy she grew into. Her mother bought her dolls and sewed tiny handmade outfits, while Lucky came home with a broken arm and a jar full of spiders. She hoped her mother would think the pansy earrings the most beautiful things in the world. And as far as her mother was concerned, they were priceless—treasured because of her love for her daughter. Lucky smiled, remembering her mother's reaction at the time to the peculiar pansy earrings. She wrapped each piece of jewelry in tissue and laid them in a small box.

Lucky opened the second drawer in the bureau and gasped. It was full of letters and cards bound with pink ribbon. Her mother had saved everything Lucky had sent to her during all the years she had been away. She couldn't hold back the tears any longer. She sat at the foot of the bed and wept quietly, hoping Elizabeth wouldn't hear her from the kitchen. When her tears subsided, she wiped her eyes and blew her nose. She placed all the letters and cards in a second box. This cleaning out project was much harder than she had anticipated.

Elizabeth hesitated at the door of the bedroom. She could tell immediately that Lucky had been crying. "I'm so sorry, honey. Maybe it's too soon for you to have to deal with all this—a lifetime of memories."

"I knew it would be, but it's got to be done somehow."

"That's true, but it's too much to do in one day. Just chip away, a little at a time. Let me know what heavy pieces you don't want to keep, and I'll have my handyman come by. We can donate them to a charity or a thrift shop—whatever you'd like to do."

The doorbell rang once and a woman's voice called out, "Hallooo." Lucky wiped her nose. "There's Eleanor now."

Elizabeth leaned over and gave her a quick hug. "I'll be on my way. Oh, one more thing. Don't forget to leave a faucet dripping—might keep the pipes from freezing. I'll leave you to Eleanor's clutches."

Lucky heard Elizabeth greet Eleanor and then felt the front door slam as Elizabeth left. Lucky returned to the kitchen just as Eleanor entered with a clipboard tucked under her arm.

"I'm glad I caught you. You have time to go over things with me?" Eleanor asked.

"Sure," Lucky replied. Eleanor reminded Lucky of a small, furry mammal, always bustling, always rushing. She had an unruly mop of curly brown hair and walked at a slightly forward tilt.

With Lucky following in her wake, Eleanor progressed quickly through each room, jotting down notes. "I'd say the square footage is probably, what, eighteen hundred?"

"I don't know for sure. My Dad would have known."

"How old is the roof, do you know?"

"I remember my parents talking about it. I think they replaced it about five years ago."

"That's good news. And do you know anything about the plumbing?"

Lucky shook her head. "Sorry, no."

"That's all right, dear. We'll have an inspection set up to go over everything before we set a price. Now, that's something I have to talk to you about. The market is down right now, as I'm sure you know. It's the economy in general, but also the plant closure and the layoffs, and even the second-home market is a disaster. Your house isn't going to appeal to the ski crowd, too far from the Resort. So . . . given that we're in the worst time of year to sell, I don't think you'd get very much, that's assuming it would even move at all. Do you know how much is left on the mortgage?"

"Not exactly. I have to go through some papers. I do know there's a second to be paid off."

"Oh. Well, then. Maybe you might want to reconsider trying to sell right now."

One more stone in her path, she thought. Maybe she'd be forced to live here and hope to make enough money to pay the mortgages. She felt a deep connection to this house, but to live here now, so soon after her parents' death, wouldn't be the best thing for her spirits.

"I'll look at the comps and get back to you with an asking price. Do you want me to schedule an inspector to come and check things out?"

"Let's talk again before you do that, okay? In the meantime, I'll talk to my Dad's accountant and find out exactly what it'll take to keep this house up and running."

"Good plan. I'll call you in a day or two, or stop by my office whenever you have a chance."

"I will. I need to get back to the Spoonful right now and relieve Jack, but I'll keep chipping away at clearing the house out."

Eleanor turned at the front door and took one last look around. "I have to say, it's very, very charming. I love the built-in bookshelves and the stone fireplace. Maybe I'm wrong. Maybe someone will come along and fall in love with it. You never know," she said in a tone that didn't sound very encouraging. Eleanor banged through the front door and hurried to her car without further comment.

Lucky checked through the house one more time, making sure the kitchen faucet was dripping slowly and all the lights were off. She slipped on her jacket and hauled several boxes to her car—a second car of Elizabeth's that she had loaned to Lucky. She said a quick prayer of thanks for Elizabeth's presence and generosity. She had no idea how she'd have been able to deal with everything otherwise.

Lucky turned on the car heater as soon as the engine fired. She could smell the change in the air—a heavy wetness. She knew from her years in New England this wouldn't be a gentle snowfall. When Arctic air rushed down from the north, it was brutal, if not deadly. Thankfully, the stove in her kitchen apartment was gas. Even if the town lost electric power she'd be able to stay warm.

By the time she reached the Spoonful, the sun had dipped behind the mountains, its last rays blotted out by roiling black clouds. A few customers still lingered, one lone man and a couple. All of the locals and most of the tourists had hunkered down. Only die-hard skiers would be happy about this storm.

"Jack. Let's close up early if you have no objection."

"None whatsoever, my girl. Time to batten down the hatches."

"I'll send Janie and Meg home. I don't like the idea of their being on the road if the storm hits early." Lucky flashed on the image of her parents dead by the side of the road in a similar storm not that long ago.

"I can swab the deck tomorrow morning. No reason it has to be done tonight." Lucky smiled at Jack's vocabulary. The floor was always the deck and the walls were the bulkhead.

She stuck her head through the hatch. "Hey, Sage. We're gonna close. I'll lock up as soon as these people leave."

"Okay," he called back. "Not much point in staying open tonight. I'll put everything away."

Janie and Meg were obviously relieved to be let off early. "You girls go ahead. I know your families will be worried if you're not in early tonight."

"Thanks, Lucky." They smiled with relief. "We can stay and help you clean up if you need us."

"No worries. You go ahead. Jack and I can handle it. We can run the dishwasher in the morning." Without another word, the two girls pushed through the swinging door into the corridor and headed for the coat closet.

Ten minutes later, Sage had cleaned up the kitchen and stacked the dishes in the washer. "I'm finished now. I'll be on my way."

"'Night," Lucky called after him.

The couple at the far table settled their bill and left. The lone man rose from his chair and paid his bill at the cash register. "Good night. Drive safe," Jack called after him.

Lucky locked the front door and turned off the neon light. "Jack, before you go, I'd like to talk to you about something." Lucky grabbed a stool at the counter as Jack sat next to her.

"What is it, Lucky? You look worried."

"It's just . . . everything right now, but I'm wondering if you have any idea about all the people who haven't been paying their bills here."

Jack nodded. "Yes, I know about that."

"You knew? You haven't said anything! Jack—we're talking about a lot of money. There isn't much in the savings account—not enough to cover any kind of emergency."

"Lucky, your Mom and Dad . . . how can I put this . . . they cared more about their neighbors and friends who were down on their luck than they did about their profits. People here have lost their jobs, their homes, some can't even afford to feed their families. Your parents told them they were welcome here anytime, and if they couldn't pay, well then they could settle up later when they had a new job or some money coming in."

"Jack, those receipts—there must be several thousand dollars."

"I know. But what can any of us do about it?"

"We should ask them to pay, don't you think?"

"We could ask, but most, if not all of them, wouldn't be able to. And then they wouldn't feel free to come here anymore. And, mark my words, in the long run, that generosity shown in a hard time will always reap rewards in the future."

"That's great, Jack, and I don't really disagree in theory, but if we don't manage to stay in business, we won't be feeding anybody—ourselves or anyone else." Lucky realized with a shock she had spoken as if she had already made the decision to keep the business.

"Lucky, I love you with all my heart, but I am not going to ask any of these people for money. We know every single one of them, and I can guarantee you that they will eventually settle up. I can't stop you, but if you take my advice, you won't be sorry." Jack rose from the stool and shrugged into his jacket. "Why don't you stay at my place tonight. If this storm wipes out the power, we can light a fire."

Lucky looked up. "Thanks. I appreciate that, but I'll be fine. Anyway, I've got some boxes in the car I have to bring home."

"I'll give you a hand." True to his word, Jack followed Lucky to her apartment and parked his truck in front of her building. Together, they lugged all the boxes up the stairs and stacked them in the hallway closet.

Jack enveloped her in a bear hug. "Don't worry, my girl.

Everything will work out fine, you'll see." Lucky managed a grin in response, hoping against hope he was right.

Once Jack had gone, she shed her jacket, boots and gloves and, carrying the box she had marked with a K, headed for the kitchen. Inside were her mother's dishes that Elizabeth had packed so carefully that very afternoon. Lucky lifted the plates out of the box and unwrapped them. She stacked them on the kitchen counter. She loved the handmade pottery her mother had used for years, their hues set off beautifully against the pumpkin-colored walls of the kitchen. All that was needed here were curtains. When she was young, her mother had insisted she learn how to sew. It was the one domestic skill she urged Lucky to learn, reminding her how valuable it was to not have to rely on what the stores had in stock. She could search for just the right fabric and create the curtains herself on her mother's sewing machine. They would be something unique that would make this apartment her own.

She turned off the kitchen light and stripped off her clothes in the bedroom, pulling on her warmest pair of flannel pajamas. The wind buffeted the building, rattling the windows in their frames and shrieking as the storm grew in intensity. She lit a candle next to the bed and snuggled under the covers as the storm began in earnest.

Chapter 9

REMY DUBOIS SLOUCHED in his chair at the corner table normally occupied by Hank Northcross and Barry Sanders. The two regulars had yet to arrive. Lucky was sure they'd be busy all morning shoveling fresh snowfall from their cars and walkways. Remy, coffee at his elbow, was doing his best to hold court. His boots jutted into Janie's path as she moved from table to table, arranging tablecloths, napkins and salt and pepper shakers. Remy had tried several times to strike up a conversation, but Janie, for her part, merely nodded occasionally without much effort to be polite. Lucky overheard Remy extolling his exploits on the slopes, and in hopes of impressing Janie, offered to show her some moves. Sage caught the drift of the conversation and, through the kitchen hatch, shot his brother a disgusted look. Janie, unimpressed, returned to the counter and began to fold fresh napkins.

The first customers finally arrived, winter visitors, brave souls who had managed to navigate through the as yet unplowed streets and sidewalks. Janie placed their orders on the clip at the kitchen hatch while Lucky manned the counter and the cash register. Jack sat at a table by the window catching up with last Sunday's newspaper. It was a slow morning.

Sage called out, "Boss, I'll be right back. This trash needs to go."

Lucky heard the back door slam as Sage headed for the Dumpster. The first customers paid for their food and left, as two more came through the door. The special today was a new tomato-based soup with carrots and spinach served over jumbo pasta shells and flavored with basil, oregano and grated cheese. Their new customers were eager to try it. Remy slouched out of his chair and returned his coffee cup and saucer to the front counter, hoping to catch Janie's eye.

"Bye," he said. "Catch you later."

"Thanks, Remy." Lucky dumped the used dishware in a plastic container under the counter. "See you later."

He shot a sideways glance at Janie, who was too busy contemplating her new green nail polish to reply.

Meg took another order from one of the new customers and clipped it above the kitchen hatch. She hesitated and turned back, rising on tiptoes to look for Sage. He hadn't returned. "Hey, Lucky, where'd Sage go?"

Lucky looked through the hatch. "He's still out back. I'll fill those." She headed into the kitchen and, quickly slicing bread, put the new orders together on a tray and carried them out to Meg. She checked the kitchen again. *What was taking him so long?* She waved to Janie to stay by the cash register and headed down the corridor. Sage was squatting by the door, his back to the wall, taking deep breaths.

"Sage!" Lucky rushed to his side. "Are you sick?"

Sage shook his head. He pointed wordlessly to the back door.

"What is it?"

He rose and took Lucky's hand, leading her out the door to the Dumpster behind the building. He pointed to a mound of snow and ice. piled next to it. Lucky stared, unsure what she was supposed to see. A tuft of blonde hair stuck incongruously out of the snow. A chill ran through her. She was staring at a death mask—a death mask of ice. It was the face of their customer, the tall, elegant blonde woman. Dark clotted blood had frozen on the side of her head. A single jeweled earring dangling from one ear flashed in the thin winter light. The rest of her was buried under three feet of snow.

Chapter 10

LUCKY LOOKED UP to see Jack standing in the doorway. "What's wrong?" he called, joining them. They stared at him wordlessly, unable to speak. Finally, Lucky pointed to the frozen head rising from the snow.

"Jack, please call the police," Lucky asked. Jack nodded once and rushed away.

Lucky shivered violently, not sure whether from fear or cold. Had the storm lasted longer, the body might have been completely buried. It could have been days or weeks before it was discovered. "Sage, can you grab my jacket? I'll stay here till the police arrive."

"I will, but then I'm staying here with you. You shouldn't be alone."

"Do you think there's a chance this was an accident?"

Sage continued to stare at the icy mask. "Not a chance."

Ten minutes later, Chief of Police Nate Edgerton, in one of the two Snowflake police cruisers, pulled up at the other end of the alley on Elm Street. He parked, blocking the alleyway, and trudged through the snow to reach them. The curious were already starting to gather around the police car.

Nate stared at the frozen, seemingly disembodied head and then turned to Lucky and Sage. "This is just great," he muttered sarcastically. "Anybody know who she is?"

"She's a tourist, that much I know," Lucky volunteered. "I forget her name—Patricia something. It escapes me now. She comes in almost every day."

Nate shook his head. "This is bad. This is real bad. Was she staying up at the Lodge?"

Lucky thought a moment. "The hotel at the Resort? No. Somebody mentioned it. Marjorie, maybe. I think she was staying in a house up on Bear Path Lane."

Nate turned to Sage. "You know her?"

Sage shook his head. "No. Like Lucky said, she was a customer here a lot. Always ordered pretty much the same thing." Lucky stared at Sage, remembering the way he had stopped in his tracks when he spotted the blonde in the restaurant. Was he lying? Did he know more that he wasn't willing to tell?

Janie and Meg flew out the back door to see what the commotion was about. Janie stared, clapped a hand over her mouth and rushed back inside. Meg was riveted by the sight. Nate turned to her. "You shouldn't be out here, young lady. Go stay inside. I'll talk to you later." Meg nodded and retreated to join Janie.

Nate scratched his head. "I'll call Eleanor Jensen. If she rented the house to this woman, maybe she'll know who the next of kin might be." He glanced down the alleyway at his cruiser, debating whether to trudge back to his radio or use the phone at the Spoonful. "Can you two stay here for a minute? I'll use your phone if that's okay."

"Go right ahead. Use the one in the office," Lucky replied.

Nate was back in a short minute to stand watch over the body until his deputy and a van could arrive. "You don't happen to know what kind of a car she drove, do you?"

Lucky was at a loss. "No—no idea."

"Well, if she was living on Bear Path Lane and going up to the Resort, she'd have to have one. We'll find it eventually. You two go inside. No point in all of us freezing."

Lucky and Sage headed back to the warmth of the Spoonful. She noticed that Jack had turned over the sign on the front door to read CLOSED, but he was nowhere in sight. Sage returned to the kitchen and stood staring at the pots warming on the stove. Finally, he turned the burners off and started to wipe down the counters. "Are we closed, boss?" he called out.

"Yes," she replied. "Probably best for now."

JACK SAT ON a small step stool in the storage pantry, his arms raised protectively over his head, his shoulders hunched, his eyes squeezed shut. He heard the screams of the men, saw the telltale flow of red beneath the waves. He couldn't get to them fast enough. If the torpedo hadn't killed them, then the sharks already circling soon would, tearing off limbs and ending lives. It was one thing to put your life on the line to fight for your country, but to die like this, torn apart by an atavistic creature of the deep—no one had signed on for this. He hadn't signed on for pulling mauled bodies out of the sea either, but it was something that had to be done.

Jack whimpered and took deep breaths. He knew what was happening to him. He knew there was some fancy name for it now—some kind of initials—something they never talked about at the time. They were kids when they signed up. After, everyone just wanted to go home and do their best to heal. He took another deep breath, struggling by a sheer act of will to shut out the screams. He had to keep going—for Lucky. If he fell apart now, she wouldn't stand a chance—and this place was all the poor girl had. No family now—only him, and he was a sad excuse for that. An old man, a widower, living alone in a cottage that had seen better days. It was that woman—seeing her and the blood on the snow—like the blood in the sea. Places blood shouldn't be.

Lucky called his name and walked down the corridor, peeking into the office. Jack wouldn't have left without telling her. He wasn't in the restaurant and there were no places to hide. Lucky walked the length of the corridor and pulled open the door to the big pantry where their supplies and nonperishables were kept. Jack was sitting on a stool, shaking all over.

"Jack!" Lucky approached him slowly. "Jack, what is it?"

"Sharks," he muttered. "Damn sharks—there's blood in the water. Couldn't fight 'em off."

Lucky stroked his arm gently. He had only once spoken about his time in the Pacific, of the nightmares he still had, of the cries of men attacked by sharks circling in the water. Tears sprang to her eyes. "It's all right, Jack. We got them all. You don't have to worry anymore. The sharks are gone." Jack's breathing slowed and eventually he turned to her.

"Lucky. I'm sorry." *That was a good sign, wasn't it?* she thought. At least Jack recognized his present reality.

"Nothing to be sorry for. Let's go out front, okay?" Lucky led him out to the restaurant and helped him into a chair.

"Sometimes . . ." he whispered. Lucky leaned closer to him. "Sometimes it all comes back." He rubbed his face with work-roughened hands.

"Stay here. I'll pour us some coffee."

Lucky returned with two fresh cups and placed them on the table. Janie and Meg were perched on stools at the counter, unsure what to do next.

Lucky heard a loud rapping on the front door. Marjorie and Cecily had come for their usual morning tea and croissants and realized something was terribly wrong. Now they were impatient for news. They stood outside the window anxiously waving to her. She sighed and opened the door for them. "Come on in. It's too cold to stay out there."

"What's going on?" Marjorie asked. "I saw Nate in the police car and the van. But that annoying deputy of his—what's his name—Bradley—wouldn't let us down the alleyway. What's happened?"

Cecily chimed in, "Why did you close? What's going on?"

Lucky started to speak. "We . . . we found . . ." Before she could complete her thought, another sharp rap came at the door. Hank and Barry had walked over to the Spoonful together. She might as well let them in and tell everyone together so she would only have to give the terrible news once. It'd be all over town in a few minutes anyway.

When they learned who the victim was, Marjorie gasped and Cecily put her hand over her mouth to stifle a cry. Hank and Barry fell silent.

"I'm sorry to close up. But under the circumstances, it was best. Sage has put everything away, but I can offer you some coffee."

"Coffee would be great," Hank replied, unwinding his scarf from his neck and rubbing his hands together for warmth. Hank was tall and scarecrow thin, partially bald, with a halo of gray hair. He wore pince-nez glasses so low on his long nose he was forced to tilt his head up to look at the person he was talking to.

"You sit down, dear," Marjorie offered to Lucky. "You've had a shock. Cecily and I will get everything." She bustled into the kitchen, her sister following in her wake.

Lucky called to Janie and Meg at the counter. "Why don't you girls grab some coffee and sit with us for a bit? I know Nate will want to talk to you." The girls slipped off their stools and pulled chairs over to the large round table.

The back door slammed and heavy footsteps echoed down the corridor. Nate entered the restaurant. He scowled at the gathering of locals.

"Folks, I'm gonna need to talk to some of you. Lucky, can I use your office?"

"Sure, Nate."

Nate leaned through the hatch into the kitchen and gestured to Sage. Sage followed Nate down the hall to the office.

Marjorie returned carrying a tray of cups, saucers and a full coffeepot. "Good thing Susanna wasn't with us. Her husband would have a fit if she were here."

"He's such a hardhead, he'd probably arrest his own wife for interfering with a police investigation," Cecily replied.

Barry stood. "Ladies, I'll do the honors." Barry was short and portly. His checkered shirt barely stayed buttoned over his midsection, but he was light on his feet and circled the table passing out cups and saucers and pouring coffee for everyone. Lucky looked down at her hands. They were still shaking. She was very grateful to be waited on for a change.

Marjorie leaned across the table and whispered, "This is so shocking! Nothing like this has *ever* happened in Snowflake. But frankly, I'm not surprised." Hank gave Marjorie a stern look as if to warn her not to speak ill of the dead.

Cecily nodded vigorously and joined in. "I told Marjorie just the other day—that woman was asking for trouble. She gave every man she saw the eye. She didn't care if he was taken or not! That woman was a genuine trollop and now she's brought trouble to our little town. We'll all be suspicious of outsiders until the murderer is caught."

Hank spoke up. "And what if it's not an outsider?"

Marjorie bristled. "Whatever do you mean, Hank? Of course it's not one of us. People in Snowflake just don't do that kind of thing."

Barry and Hank exchanged a careful dubious glance.

Cecily asked, "Did she come in yesterday? Remember? We've noticed on Tuesdays, she always gets food for two."

"She was here, as I recall, but yesterday was Monday. Jack? Did you notice her order?"

Jack rubbed his chin. "I don't remember what it was. The girls will. Janie packed it, I think."

Sage reappeared with his coat slung over his shoulder. "Nate wants to see Janie and Meg next—together." The girls rose from their seats, obviously nervous. "Boss, if you're closed, do you still need me?"

Lucky pushed back her chair and walked over to him. "No. I'll be fine. Thanks, Sage."

"For what?"

"For staying with me out there. I appreciate it. We'll open again tomorrow as usual. And let's hope things get back to normal."

Sage nodded and headed out the front door without another word. Lucky noticed he avoided his usual exit at the back. She rejoined the group at the table.

"I heard she was seeing one of the young ski instructors

up at the Lodge," Barry said, slowly stirring cream into his coffee.

"Where'd you hear that?" Hank demanded.

"My neighbor works up there—bartending. He tells me all the news."

"Hmmph." Hank snorted. "Some people have nothing better to do than to mind other people's business."

Barry bristled. "You just wait. The Chief will be asking lots of questions and that's exactly what he'll want to hear."

Janie and Meg hurried down the hall and came through the swinging door. "Nate says we can go now. Is that all right with you, Lucky?"

"Yes. Please. Go on home. There's nothing much we can do here today. See you tomorrow morning, all right?"

Both girls nodded and slipped out the front door, not waiting for any further instructions. Lucky wondered if their families would object to their returning. If they did, she couldn't imagine how she'd manage a full house without them.

Nate returned to the front room and glared at the visitors. Marjorie and Cecily busied themselves putting on their coats and hats, obviously taking the hint they weren't welcome at the moment. Marjorie turned to Lucky. "You stop down to see us soon, dear. Those nice things are going fast."

Nate jerked his head at Barry to indicate it was time to go, and he and Hank rose from the table. When everyone had said their good-byes, Nate grabbed a mug and poured himself a cup of coffee, sitting heavily in the seat Hank had just vacated.

"Now. What can you tell me about this woman?"

Jack spoke first. "Not much, except she came in just about every day either for lunch or to pick up orders to go. Never really spoke to her. She always created quite a stir when she came in, but other than her name, I don't know much."

"You ever see her up at the Resort?"

"I never go there, Nate, you know that."

"Hmmm. I gather she was pretty friendly with a lot of men in town."

Lucky shrugged her shoulders. "To tell you the truth, I've

never seen her with anyone. Sometimes tongues wag just because someone's a stranger. You know how that is."

"Any idea how she ended up in back of the Spoonful?"

"No," Lucky answered. "We closed up early last night because of the storm. The last customers left about five o'clock. No one else was venturing out so I sent everyone home."

"So nobody went out the back way when you closed up?"

"Well, I guess we all did. Jack, me, Sage."

"And you didn't notice anything unusual then?"

"I didn't. But it was dark and I wasn't looking for anything. Sage generally puts the last of the garbage in the Dumpster before we close, but I don't think he did last night. That's why he was out there this morning. Are you saying you think she was already there when we left the Spoonful?"

"Won't know that for sure till we have a better time of death. The cold has thrown everything off, but we'll know more after an autopsy. What about this morning when you all arrived? Did anyone notice the body then?"

"No. I came in through the front. The alleyway hadn't been plowed. Just easier to use the front door—we probably all did. Nate, this couldn't have anything to do with us. Nobody here would have wished her any harm. And I can't imagine what she'd be doing in the alleyway at all."

"Did she come into the Spoonful yesterday?"

"We were just talking about that. She did—and picked up an order to go."

Jack said, "That's right. I remember now. She didn't take her change."

"Okay then." Nate lumbered to his feet. "We should have things cleared up back there pretty soon." Nate looked from Jack to Lucky. "If either of you think of anything at all, you give me a call, all right?"

Lucky nodded. "We will, Nate. I just hope this doesn't scare our customers away."

"Be a lot better for your business if she hadn't been found here, I'll tell you that." Nate turned and headed back to his duties in the alleyway.

As soon as he was out of earshot, Lucky turned to Jack. "This is not what we needed."

"I know it isn't. But there isn't much we can do about it now, is there? Why don't we close up, take the day off and start fresh in the morning?"

Lucky sighed. "No choice, I guess." She double-checked that the front door was locked, turned off the lights, checked the stove in the kitchen and followed Jack down the hallway to the back door, locking it behind her.

Nate, his deputy and another officer were gathered around the body of Patricia Honeywell. Lucky was surprised to see Elias with them. He looked up and walked over to where she stood.

"Lucky, I'm sorry you had to see this."

"Why did they call you?"

"They wanted me to have a look before they moved her."

"Oh." Lucky glanced over unwillingly. The fresh snow had been shoveled away from the body. The rest had been carefully brushed aside to reveal the blonde woman propped with her back against the Dumpster, dark blood frozen on one side of her face and neck, her legs splayed out in front of her. She was dressed all in black with a short fur jacket, not the expensive ski outfit Lucky had noticed at the Spoonful.

Nate grumbled to his deputy, "Keep looking . . ."

Elias shifted his position, attempting to block the dreadful sight from her. "Lucky, you should leave. You really don't want to be here for the rest of this."

Chapter 11

LUCKY STOOD BEHIND the counter staring disconsolately at an empty restaurant. Janie's mother had called that morning to say that Janie would not be returning—at least for the time being. Meg had turned up, but against her family's wishes. Lucky was sure her crush on Sage had been the driving force.

Sage, realizing very quickly that they wouldn't be overwhelmed with customers this morning, had prepared only smaller batches of soup in three Crock-Pots. One lone bakery loaf was warming in the oven. A layer of ice had formed on the sidewalk overnight. Jack had patiently scraped it away, then returned to his newspaper and the warmth of the restaurant.

To Lucky's dismay, not one customer arrived. Obviously, the discovery of Patricia Honeywell's body was the talk of the town and news of it had reached the winter visitors. It wasn't a surprise that tourists might stay away, but where were Barry and Hank or Marjorie and Cecily at least?

Through the steamy windows Lucky spotted a figure in a long red scarf approaching the front door. Her spirits lifted—perhaps a customer to break the spell. The front door banged open and Janie rushed in.

"Oh, Lucky, I'm so sorry. I can't work right now. My mother had a fit, but I wanted to stop by anyway."

Lucky shrugged. "I understand. You can't really blame her. She must be frightened out of her wits. I'd feel the same if I were her."

"She's just so stubborn," Janie grumbled. "She wouldn't even listen to me. I know this had nothing to do with the Spoonful."

"I agree. It couldn't have anything to do with us. Unfortunately, it's landed on our doorstep, if you'll pardon the pun."

"Is it okay if I hang out and talk to Meg?"

"Go right ahead. We're anything but busy."

The girls grabbed the corner table usually occupied by Hank and Barry and began a whispered conversation.

Lucky returned to scrubbing the work space behind the counter. This was a good opportunity to catch up on chores if nothing else. She caught movement out of the corner of her eye. Nate's police cruiser had pulled up in front of the Spoonful. If Nate and Bradley wanted coffee or breakfast, she had no objection, but she couldn't help but wish they had parked somewhere else. A police car at the front door wouldn't help their image one bit. Lucky watched as Nate heaved himself out of the passenger seat and headed for their front door, Bradley bringing up the rear. The bell over the door rang as they entered.

Nate approached the counter. "Hello, Lucky."

"Nate. Any news for us?"

"Unfortunately, yes. Is Sage here now?"

"Sage? Yes, he's in the kitchen."

"Lucky, I want you to know, I'm real sorry about this." Nate turned away and headed toward the doorway to the kitchen with Bradley following behind him. Sage stopped his work at the counter and looked over at Nate looming in the doorway.

Nate cleared his throat. "Mr. DuBois, you are under arrest for the murder of Patricia Honeywell. You have the right to remain silent. Anything you say or do can and will be held against you in a court of law. Anything you say can and will be used in evidence against you . . ."

Lucky dropped the silverware she was holding. It clattered on the counter, half of it falling to the floor. She turned to Jack in astonishment, unable to believe her ears. Jack bolted out of his chair and rushed into the kitchen. "Nate, this can't be right. You're making a mistake."

Janie and Meg sat in shocked silence and watched. Meg's face had turned a ghastly white. Janie jumped up and attempted to follow Jack. Lucky held up a hand to halt her and peeked through the hatch into the kitchen. Sage's shoulders slumped. He dropped the utensil he was holding and stood, hands at his side, his expression blank. He made no protest. He didn't even look surprised. Lucky had the strange impression he had been waiting for this. Silently, he turned and pulled his coat off the peg on the wall and slipped it on. Bradley led the way through the restaurant with Nate following after Sage. Sage kept his gaze lowered, never meeting anyone's eyes.

Jack stepped around them to block their path. "Nate, what's this all about?"

"Jack, I'm sorry. Please step aside. There's just nothing I can tell you at this point." With no word of explanation, the three men exited through the front door of the Spoonful. Once outside, Bradley held open the back door of the cruiser and waited while Sage climbed in. Nate returned to the passenger seat and Bradley climbed in behind the steering wheel.

Janie and Meg pressed up against the frosty window watching as the cruiser drove away. Lucky reached for Jack's hand. He squeezed it to acknowledge her. No one had spoken a word. The girls turned to Lucky as if she could explain what had just happened, but she was as stunned as they were.

"Oh God, it's all my fault," Meg wailed and burst into tears.

"What are you talking about?" Lucky asked. Jack stared at the young girl in complete confusion.

"It's all my fault!" Meg cried again.

"Come sit down and tell me what you're talking about." Lucky caught Jack's eye and made a slight gesture to indicate this would be girl talk and he should make himself invisible. Janie threw an arm around Meg and led her back to the counter. She pushed her gently down onto a stool and sat next to her. Jack returned to his newspaper at a corner table, discreetly feigning a lack of interest in their conversation.

They had Lucky's full attention. Janie spoke first. "The other night . . . we left with Sage."

"Yes, I remember," Lucky replied.

Janie reached out and put her hand protectively over Meg's. Meg was trying hard to regain control. ". . . Sage said he had to come back to the Spoonful. He had forgotten his keys."

Meg took a deep breath and stifled another sob. "He doesn't know it, but we followed him." Lucky nodded sympathetically and waited for Meg to spill out the rest of her story. Meg looked up, her face stained with tears. "Lucky, he was lying, because he didn't go back inside the Spoonful. He hung around outside, like he was waiting for someone."

"What night was this? The night of the storm?"

"No. A few nights before. I'm not sure exactly. It was the night you were working in the office."

"Did you see him meet anyone?"

"No. We waited as long as we could. We didn't want him to know we had followed him, but nobody else turned up."

"That's hardly incriminating. I'm sure Nate wouldn't jump to any conclusions based on that."

"That's not all," Janie offered. "The night we closed early—the night of the storm—I usually give Meg a ride home—but instead we parked down the street and waited for Sage to leave."

Lucky marveled at the craftiness of young love. "Did you hope to talk to him and hang out?" Meg nodded sheepishly, her face bright red. "What happened then?"

"We saw him come out to Broadway. He started walking away from us toward Maple," Janie responded.

"I'm sure he was just walking home. He only lives a few blocks away."

"Maybe he was, but then a red Jeep passed by and pulled up next to him. The driver must have called out to him, because Sage stopped and looked at the car. First, we thought somebody was asking him directions. But then Sage turned away and started walking faster."

Meg, more excited than upset now, said, "It was really weird. The red car started up, passed him and pulled over ahead of him. That woman jumped out. She left the car running in the street and got right in his face."

"You mean Patricia Honeywell?"

"Yes."

"Really!" Lucky wondered once again what the connection between Sage and the blonde woman could be. There had to be some history. "What did Sage do then?"

"They were kinda far away by then. We started the car and drove real slow to catch up. We wanted to see what was going on, but we were trying not to be obvious. Sage said something to her—we couldn't hear—and then it looked like her hand came up, like she was reaching for him. He backed away quick and held up his hands, like 'Don't touch me.' Something like that—at least that's what it looked like, and then he took off really fast."

"What happened after that?" Lucky asked.

"Nothing. That woman got back in her car and drove away," Janie said.

Lucky shook her head. "Weird. I wonder what that was all about," she said more to herself than to the girls. Where was Patricia Honeywell heading when she spotted Sage? And why had she felt it necessary to accost him like that in the street? Could there have been a later altercation that night? The night of her death? No—Lucky shook her head. Whatever was behind that confrontation, it sounded like Sage would have done anything to avoid running into the blonde woman.

"There's more, Lucky," Meg spoke softly. "We saw him with the dead woman before—up at the Lodge. We help out there sometimes. She was at the bar with one of the ski instructors—I think it was Josh. It was so disgusting. He was mooning all over her . . . Josh I mean, but then she spotted Sage and she told Josh to get lost. She walked right over to Sage as if she knew him."

"What was Sage doing up at the Lodge?" Lucky asked.

Janie dug through her purse and passed a wad of tissues to Meg. Meg took off her glasses and wiped them carefully. Her round face looked doughy and forlorn. "Don't know. Maybe he was there to meet that Sophie—she's such a cow! Or maybe he was meeting his brother. Remy sometimes does odd jobs up there."

"Janie . . . Meg . . . even if he knew this woman—Patricia Honeywell—even if there's some story behind all this, it might not mean anything at all." Lucky remembered Sage's reaction at the restaurant when he saw the blonde woman at the counter. It certainly did appear as if they knew each other, or at least Sage recognized her, but she cautiously decided it was best not to offer any more information to the girls.

Red blotches covered Meg's face. "I shouldn't have told the police any of that stuff. I got so scared when Nate started asking me questions, it just all came out. If I had just kept my mouth shut, they never would have arrested him."

Janie put an arm around Meg's shoulder in an effort to console her. "Lucky, can Meg go home now? There's nothing for her to do here anyway."

"Sure. Go ahead—both of you. We might as well close for the day. Again, no one's turned up and now Sage is gone. There's not much we can do for him right now, but I intend to find out just why Nate's arrested him."

Chapter 12

LUCKY WAITED IMPATIENTLY at the counter, shifting from one foot to the other, as Bradley rummaged through file drawers.

"I know that form is in one of these folders. I'll find it in just a minute, Ms. Jamieson."

Lucky heaved a sigh. "Bradley, it's me. Just call me Lucky, okay? You know me. Why do I need to fill out a form to visit a prisoner?"

"It's required, Ms. Jamieson . . . Lucky. It's Department of Corrections Policy No. 327 and the Administrative Procedure Act, Rule No. 79.26, commonly known as the APA rules. 'Each visitor shall, upon entry, register his name, address and relationship to the resident.' I am entitled to ask you to submit to a search, but since it's you, I won't insist."

Lucky bit her tongue. "I appreciate that, Bradley." If he dared to lay a hand on her, she'd slug him. "I just want a chance to talk to Sage. He works for me. I'm concerned about him."

"Found it." Bradley triumphantly held up a one-page form, slightly wrinkled at the corners, and carried it to the long counter. "It's just . . . well, we haven't had a prisoner for a long time. Actually, I can't remember when we last had one . . . except for old Arnie Hicks. He gets drunk and disorderly once a year on his birthday. But we just lock him up so he won't hurt himself. He's sober by the next morning."

Lucky reached for the form and pulled it from Bradley's fingers. She thought he looked quite pleased that his jail cell was actually accommodating an alleged criminal.

"Where do I sign?" Lucky scanned the form.

"I'll have to see some ID." Bradley drew himself up to his full height of five feet seven inches. "All visitors must identify themselves and state their relationship to the prisoner."

"Bradley! That is ridiculous."

"Sorry, it's just APA rule 79.26."

"I thought it was rule 327."

"No, 327 is Department of Corrections Policy. Rule 79.26 is APA."

Lucky blinked slowly, ready to reach across the counter and throttle the deputy, but thought better of it. Bradley might arrest her. She was sure there was a penal code to cover assault on a police officer, and sure that Bradley could quote it chapter and verse. She took a deep breath to control her impatience and calmly replied, "Will a driver's license do?"

"That would be fine. Please remove it from your wallet. I'll have to make a copy."

"Okay." Obviously, the quickest way to get past Bradley and actually speak to Sage was to comply with all aspects of the APA rules. She hurriedly filled out the one-page form and signed it, as Bradley returned her driver's license to her.

"Follow me, please." Bradley opened a heavy door and led her down the hallway. "I have to ask, are you carrying any weapons?"

"Not today, Bradley." *But next time I see you . . .* She followed him down the short corridor and waited while he unlocked the security door. At the end of this area were two cells, each one equipped with a cot and a hard wooden bench.

Sage sat on the bench, his eyes closed, leaning against the concrete block wall. Lucky spotted a row of stools and pulled one closer to the locked cell.

"Ms. Jamieson . . . Lucky . . . please do not move any closer to the cell, and do not touch the prisoner or pass any items to him. Do you understand?"

"Yes, thank you, Bradley. I only want to talk to Sage." Lucky waited, but Bradley continued to stand next to her. She looked up at him. "In private, please."

Bradley sniffed and reluctantly retraced his steps to the front counter. Lucky waited until she heard the door close behind him. She watched Sage carefully, trying to gauge his mental state.

His arms were crossed against his chest. He opened one eye and stared at her. "You shouldn't have come here, boss."

"Don't you start. I've had enough difficulty with Bradley."

"Don't waste your time with me. There's nothing you can do." A muscle in his jaw clenched and unclenched.

"Why not?" Lucky's heart skipped a beat. "Are you saying you're guilty?"

Sage shook his head negatively. "That's not what I'm saying."

"Then talk to me. Maybe we can find a lawyer to help you. What was there between you and this Honeywell woman?"

Sage leaned back against the concrete wall and closed his eyes once again. "Go away, boss. I've got nothing I want to say—especially to you," he replied bitterly.

Lucky felt as if she had been slapped across the face. His bitterness was directed at her, and she was at a loss as to why that would be, or how she could reach him. She patiently waited a few minutes more, willing Sage to talk, but he refused to look at her or offer any explanation.

"Okay," she finally spoke. "Have it your way—for now. But I'll be back. You've gotta let somebody help you, Sage." Lucky pushed the stool against the wall and returned to the front counter where Bradley was pretending to be absorbed in a clerical task. He looked up as she approached.

"Bradley, is Nate around?"

"No. He's up at that house on . . ." Bradley clamped his mouth shut, suddenly aware he was about to say too much and he'd be in trouble with Nate. Lucky noticed that his high school acne had never quite cleared up. Blemishes stood out against the paleness of his skin, particularly when he was embarrassed.

"The house on Bear Path Lane?"

Bradley stood up straighter. "I didn't say that."

"Never mind, Bradley," Lucky replied sweetly. "I won't tell Nate you told me."

Bradley sputtered, "I never did, Lucky, you know that."

"Of course you didn't," she replied neutrally, enjoying a delicious moment of needling him.

Bradley quickly shuffled the papers in front of him into a neat pile while he regained his composure. He turned back to Lucky and asked blandly, "Did Sage have anything to say?" Lucky caught the hint of a crafty gleam in his eyes. Did he really think she was so naïve she would confide in him?

"Not much. What has he told you?"

"He won't say a word to us," Bradley blurted out quickly. "He . . ." Then he stopped himself in midsentence, realizing the tables had been turned and Lucky was attempting to extract information from him.

"I'll be back tomorrow to see him. But can you let Nate know I stopped by? I'd like to talk to him when he has a minute."

"I'll tell him. By the way, we have to feed our prisoner until the arraignment. We're not set up for that kind of thing. We can bring him breakfast in the morning, but we won't be able to feed him lunch or dinner. If the Spoonful can take care of him, the County will reimburse you."

"Not a problem. You have a refrigerator and a microwave?"

Bradley nodded. "Sure. In our lunchroom."

"We'll take care of it then. Jack or I will be back later," she called out as she pushed through the front door. She had kept up a front for Bradley, but her spirits were somewhere down around her boots. There was no way she would confide any of her fears to Bradley. Anything he learned would be all over town in no time flat. Try as she might to be compassionate, Bradley always seemed to bring out the worst in her. She had to make a conscious effort not to react. After all, it was so easy to puncture his pomposity, like sticking a pin in an overinflated balloon. She wasn't sure if that qualified her as mean-spirited, but most of the time Bradley had it coming.

WHEN LUCKY REACHED the Spoonful, the neon sign in the window was glowing, a beacon against the cold and the fear. The restaurant was empty. She entered through the front door, flung her jacket on one of the chairs and called out to Jack.

"In here, my girl," he answered.

She slipped behind the counter and peeked through the hatch into the kitchen. Jack was heating one of Sage's containers of soup on the stove. A baking dish of cornbread sat on the counter, with squares already sliced.

"You hungry?" He looked up and smiled.

"I'm starving. That smells wonderful."

"It's the zucchini parmesan, and we can have some with cornbread. I'm not Sage, but I thought the least I could do is fix us some lunch. There are several more containers in the freezer—so we'll be okay until Sage is released."

Lucky heaved a sigh. "I wish I could be as optimistic." She did a slow turn, looking around the restaurant. She loved this room—the yellow-checked café curtains at the big window, the framed photos of historic Vermont sites and snapshots of skiers on the slopes and regular customers covering the upper walls. The wainscoting was dark polished wood and the floor was constructed of old wide pine boards. Everything here spoke of the presence of her parents. She could feel them as if they were just at the edge of her vision, still here, watching over her and Jack. If she could only turn quickly enough, she'd be able to see them again.

She knew she was feeling sorry for herself, but she couldn't help but remember times in her life when she had worked so hard and something out of her control dashed her plans. There was the spelling bee in junior high with a prize of a new cherry red two-wheeler. She stayed up studying for three nights only to wake with laryngitis, unable to speak the day of the event. Then there was the time she fell out of a tree and broke her ankle the day before the senior prom. Maybe she was the jinx—Jack should have named her "Unlucky." She'd had her doubts about keeping the restaurant open. Now it looked as if that choice might be taken out of her hands. But all that aside, currently the important thing was to convince Nate that Sage wasn't guilty and that the murder had nothing to do with the Spoonful.

She gathered two place mats with silverware and napkins and laid them on a table by the window. Jack returned from the kitchen with the soup bowls and cornbread on a tray. "We're sitting by the window?"

"Yes. Maybe people will mistake us for customers and come in."

Jack smiled. "Eat up. What did you learn from our boy? How's he doing?"

"Not good." Lucky looked across the table at Jack. His complexion was gray, and the long lines that scored his face were deeper. "He wouldn't talk to me at all. Told me I shouldn't have come. Oh, before I forget, we're in charge of feeding him—at least until he's arraigned—lunches and dinners."

"Good. I'll fix him a steak and a baked potato tonight and bring it over with a few containers of soup. I just hope you can cook something besides steak—that's all I know how to do."

Lucky smiled. "I'm no chef, but he won't starve. I have some chicken recipes and I make wonderful mashed potatoes. We'll figure it out. We can take turns. If you want to bring food today, I'll do the honors tomorrow."

Lucky broke off a chunk of cornbread and dropped it in her soup. "Maybe you'll have better luck getting Sage to open up. You know, I noticed something the other day and I didn't know what to make of it." Lucky recounted Sage's reaction when he spotted the blonde woman in the restaurant. "Jack, there had to be *something* between Sage and that woman."

Jack, stirring his soup, looked up. "I didn't notice that. But come to think of it, I don't recall seeing him around at all when she came in. Maybe you're right."

"Wish you could have seen it. He just looked thunder-struck. Clammed up and dashed right back to the kitchen. It was very weird."

"Like he knew her from somewhere else and didn't expect to see her here?"

"Exactly like that. There's something there—between him and that woman. But he's not about to tell me, at least not right now. Hopefully, you'll have better luck."

"Hmmm." Jack wiped his chin carefully with a napkin. "I'll give it a shot. We'll find out eventually, whatever it is."

"I don't want to wait for eventually. This couldn't have happened at a worse time. Now the Spoonful is associated with murder in everyone's mind. The more I think about it, the angrier I get. We don't deserve this."

"Deserve has nothing to do with it, my girl. We'll get through. And if not, well, we'll both figure out something else to do. After all, you've got a college degree. Must be lots of things you can do."

Lucky chuckled. "Oh, sure—a degree in theatre arts. That'll be very useful in Snowflake."

Jack reached across the table and grasped her hand. "You never know. Give me a smile now."

Lucky looked across the table at Jack and tears rushed to her eyes.

"What's that?" Jack asked. "Tears? No tears, now. Nothing to cry about."

"Just once, I want something in my life to go smoothly."

He squeezed her hand. "It will. Never drag the past into your future. Remember that."

She nodded disconsolately. "Any customers while I was gone?"

"Just Hank and Barry. They stopped in to see how we're doing, but that's all. I guess everyone's afraid to come near us." Jack turned to look out the window. "Don't tell me . . ."

Lucky followed his gaze. A white van topped with an apparatus that looked like a satellite dish slowed to a stop in front of the Spoonful. Across its side in red and blue were large letters—WVMT. Two men jumped out of the rear of the van, followed by a tall woman with long dark hair wearing a red coat. She stood on the sidewalk, directly in front of the blue and yellow neon sign, while a man in a parka hoisted a camera onto his shoulder. Another woman climbed out of the rear of the van. She wore jeans and a jacket and carried a bag with many small pockets on the outside. She whipped out a large makeup brush and quickly touched up the face of the woman in the red coat.

Lucky gasped, dropping her spoon in the soup. "Jack, are they doing what I think they're doing?"

The second man, standing next to the cameraman, held up three fingers, counting silently . . . three . . . two . . . one . . . The dark-haired woman held the microphone in front of her, and her lips moved while she gazed intently into the eye of the camera.

Jack jumped up from his chair. "We'll see about this . . ." He stomped into the kitchen and returned with a broom in his hands. In a moment, he was out the door and onto the sidewalk, charging the cameraman with his broom. Lucky jumped up and rushed outside. The cameraman's assistant was doing his best to run interference between Jack and his boss while the dark-haired woman had a terrified look in her eye. Lucky grabbed Jack's arm just as he was about to smash the broom over the cameraman's head.

"Jack, please, don't," she begged. "This'll just make things worse."

Jack looked at her, his face flushed. "These *vultures* are gonna make things worse. We don't want this kind of publicity."

The dark-haired woman spotted her opening. She moved quickly and stood next to Lucky, who was struggling to extricate the broom from Jack's hands. The camera followed the movements of the newswoman as she turned to the camera again.

"I'm here with the owners of the By the Spoonful Soup Shop, a thriving Snowflake business—thriving, that is, until the discovery of the body of Boston socialite Patricia Honeywell who was brutally murdered at this very restaurant."

The dark-haired woman stuck the microphone in front of Lucky's face. "Do you have anything you'd like to add, Miss Johnson? I understand your chef has been arrested for this murder."

Lucky was shivering from cold, but nevertheless, the words came. "No one—absolutely no one—was murdered at our restaurant. We're shocked by all this, but we firmly believe our chef is innocent. This had nothing to do with By the Spoonful." Her anger building now, she added, "And by the way, it's Jamieson—J-A-M-I-E-S-O-N—*not* Johnson."

The dark-haired woman ignored her last statement. Smiling, she turned to the camera. "Well, there you have it, folks. The owners of the By the Spoonful Soup Shop are standing behind the accused murderer. Let's hope their faith is not misplaced."

The cameraman yelled, "Cut," and the woman in the red coat turned her back on Lucky and threw the microphone at her assistant. She grabbed the door handle of the van, climbed into the front seat and locked the door. The cameraman and the makeup woman hurried into the back of the van. As soon as all the doors slammed shut, the assistant revved the engine and the van pulled quickly away.

Lucky and Jack stood rooted to the sidewalk watching as the van took off down Broadway heading for the highway out of town. Jack, muttering to himself, turned and headed back to the warmth of the restaurant, broom still in hand. Lucky followed.

Jack threw the broom in the corner. "I'm sorry I lost my temper like that. But the way they're making it look, Sage is guilty and we're running some kind of a murder factory." His cheeks were still flushed with anger. He swayed as though about to lose his balance. He leaned against a chair and clapped a hand to his chest.

Lucky was instantly alarmed. She rushed to his side. "Jack, what is it?"

He took a very deep breath. "Nothing, my girl. I'm fine." He smiled weakly at her.

Lucky took him by the arm and led him back to his chair. When he was seated, she asked, "Are you having chest pains?"

"Oh no," he answered. "Just sometimes . . . sometimes it feels like . . . a little pitter-patter."

"Like palpitations?"

Jack shrugged. Lucky squeezed his hand. "Let's finish our lunch before it's completely cold."

Chapter 13

"WELL, THAT'S IT then," Eleanor announced as she slid the last document across the desk toward Lucky. "Sign right there, dear, and your listing will be official. Now, you know, you don't have to accept any offer you don't like, but once you accept, you're committed, even though the buyer can still back out."

Lucky nodded. "I understand." She pulled the pages closer and signed and initialed in all the spots Eleanor had marked.

"And if you change your mind, I won't be the least bit upset. I'd frankly like to see you hang on to your house."

"I don't think I could change my mind, even if I wanted. Especially now, with business going so badly."

Eleanor laughed mirthlessly. "Tell me about it." She waved a hand toward the large bulletin board on the wall covered with flyers of properties for sale or for rent. "I've had three cancellations so far this morning. I doubt the Resort has been affected, but since this horrible murder, no one wants to be anywhere near town."

Lucky looked at Eleanor thoughtfully. "Tell me something. Did you rent that cabin on Bear Path Lane to Patricia Honeywell?"

"Yes, I did."

"What can you tell me about her?"

"Not much, really. She rented that same cabin this year and last winter. Both times after the holidays, for maybe two or three months, depending."

"How come she didn't stay up at the Lodge?"

"I asked her that. She said she wanted to be away from the crowds and she liked her privacy."

"She stayed there all alone?"

Eleanor let out a peal of laughter. "Well, I wouldn't say that. I'm sure she had lots of company from what I've heard."

"Anybody special?"

Eleanor shrugged. "Not that I know of, nor did I want to know. She was a good tenant, paid her bills ahead of time. No damage to the house. Not a spot of trouble in that regard."

"You don't suppose I could have a look around, do you?"

"What for? Are you interested in renting it?"

"No. I'm just wondering if she left anything behind that might give us an idea who killed her."

"Us? Who do you mean?" Eleanor asked sharply.

Lucky stammered. "I guess I mean all of us. This has hit the Spoonful hard. And if people are afraid to come into town, other businesses will suffer too. We haven't had one customer since the body was found—not one. Well, Hank and Barry, but they're there so much it almost doesn't count. And now with Sage in jail, I don't know how I'll keep the place going anyway."

"I sympathize. But it's nothing you should be meddling with. That's Nate's job, and I know he's searched that cabin."

"Are her things still there?"

"Right now they are. Nate finished up but I'll have to arrange to have her things packed up."

"Did she have any family?"

Eleanor shook her head. "Just a brother and he lives out West somewhere. So I guess whatever was hers in Snowflake will get shipped to him."

"So there's no harm done if I have a look around, is there?"

"Lucky, I can't let you do that. Bad enough the owners have lost all that rent, and I had to tell them we couldn't list it yet because of the investigation—plus they'll probably lose out on the rest of the season."

"Who owns that cabin?"

"A retired couple from New York. Nice people. They used to ski a lot but don't get up here very often now, so they rent it out."

"Can you let me have a key?"

Eleanor groaned. "Lucky, if you want my honest opinion, I don't think it's a good idea for you to be involved in this."

Lucky stared at Eleanor and said nothing. Eleanor blinked first. "Oh, all right. Fine. I will loan you the key just for today. And whatever you do, don't move anything around or take anything away. I can't even imagine what Nate would say if he knew I did this."

"I swear. I won't say a word. No one will ever know I was there."

"You have to get this key back to me by the end of the day. If I'm gone, just slip it in the mail slot, but don't you *dare* tell anyone I gave you this."

"I won't tell a soul. Cross my heart." Lucky made a quick cross over her heart with her finger. For a moment, she almost laughed, remembering schoolgirl promises made with solemn vows. "And maybe I'll find something that will point me in the right direction. Somebody killed her, but I don't for a minute believe it was Sage."

Eleanor shrugged. "I hope you're right. For your sake, at least."

THE DRIVEWAY HAD been cleared of snow with a shoveled path that led to the front door. Lucky pulled up to the garage and turned the engine off. She wondered if Nate had located the murdered woman's rental car—a red Jeep from what Janie and Meg had told her. The house was positioned near the top of the hill, within a short walking distance to other homes, but no house was close enough to observe the front door or driveway. Patricia Honeywell had wanted to guard her privacy well.

Lucky climbed out of her car and walked slowly up to the front door. The original house had been a cabin constructed of logs, but modified and remodeled over time. She turned the key in the lock and stepped inside, resisting the urge to call out—after all, no one could answer now. From the street, the house appeared a modest size, but inside, it was spacious with wide floor-to-ceiling windows at the rear offering a view of the mountains. A stairway led down to a lower level. Eleanor had mentioned there were two more bedrooms, a bath and a laundry room downstairs. This was a lot of house for one woman. A deeply cushioned sofa faced the stone fireplace, and an antique clock ticked softly on the mantel.

Lucky walked slowly down the hall, all her senses on alert, hoping to absorb the atmosphere of the house, hoping to gain some understanding of who Patricia Honeywell was and why someone wanted her dead. A faint wisp of perfume hovered in the hallway. There was only one bedroom on the main floor. The scent of perfume was stronger here. This had definitely been the room she used. A pale green silk robe was tossed over the end of the bed. The bedcovers were rumpled, half on the floor. More than one person had slept there last. Several ski outfits, two pairs of wool slacks, a black pantsuit and two cocktail dresses hung in the walk-in closet. Heavy boots and slender black leather ones, along with three pairs of high heels, were lined up on the floor of the closet. On the upper shelf were sweaters in varying shades of blues and greens, folded neatly. A heavy red cable-knit sweater took up the rest of the shelf. Lucky reached up to feel the material. A few of the sweaters were definitely cashmere. She closed her eyes for a moment, trying to visualize Honeywell's clothing the day her body had been found. She had been wearing a black outfit, slacks, sweater and a black fur jacket.

Had Nate found a cell phone on her body? Lucky couldn't remember seeing a purse, but she couldn't be sure. Possibly it was buried with her under the snow. And where was her rental car? Maybe Nate would discover she had been killed in her car and her body dumped behind the restaurant. That might go a long way toward dusting off the Spoonful's reputation. She immediately felt a pang of guilt for the thought. A woman had been killed and here she was worrying about the Spoonful's reputation—not to mention the fact that a murderer was probably still on the loose.

Lucky spotted a thin laptop case on top of the desk. It was empty inside. Nate must have taken the laptop to examine the contents. Hopefully the police—Nate or others—would check her e-mails. Those could lead them to someone who had a motive to kill her. A black leather datebook was tucked into the side pocket of the laptop case. Lucky pulled it out, riffling through its pages. She spotted a notation for the starting date of the lease in January, and the address of this house. Eleanor Jensen's address and office numbers were jotted in the margin next to that in a bold scrawling hand. Inside a pocket of the datebook were several receipts. Lucky pulled them out and laid them on the desk. All local receipts—for clothing and restaurants at the Snowflake Resort.

She checked the calendar from the end pages at the back where a section was empty for notes. On the last page at the back was another Snowflake address, with no name. Lucky recognized it as one of the streets in the Lexington Heights area. She grabbed a notepad from the drawer of the desk and jotted the address down—201 Brewster. The address of a friend or some other connection she might have had in town?

Lucky quickly scanned the pages covering the next few months where Patricia Honeywell had made entries for dinner dates, a ballet and a party she would never be attending. Turning back to the page for the day of the murder, she worked back in time. Other than a notation for the start of the lease, the pages were blank.

She shivered suddenly, aware of the emptiness of the

house. She couldn't shake the feeling that someone was hovering. *I'm imagining ghosts,* she thought.

Lucky carefully opened each of the drawers. They were filled with skimpy lingerie, gloves, hats and scarves. *Nothing like looking in someone's underwear drawer to glean information about them,* she thought. The top drawer held jewelry, gold earrings, a bracelet dotted with diamonds, a gold watch and several necklaces. All these things spoke of a careless elegance, a woman who never worried where the next expensive outfit or dinner was coming from.

In the desk drawers, she found lift ticket stubs, brochures from the Lodge and a business card from the Snowflake Clinic. Had she been a patient there? Gone for a flu shot? That would be something she could ask Elias. A large, soft leather purse with multiple side pockets was thrown carelessly in a corner on the floor. Inside was the slim wallet Lucky had seen at the Spoonful on the day she picked up her order. Lucky opened it—no photos, several credit cards in the slots but no driver's license. Was her license with her the night she was murdered? A small tapestry pouch with a zippered top held a comb and lipstick. Had she gone out that night with only her driver's license, keys and a cell phone in a pocket of that beautiful fur jacket? Had Nate found those items on her body? Or were they somewhere in her missing car?

In the bathroom, bottles and jars of lotions, creams, nail polish, lipsticks and rouge containers littered the counter. Lucky recognized several expensive brands. The wastebasket held a few tissues and clumps of blonde hair cleaned from a brush. If Marjorie and Cecily were correct, Honeywell had a secret lover and perhaps had carried on more than one affair. Would there be DNA evidence in the house linking her to other men? Would Nate be able to conduct such a high-tech search? Or with Sage in jail, would he even consider it? If there was something here that pointed to another person with a motive, maybe Nate would listen and rethink his decision to arrest Sage.

Lucky diligently opened each drawer and cabinet in the

bathroom but found nothing other than a toothbrush, a box of tissues and some rolls of toilet paper. Had Patricia Honeywell not left a single clue as to who she was seeing, and who dined with her every Tuesday? Or had her killer returned here after the murder and methodically removed any evidence of his existence? Perhaps, she thought, the kitchen might yield something—a pad of paper with a phone number, anything. She stepped out of the bathroom and walked down the hallway. She glanced at the stairs leading to the downstairs bedrooms. As long as she had the key, she might as well leave no stone unturned. She felt for the light switch. The stairway was immediately illuminated with recessed lighting. She grasped the banister and took a step. Something hard pushed against her upper back. She gasped and tried to turn—too late—as she tumbled headlong down the stairs, landing on her side before everything went black.

Chapter 14

SOMEWHERE FAR AWAY someone was crying—a woman. Lucky was certain her eyes were open, but everything was coated in a gray mist with shifting shapes. She couldn't remember where she was, and the woman's crying was hurting her ears. Lights came into focus. It was a chandelier, but how strange it should be hanging like that on the wall. No, it wasn't a wall, it was a ceiling. The light was hanging from the ceiling and she was on the floor. The house on Bear Path Lane. That's where she was. At the foot of the stairs. But for heaven's sake, if only that woman would stop her crying.

Her eyes were finally able to focus. Someone was moving her head and something cold was pressed against her temple. She shivered violently and tried to sit up but her legs wouldn't cooperate. The crying stopped suddenly and a face appeared surrounded by a cloud of intensely orange hair like a psychedelic halo, inches away from her face. The face was familiar, but Lucky couldn't place her right away.

"Oh, Lord, I thought you were dead," the woman cried. "I never had such a fright in my life."

Lucky tried to speak but only a croak came out. She recognized the voice—Flo. It was Flo Sullivan. "Flo? What happened?"

"Lord in heaven, Lucky, when I realized it was you—I thought somebody had killed you—just like that other poor woman. What are you doing here?"

Flo Sullivan had worked for her parents for several years, off and on, at the Spoonful. She had been widowed many years earlier, when Lucky was still in grade school. Lucky knew Flo sometimes did light cleaning at many of the winter rentals. Eleanor must have forgotten that Flo would be at the house today, or more likely, Flo made her own schedule and turned up when it suited her.

Lucky managed to speak. "I was just starting down the stairs when . . ." She hadn't imagined that hand on her back, shoving her forward. She had turned, but whoever it was had crept silently behind her. She hadn't seen a thing. "Somebody was here. Somebody pushed me."

"Oh, Jaysus." Flo quickly made the sign of the cross over her breast. "That's it then. I quit. They can get somebody else to clean this place. I should have quit right away when I heard about that murder."

Lucky sat up slowly. "How long . . ." She couldn't form the words correctly. She had no idea how long she had been unconscious. Had someone meant to kill her or only put her out of commission for a while? Someone must have been in the house when she arrived. Or perhaps they had entered with a key when she was busy searching the desk and the bedroom. "Flo, when did you get here?"

"Just a few minutes ago. I come by twice a week for the cleaning. The bedroom upstairs is a mess—it's all torn up. I thought someone had broken in and I was that terrified, I was—especially after what happened to that Mrs. Honeywell. And I didn't realize it was you till I took a good look."

"Can you help me up?" Lucky winced as she struggled to her feet and a sharp pain flooded her head.

"I couldn't believe my eyes it was you. I haven't seen you for almost . . . what? Five years? Whatever are you doing in this house?"

"Snooping, I guess you'd call it."

"Well, it's wonderful to see you—even like this. I heard about your parents, dear. I'm real sorry. They were such nice people."

"Flo, I didn't really break in. Eleanor Jensen gave me the key. I just wanted to have a look around. But you can't tell anyone. Please? I don't want Eleanor to get in trouble with Nate."

"I won't, dear, if you don't want me to. But let me make us some tea and we can sit and have a good chat and catch up. Just keep this ice on your head, now."

Flo led Lucky slowly up the stairs. Lucky clung to the banister, trying to push the dizziness away. Flo led her to the sofa in front of the fireplace and made sure she was settled.

"You stay right here. I'm going through this entire house. I just want to make sure nobody's lurking around. Then I'll make us some tea." Lucky listened to the clock ticking softly while Flo moved from room to room, checking under beds, opening and closing closet doors, checking the shower stall. Finally, she turned the lock on the front door and the kitchen door and a few minutes later returned with two cups of hot tea with honey.

Lucky reached for one of the cups. "Thank you, Flo. This is just what I needed."

"Now, tell me. What are you looking for?"

"You've heard they arrested Sage?"

"No!" Flo gasped. "Never! That nice young man? Whatever for?"

"That's just it. We—Jack and I—we just don't know, and I don't have any information from Nate. And when I went to the jail to see Sage, he wouldn't tell me anything either."

"And how is your grandfather these days, dear?" Flo asked neutrally.

"Oh, he's fine." Lucky recalled a time years before when Flo had set her cap at Jack and made numerous attempts to interest him. Jack was having none of it and was terribly

relieved when Flo found other employment. He'd be anything but thrilled to hear that Flo was still asking for him.

"You're sure your young man at the restaurant is
innocent?"

"Just instinct, Flo, but I can't imagine Sage—he's shy
and really gentle—I can't imagine him hurting anyone,
particularly a woman. I don't believe he killed her. In fact,
I'm sure he didn't. But everyone's staying away in droves,
and we've lost a chef. I guess I was hoping that I'd find
something here that would tell me who else was in Patricia
Honeywell's life. Who else might have had a motive to murder her."

"Well." Flo took a deep breath, gathering herself for a
gossip fest. "She was the talk of the town. There were a few
men buzzing around. A lot more than just buzzing, but I
can't tell you who. I wish I could, but I can't. I only come in
during the day, and that woman—Mrs. Honeywell—she was
always out—skiing, I guess, or doing who knows what. But
I can tell you this—she had a man in her bed most nights.
Whether it was one or more than one, I can't say. But I could
tell. One skinny blonde woman couldn't make such a mess
of a bed as she did. She had company, believe me!"

"That seems to be the general consensus around town.
But who? Who was she seeing? Somebody wanted her out
of the picture and had to have a good reason."

"I don't know, dear. Whoever came here to spend the
night with her—if they actually did spend the night—I never
saw them. I come in late mornings and I'm gone in an hour
or so, so I have no idea. There's a landline here, but I doubt
she ever used it. She had her cell phone."

"Speaking of which—I've looked all over and I don't see
one. She must have had it on her when she was killed."

"Between you and me, if I were the murderer, I'd make
sure that cell phone was in tiny pieces and never found."

Lucky nodded. "You're right. But I'm afraid that if Nate's
convinced Sage is guilty, he won't do a real investigation—
find her cell number and examine the records. For whatever

reason, he's sure that Sage had the best motive of all. It's not that I know him so well, because I don't. But he's worked for my parents for several years and they thought the world of him."

"Then he must be a good person. He couldn't have pulled the wool over their eyes all this time."

"Flo, if you can think of anything—anything at all that might lead to someone who did have a motive, please let me know."

"There was something odd . . ." Flo took another sip of her tea and replaced her cup on the saucer. "Nothing definite, but she wasn't quite the same these last few days. Something was making her very nervy."

"Do you know what?"

"I don't, I'm sorry to say, but I thought maybe somebody was threatening her. Several times when I was here the last couple of weeks, the phone rang. Normally, I wouldn't pick it up, but I thought maybe it was the realty office trying to reach me."

"Who was calling?"

"Have no idea. The first time, a man's voice said, 'Get out of town and don't come back.' Made me jump out of my skin, I'll tell you."

"What did you do?" Lucky asked.

"I yelled right back at him and said, 'Whoever you are, you leave this house alone.' I think the call was to scare her and whoever it was realized then that I wasn't her at all. It happened a few more times, but there were no words. He just breathed heavy and hung up." Flo folded her fingers around her teacup and leaned closer, almost whispering, "And she had a gun."

"A gun? Whatever for?"

"I tell you, she was scared of somebody. I came here late in the day one time. It was already dark. She wasn't expecting me that late. She was fine once she realized it was only me, but she was real jumpy nonetheless."

"Did you tell her about the phone calls?"

"I most certainly did." Flo sniffed.

"What was her reaction?"

"She looked a little strange, a little white around the lips if you know what I mean. At first she didn't say anything, just stared at me real cold like the eyes of a dead fish, and then she laughed. Not a happy laugh neither, more like a 'we'll see about that' kinda laugh, and she said something then."

"Do you remember what it was?"

Flo shook her head and looked off in the distance, thinking for a moment. "I don't remember exactly, but something like 'We'll see who gets out of town first, won't we.' Fair sent chills down my spine, something in her eyes."

Lucky's head was finally clearing. "Flo, what did you say earlier about the bedroom being torn up?"

"It's a complete mess. I'll have to straighten it all up, but I tell you I'm not coming back here—never! Come on, have a look."

Lucky followed Flo down the hall and stopped in shocked silence when she saw the room. Every drawer, every item of clothing had been pulled out of the closet. Every box and its contents had been dumped on the floor. Diamond jewelry embedded in the carpeting glittered in the overhead light. The bedclothes had been pulled off the mattress, and the mattress and box spring were tipped on their sides.

"Flo, it looked nothing like this when I got here. I rummaged around, but I didn't disturb a thing."

"I believe you, dear. Somebody pushed you down the stairs and somebody was desperate to find something she had."

Lucky shook her head in disbelief. "But what? There was nothing here except some expensive jewelry and clothing. Nate must have taken her laptop and any papers she might have had. Whatever they were searching for is probably at the police station."

Lucky bent down and picked up the scattered pieces of jewelry before they were stepped on and crushed. "Here, Flo, I'll give you a hand. This bedding is way too heavy for one person." She moved to the other side of the bed and together they maneuvered the box spring back on the bed frame and finally the mattress.

"Just dump all those linens in the hallway. I'll have to wash those and put them away for whenever they get the next tenant."

"Okay. I'll hang the clothes back up in the closet. I think Eleanor's arranging for someone to pack up all this and ship it to her brother."

"That's fine, but it won't be me. I'm taking all this to the Laundromat. I don't want to be in this house one more minute than I have to."

"You never saw any men up here with her?"

"Nope. Never saw anyone, even though I could tell they were here and had spent the night—if you know what I mean."

Flo stood with bed linens piled high in her arms and gave Lucky a dark look. "You be careful, Lucky. For all you know this was a narrow escape. Whoever killed her wouldn't hesitate at killing again."

Chapter 15

WHEN LUCKY WOKE the next morning, the throbbing had stopped, but a small egg had formed on the back of her head. Wincing, she reached up and touched it gingerly. Her shoulder was bruised and stiff. She limped to the bathroom, downed two aspirin with water and made a cup of strong coffee. As soon as she felt the coffee take effect, she climbed into a hot shower and let the water run over her until her muscles loosened up.

With a towel wrapped around her, she opened the closet door and stared disconsolately at her wardrobe. It was so limited. She owned one good suit that she had worn for job interviews, a dressy black number that would never do for a casual dinner, a serviceable black wool skirt, a pair of slacks and slightly worn leather boots. The rest of her clothes were more suitable for a college frat party. She needed to get dressed for work soon, but she wanted to plan what she'd wear for her dinner that night with Elias. Was she being terribly vain to be worried about one outfit when everything around her was falling apart and a murdered woman had been found behind the Spoonful? The truth was, she was terribly nervous about spending time with him. She couldn't ignore the fact that his presence, even after such a long absence, still had a powerful effect on her.

She slipped out of her robe and pinned her wet hair up. She pulled several items out of the closet and tried them on. She really did need to treat herself to something new. Marjorie and Cecily had suggested she stop in at the Off Broadway. No better excuse than wanting something a little nicer to wear for a dinner invitation. She hung her robe on a closet hook, pulled on a pair of socks, underpants, warm slacks and a sweater, then rehung all the clothes in the closet, folded up the rest and placed everything back in the drawers. She had much more pressing things to deal with than worrying about one dinner date.

She opened the hallway closet where she had stacked the boxes from her parents' house. The first was full of books she had decided to keep, and since she didn't have a bookcase as yet, they would have to wait. She lifted that box aside and opened the next. This one held framed family photos. She unwrapped them carefully and carried her two favorites to the bedroom, placing them on top of the bureau. One was a snapshot of her parents on ice skates on a pond in the woods. They were smiling widely at the camera, her father's ankles buckling slightly on his skates. Even though his arm was draped protectively around her mother, she was sure it was her mother holding him steady on the ice. As hard as it was dealing with their death, it was easier than imagining one of them without the other. Her father would never have been able to cope with the loss of her mother. And even though her mother may have been the stronger of the two, the joy in her eyes would have faded. Lucky kissed the photo gently and placed it on the bureau. The other photo was of Lucky and her mother at her college graduation, their arms around each other. Lucky beamed at the camera—was she ever so young only six short years ago—while her mother leaned her head gently against Lucky's cheek. A sob rose in her chest for all the years she had taken her parents for granted.

She took a deep breath to quell the grief that threatened to rise up again.

She pulled her old CD player out of the next box. It was one she had used in her bedroom all through high school and still used when she had come home for visits. Tucked in next to it were several CDs she had cherished. They probably wouldn't be Jack's taste, but she wouldn't mind hearing them again. She left the player and CDs on the floor in the hallway to take to the Spoonful later. It might be nice to listen to music—with or without customers. If nothing else, it would lift their spirits a little. The next box held her mother's sewing machine and yards and yards of fabric. She carried the sewing machine to the kitchen table. There must have been projects her mother had never gotten around to, but perhaps she could use this fabric to make curtains for the apartment. She smiled, hearing her mother's words in her head. *I just knew this would come in handy.*

She lifted out the various folds of material and carried them to the bed. One was a white and blue plaid fabric, mostly white with a thin dark blue plaid pattern—perfect for curtains for the kitchen window. She measured it, stretching her arm out and holding an edge to her chest— about four yards, just right for café curtains. Another was a muted floral print in rose tones with a chinoiserie feel to it, as though copied from an oriental print. The bedroom, she thought. She quickly measured and refolded it—more than enough for bedroom drapes and even pillow covers. For the first time since she had returned home, she looked forward to creating something new that would help her feel she belonged. What could be better than using fabric her mother had chosen?

She quickly checked the clock. She'd have to hurry if she wanted to find something at the sisters' shop and then get to work. She refolded all the fabric and carried it to the linen closet. Running her hands over the cloth, she held it to her face, relishing the aroma and imagining her mother's hands caressing it as she picked it out.

* * *

THE SISTERS WERE sitting on stools behind the glass display case when she arrived. Cecily waved. "Oh, it's Lucky! Come on in, dear. We were just talking about you."

"I hope it was all good."

"Don't be silly. Of course it was," Cecily replied, looking a little sheepish. "Sorry we haven't been in lately."

"I noticed. I was hoping you'd come back and break the evil spell. We've opened every day since the murder, but no one seems to want to come near us. And of course, now with Sage . . ."

"Ooooh, we heard. That's just terrible. Do you think . . . ?"

Lucky was sure what the unspoken question was, and she stated emphatically, "No. I do *not* think Sage is guilty. Quite the opposite, and I'm going to try to do everything possible to get him out of this situation and back to the Spoonful. We'd fall apart without him."

Marjorie looked at Lucky over the rim of her glasses. "You seem very sure."

"I am. I really am. I think Nate jumped the gun. And I think the murderer is still out there somewhere."

"Well, dear, I certainly hope you're right—about his innocence, that is." Marjorie's words held a dubious tone. "But I don't like the idea of a murderer being among us. Even if Sage is innocent, who do you think killed that awful woman?"

"Everyone around seems to have taken a great interest in her. Janie and Meg said they've seen her with one of the ski instructors up at the Lodge."

"Oh yes," Cecily said. The sisters nodded in unison. "I'm sure that's true. And I don't think she was ungenerous with her favors, if you know what I mean."

"That's just it. Who else was she seeing?"

"Well," Cecily said breathlessly, "we all know about the double order on Tuesdays."

"What's the significance of Tuesday, do you think?"

"Someone who could only get away one night a week?

Someone who had to make excuses. Perhaps a married man?" Marjorie sniffed.

Cecily replied, "What a scandal that would be if it came out."

Marjorie cast a withering look at her sister. "Enough of that dreadful subject. That's all anyone can talk about, it seems." She rearranged her face and smiled at Lucky. "We're so glad you came by. Let me get some of those sweaters from the back—I think you might really like one or two." She slipped behind the curtain separating the shop from the storage room.

Once she was out of earshot, Cecily leaned over the counter and whispered, "I am sorry we haven't stopped in. I think Marjorie's afraid."

Lucky leaned closer. "Afraid of what?"

"Of being associated with a murder—afraid it might hurt our business. But frankly, I'm going to have a word with her. This just isn't right, not supporting your friends." She reached across the counter and squeezed Lucky's hand. The gesture brought tears to Lucky's eyes.

"Thank you, Cecily. I mean that—from the bottom of my heart. I'm really worried about Sage, about Jack, about the restaurant. If the real killer isn't found, and something happens to Sage, we could go under. It's bad enough tourists are staying away, but we need our regular customers to support us too."

"I know, dear. If Marjorie wants to be standoffish, that's fine, but I'll be there every morning from now on for my tea and croissant."

Marjorie pushed her way through the curtain and laid a pile of neatly folded sweaters on top of the display case. One in particular caught Lucky's eye. It was a soft periwinkle blue with a scoop neck and long sleeves. She placed her carry-all containing the CD player on the floor and picked up the sweater. She moved to a full-length mirror and held it under her chin.

"It's your size. It'll be beautiful—bring out your eyes."

Cecily smiled. "Are you looking for something for your date with Elias?"

Lucky felt her cheeks grow warm. "Oh no. Not really. And it's not a date," she declared emphatically.

The sisters nodded knowingly in unison. "Of course it's not, dear."

Cecily was right. The color accentuated the deep blue of her eyes. "I think I'll take this."

"Good choice. I'll wrap it up, and we'll knock off twenty percent—very reasonable. And I'm sure that nice doctor will appreciate it too."

Lucky bit her tongue, tired of having to convince people that her interest in Elias was merely platonic, afraid to reveal her feelings if Elias's interest in her was only platonic. She just smiled and said, "Thank you."

"Don't you want to look through the rest of our new things?"

"I'd love to, but I have to get to the Spoonful. Jack's alone. We might not have any customers, but I feel I should be there."

Marjorie nodded. "Of course. Come back soon, though."

"And I'll see you tomorrow for my tea and croissant," Cecily chimed in, shooting a meaningful look at her sister.

"Great—see you then." Lucky smiled and pushed through the door, heading up Broadway toward the Spoonful. Her thoughts were focused on the upcoming dinner with Elias, and she realized her stash of cosmetics and toiletries was woefully thin. She needed shampoo and some moisturizer, and a little clear nail polish wouldn't hurt. She pulled off her gloves and studied her hands—red and raw, with nails that needed help.

Being "feminine" had never come naturally to her. Was the ability to wear makeup and play with dolls a genetic trait? If so, she had been left behind the door when those gifts were given out. Her college roommate had taken pity on her, teaching her to apply makeup and experimenting with updos for her hair. She insisted that Lucky go shopping with her and bored her to tears with fashion magazines. She now knew the difference between a pencil skirt and a dolman sleeve—for all the good that would ever do her. Flagg's Pharmacy was on the way, and there was no time like the present to get her life as organized as it could be for now.

She waved to Jerold Flagg as she entered. He was standing behind the glass partition above the pharmacy counter. He smiled and nodded at her in return. She picked up a plastic basket and wandered down the aisle devoted to hair and skin care. She dropped a small container of moisturizer and a bottle of shampoo in her basket, adding a tube of lip balm to keep her lips from chapping in the winter air. At the end of the aisle was a revolving rack of CDs. One caught her eye—she knew Jack would love it—a compilation of famous bands from the forties. She dropped the CD in her basket.

Nail polish was on the other side of the pharmacy along the wall. Two women were chatting as she approached. She maneuvered around them and found a display case of products that claimed to guarantee an end to split nails—*if only,* she thought. The two women didn't appear to be tourists, but neither did she recognize them as locals. She hadn't intended to eavesdrop, but she was so close it was impossible not to overhear.

"I can hardly believe it—that something like this could happen here . . ."

"Isn't it just awful?" the second woman exclaimed. "We left the city because of things like this and now here we are. It's as though the crime spree has followed us."

Lucky had no doubt they were discussing Patricia Honeywell's murder.

"And that restaurant . . ." The words were said in a tone of complete disgust. "Why, we almost ate there one night."

The other woman snickered. "Good thing you didn't, with a murdering chef."

Lucky's face was on fire. Hot anger swelled in her chest. Who were these women that they could speak so disparagingly of the Spoonful and of Sage? They knew nothing, but had already made up their minds. There it was—in a nutshell—the reason everyone was staying away.

Before she could stop herself, she turned, her face bright red. "Excuse me."

The two women stopped in midsentence and turned to her, smiling.

"I couldn't help but overhear." They continued to smile as though meeting a stranger who'd agree with their opinion.

"I'd like you both to know that the restaurant you speak so judgmentally of happens to be *my* restaurant. And in case you don't already know, it's really an excellent place that my family has spent years building. More importantly, our chef, contrary to some opinions, is *not* a murderer." Lucky sensed rather than saw Jerold's attention focused in their direction. He likely couldn't hear their conversation but was definitely aware something in the atmosphere had shifted.

"So"—Lucky took a deep breath to calm herself—"I, for one, would appreciate your being a bit more circumspect with your comments and your gossip."

"Well . . ." one woman breathed. They weren't smiling now.

"Well, nothing," Lucky replied. "Please remember that no one has been convicted of a crime—least of all our restaurant, and your casual speech could actually hurt people." She turned on her heel and headed to the counter where Jerold was waiting. She plopped her basket down and reached for her wallet. She was sure her face was flaming. Jerold said nothing as he rang up her purchases. Lucky handed him a few bills and said, "I'm sorry. I hope I haven't scared away your customers, but I'm sick and tired of wagging tongues."

"That's quite all right, Lucky. If anyone deserves to speak her mind, it's you." He smiled and winked. Lucky turned and headed straight for the door without another look at the two women who stood speechless, watching her.

Chapter 16

LUCKY BRUSHED OUT her hair and let it flow over her shoulders, adding a touch of lipstick and a little blush. She was worrying far too much about this dinner. She needed to keep things in perspective. No matter what Elias said, he was being kind and trying to be a friend, maybe the only friend she had in town other than Elizabeth and Jack. And she sorely needed friends.

For all she knew, Elias could already have someone in his life. She was sure he must have dated many women in the past several years—women who were undoubtedly far more sophisticated than she. If so, he had been discreet, since she hadn't heard a word of gossip about him since she'd been back in town.

She slipped on a long winter coat and wrapped a scarf around her neck. His house was only a few blocks away. It was silly to take the car. She grabbed her purse and headed down the stairs to the sidewalk. Outside, the temperature had dropped and the air was dry and crackling. She tucked her scarf closer to her neck and turned north toward Hampstead Street, her boots crunching in the freezing snow.

When she reached the house Elias had described, the one she remembered, she stood for a moment admiring it. An old brick path, cleared of snow, curved up to the front door. Lilac bushes, her favorite, lined the side of the property, now blanketed with mounds of snow like melted marshmallow. Their bare branches poked out from under and glittered with encrusted ice in the moonlight. She imagined them in May, their heady scent filling the air and bursting with voluptuous purple blooms.

The house itself was white, its doors and shutters painted a soft grayish lavender. She wondered if the color had been chosen to match the lilacs in bloom. The house was three stories tall and topped with a peaked roof. Narrow front double doors held long panes of etched glass. Each window was rectangular except the one window at the top just under the eaves. It was curved in a half-moon shape, and below that on the second floor was a rounded window of stained glass that probably overlooked the staircase. The side porch had been enclosed at some point in time with large windows in keeping with the architecture of the house. All in all, it was lovely, more beautiful than she had remembered.

Lucky hurried up the path toward the front door and ducked into the vestibule, protected from the cold night air, and rang the bell. A figure approached, outlined against the etched glass of the inner doors. Elias opened one side, a broad smile on his face.

"You made it. I was feeling very ungentlemanly for not picking you up."

Delicious cooking smells filled the hallway. Lucky smiled. Why, oh why, did he engender such warm feelings in her? "That's quite all right. I'm a big girl." She almost said, *It's better that you didn't. It would have been the talk of the town and I wouldn't have been able to keep a straight face.*

"Come right in. Here, let me take your coat." He slipped it off her shoulders and hung it on a mirrored coatrack by the front door. Lucky looked around the entryway. To the right was an old-fashioned parlor, a formal dining room to the left. "Let's get back to the kitchen before I burn everything or we'll have to go back to the Spoonful for food."

She followed Elias through the swinging door into the kitchen and stared in awe. "This kitchen is huge. It must be the largest room in the house."

"Now you see why I need company. It's too big for just one person. I had it partially remodeled to bring it up to date, but kept the original oak cabinets and as many fixtures as I could."

"I really like what you've done."

"Let me get you some wine." Elias reached into the refrigerator and uncorked a chilled bottle of Pinot Grigio, pouring a small amount into a crystal wineglass.

"Tonight, *mademoiselle*, we're having wild salmon with grilled red potatoes and an arugula salad. I hope you like all of this."

"It sounds divine. I can't remember when I last had a complete home-cooked meal."

"Just happy to have a free night. My on-call schedule varies from week to week, but I'm off the hook tonight." Elias separated the salmon onto two plates already warmed in the oven. He carried the dishes to the kitchen table. The salad was dressed and chilled and the potatoes were hot in their serving bowl. "Please have a seat."

"You work Monday through Friday?"

"And half a day on Saturday—it varies. We're closed on Sunday, but we switch days off. Friday's my day off this coming week. But that's a lot easier than your schedule. I'll bet there are no days off in the restaurant business."

Lucky laughed. "Absolutely right." She sat at the round kitchen table and spread a linen napkin over her lap. Elias turned off the overhead light and struck a match, lighting two candles that stood in holders on the table.

"Elias, this is absolutely wonderful. I had no idea you were so talented."

"You should see what I can do in the lab! But then again, you might lose your appetite."

Lucky smiled at the witticism and dove into her meal, embarrassed that she was so hungry.

"There's something I've always wanted to ask you."

Lucky, surprised, looked up. "What's that?"

"Your real name. What's Lucky the nickname for?"

Lucky suppressed an embarrassed laugh. "It's not a nickname. Jack named me. It's my real name."

"You're lying. Tell me."

Lucky burst out laughing, almost spilling a potato on her lap. "No!" She had no intention of telling Elias how her name came to be.

"Why? It can't be that bad!"

Lucky shook her head.

"Come on. What is it? I promise not to laugh."

"Not a chance." Lucky flashed on a memory of Jimmy Pratt from grade school, a bully who terrorized every kid he could. For a solid year, he taunted her mercilessly about her real name, following her all the way home from school, laughing and hollering out her name, just to annoy her. One day a crowd followed them and the rest of the kids joined in on the joke. Her given name was old-fashioned, but it wasn't so horrible that Jimmy Pratt should make her the butt of a joke.

She had spent months ignoring him, but on that day, something inside her snapped. She turned and decked him with a terrific right hook. Blood spurted from his nose and poured over his shirt. The crowd fell silent. She hit him again for good measure and heard a sickening sound. She had broken his nose. Jimmy's nose never healed right. It stayed lopsided, and Jimmy never teased her again. In fact, he never spoke to her again, which was just fine with her. Her parents were horrified, but when Jack heard the story, he gave her a thumbs-up and said the kid deserved what he got. He would honor her by calling her Lucky, after a Navy boxer he admired. She had no intention of recounting the real story to Elias. No way.

"Okay. Okay. Truce. I promise not to hound you." Lucky

thought for a moment that it might be quite nice to be hounded by Elias.

His expression became more serious. "How are you adjusting?" He watched her carefully.

Lucky's smile faded. She thought for a moment before answering. "It's as if everything is exactly the same, and yet nothing is the same. I feel like Dorothy, swept up by a tornado and deposited in a very strange country. The hardest part is dealing with the loss of my parents. I still . . . I have to struggle with that every day. It's just so unfair for them to end like that. Unfair for them and unfair for me."

"That's a pretty normal reaction."

"I look around and sometimes feel as if my life in Madison was something I imagined and sometimes being here feels like the dream. I suppose it will get better, at least that's what I keep telling myself."

"It will. The old adage is true. My personal belief—when the tornadoes hit, whatever may have caused them, they put you down on the path that you're supposed to be on."

"Let's hope you're right." She chewed thoughtfully on a grilled potato. "You sound like you've had a few tornadoes yourself."

Elias smiled. Lucky did her best not to stare at the dimples in his chin. "I suppose you could say that. I certainly could have ended up in some specialty practice at Tufts or one of the bigger institutions in New England."

"Didn't appeal?"

"Well, I wouldn't say that. That was my original plan, but I realized I wanted the type of practice that would give me more of a connection to a community. And when I first saw Snowflake, I fell in love with the place. It was just luck that the opportunity fell in my lap when Dr. Stevens retired. And then the practice grew, so we added Jon."

"I know I've never met him. How long has he been here?"

"Let's see, when Dr. Stevens retired—you remember him, I'm sure—that was eight years ago, so Jon moved up about a year and a half later."

"Where from?"

"His practice was in Boston—family medicine. I think he and Abigail, his wife, both felt they needed a change of pace, and they loved it up here, so when he heard about the position, he was eager to take it. Frankly, I've been afraid he might become bored, but he seems very happy with his work."

"Kind of easing into retirement for him and his wife?"

"Oh, hardly. He's only in his midfifties and certainly not ready to retire. I think the pace of the city and big hospitals got to him. Wanted to enjoy life a bit more before hitting the speed limit. Everyone loves him at the Clinic. You'll meet him soon." Elias held out the bowl of potatoes. "More?"

"Mmm." Lucky shook her head. "You finish them."

Elias ladled the last few potatoes onto his plate. "So now it's just the two of us, one medical assistant, one RN, two receptionists and a records clerk. Oh, and we have an orthopedic specialist we can call in if need be, just in case we end up with casualties from the Resort."

"Doesn't the Resort have resident doctors?"

"Yes. Very good ones—two orthopedic surgeons, and a trauma specialist, which is mostly what's needed at a ski resort, unfortunately." Elias grimaced. "And I have some other duties as well. I'm the official . . ." Elias stopped himself in midsentence. His face flushed slightly and he popped a piece of potato into his mouth.

"You're the official . . . what?" Lucky asked.

"Nothing. Tell you some other time. More salad?" He reached over to the serving bowl.

Lucky stopped with her fork in the air, suddenly understanding. Her face grew pale. "You're the coroner for the County."

Elias nodded in return. "I'm sorry. That was careless of me."

Lucky sighed. "I don't know what's worse, knowing exactly what happened to my parents in the car that night, or imagining what might have happened."

"Lucky, I am truly sorry. I wanted to cheer you up and get your mind off of that, not dredge it up."

"It's not your fault. It's never far from my mind anyway."

"If you ever decide you want to talk about this, you just let me know. I will tell you one thing—if it's any help—it all happened very quickly. They did not suffer."

Lucky felt her shoulders relax. She took a shaky breath. She realized she had been bracing herself in case she heard details she wasn't sure she'd be able to handle. She breathed a sigh of relief. "Well, that's something. Thank you."

Elias nodded in response. "I'm sorry I haven't had a chance to come down to the Spoonful in the past couple of days. My schedule's been so tight. Have people been staying away?"

"You've heard about Sage, I'm sure."

"Yes, but do you know why he's been arrested?"

"I haven't had a chance to talk to Nate yet. Not that he'd confide in me, but I can at least try. And I tried to talk to Sage at the station."

"What did he have to say?"

"Nothing. He was completely closed down. Upset, really—that I went to see him. I just wish . . ." Lucky trailed off. "I just wish I knew more about this woman—this Patricia Honeywell. Somebody obviously had a motive to kill her, but I cannot believe it was Sage."

"How can you be so sure?"

Lucky speared the last piece of salmon on her fork. She was quiet for a moment before speaking. "I saw him a few seconds after he discovered the body. He couldn't even talk, he was so upset. And just before that, he had been his usual self, quiet, in good spirits."

"I hate to say this, but how do you know he isn't just a very good actor?"

Lucky shrugged. "I don't. I guess I'm just trusting my instincts, and Jack's opinion of him too. He's known him well for the past few years while I've been gone. He has good insight when it comes to people."

Lucky remembered the card for the Clinic that she had found in the murdered woman's bedroom. "Elias—I have to ask you something. Do you happen to know if she was a patient at the Clinic?"

"Who? The victim?" Elias stared into space, lost in thought. "I was about to say 'no,' but it's perhaps possible she was. I can check with our receptionists. To tell you the truth, I just assumed she was a tourist, but she might have come to the Clinic for some reason and I never knew about it."

"How did she die?"

Elias put down his fork. "She was hit right here," he said, pointing to the left side of his head just above the temple. "The blow caused a fracture and internal bleeding. Look, I don't mean to cut you off, but I really shouldn't be talking about this."

"Come on, Elias." Lucky persisted. "What was she hit with?"

Elias sighed. "This is between you and me, okay? I have no idea, but I'd guess a heavy object with maybe a rounded edge. What it was I can't say for sure unless the object is found."

"So—no chance this was an accident?"

"No." He shook his head. "She was hit with a great deal of force."

"I just want to know how and why she ended up behind the Spoonful. I'm thinking she wasn't killed there, and worse yet maybe she was still alive and left there to freeze and die in the storm." She shuddered involuntarily. "Nate was there with a technician, and I suspect they were looking for something to indicate one way or the other whether . . . if that was where it happened."

"We'll know eventually, and in her condition—" Elias stopped in midsentence.

Lucky looked up from her dinner. "What did you say? What condition?"

"Nothing. I'm sorry. Let's change the subject—this is no conversation for dinner."

"No, Elias. Really. I want to know. What did you mean?"

He sighed. "Can you keep this to yourself? It will come out eventually, but I'd rather not have it known it came from me. I'm the coroner, but I'm not a pathologist. We called in someone from Lincoln Falls and I attended. Please don't mention this to anyone just yet."

Lucky nodded. "Of course."

"She was pregnant."

"Oh," Lucky breathed. "Oh," she said again, thinking of the implications. "So who was the father?"

"We may never know. And that doesn't necessarily mean it has anything to do with why she was killed."

Lucky thought about the house on Bear Path Lane, the rumpled bed and silk robe and aroma of perfume. She thought of telling Elias about her search of the house and the attack, but held back. She had promised Eleanor not to breathe a word about being given the key, and she could imagine Elias's reaction if she shared the information.

"I follow your logic, but it also could have everything to do with why she was killed." Lucky scooped up the last piece of potato on her plate. It melted in her mouth. "This is so delicious, by the way. Thank you."

"Don't thank me yet. I expect help loading the dishwasher." Elias smiled. "Hey, let's throw a log on the fire and keep it going. And I promised you a tour."

Lucky waited at the foot of the stairs while Elias lifted another log onto the already blazing fire. He prodded the embers with a poker, wiping his hands on a small cloth, and turned to her, smiling. Her heart skipped a beat. She was enormously attracted to him, and embarrassed that her feelings might show. If only she could be the kind of woman who could appear reserved and aloof.

Elias led her into the dining room and turned a knob, illuminating a glittering crystal chandelier that sent sparkles of light dancing around the room. "I built this seat into the window area myself and had these seat cushions made."

"I'm impressed. When and where do you find time to do all this?"

He laughed. "Every chance I get. I have a small carpentry workshop in one of the garages. It feels good to be actually building something by hand. The craftsmanship is what appeals to me." He turned the knob, dimming the chandelier. "Let me take you upstairs."

"This house needed a lot of TLC when I bought it. A lot of the plaster was old and cracked and had to be redone. It was a messy job, but it's finally over. I started at the top with the roof and then had the bedrooms upstairs replastered and the floors refinished. Finally, after what seemed like years—maybe it was, after all—I managed to work my way down to the first floor. Whatever I could do myself, I did, but when it came to plumbing and electrical, I was lost and had to hire people."

Lucky peeked in each bedroom; one was obviously Elias's room, and another had been put to use as an office, with a small sofa, desk and file cabinets. The other two bedrooms were minimally furnished with beds and bureaus, obviously for guest rooms. "I love the colors you chose. They're subtle, but warm." She turned to him. "You must love this house very much."

Elias grinned, proud of his handiwork. "I do. I grew up in the city and always dreamed of owning a home. All my living quarters have been cramped dorms or apartments. Believe me, I never planned on buying an antique that required so much work, but it has good bones. It's built with wood and details you couldn't even find or afford to buy today. And I've enjoyed restoring it. I guess it's been my avocation for the last few years—an escape from work. Don't get me wrong, I love my work, but everyone needs variety in life."

They descended the stairs and returned to the parlor. "Have a seat. Would you like more wine?"

Lucky nodded. "A very small glass would be nice."

Elias returned from the kitchen carrying two glasses and the bottle he had opened earlier. He poured a small glass for Lucky and sat on the sofa. This was the most heavenly evening she had enjoyed in a long time, she thought. After her initial nervousness, she had come to feel almost as if she and Elias were equals—compatriots, not an older man and a too young schoolgirl. She still didn't know quite how to evaluate the evening that she was in the middle of. It had all the makings of a romantic tête-á-tête—a wonderful dinner, wine, a blazing fire. Yet Elias sat at the other end of the sofa and made no move to draw closer. Eventually they lapsed into a comfortable silence, both of them staring at the fire.

"Have you made any decisions about the Spoonful yet?"

She turned to him. "I haven't had a chance to even think lately, what with Sage being arrested. I feel terrible that Jack's had to shoulder the burden for so many weeks, and now, with business the way it is, how could I even think of selling? I just don't know what I can do."

"If your parents were still here, would you have considered coming back?"

She smiled. "If only. I honestly don't know. Even before I got the news I was at a loss as to where my life was going. My major was theatre arts—without a graduate degree in something, I wasn't really qualified for very much. I held jobs—some of which were interesting but paid very little. Madison's a really nice town, with the University and all, but it wasn't the same once I finished college. I was thinking of a teaching credential for lack of anything better, and then all this happened."

Elias nodded. "I guess I was lucky. I always knew what I wanted to do, even when I was very young. I've never been in doubt about it. How I was going to get there was always the struggle. But I got through and here I am, and very happy in Snowflake."

"You never get bored?"

"Never. Although rattling around this big place gets lonely sometimes, I still wouldn't trade my life for anything."

Lucky stifled a yawn.

"Sleepy?"

"Yes. I'm sorry. How rude of me. It's been such a long day. I should be going."

"I'll walk you home." Elias rose from the sofa.

"There's no need. I'll be fine."

"Not a chance. I invite a lovely lady to dinner and allow her to walk home alone in the dark and cold? What kind of a cad would I be?"

He left the room and returned with her coat and his own. He held her coat while she slipped it on. A freezing blast of air hit their faces when he opened the outer door. Lucky followed the winding brick path, and when they reached the sidewalk, Elias tucked Lucky's arm under his. Their boots crunched on ice crystals as they walked. For a moment she wondered what it would feel like to be enfolded in his embrace, to be held close. She had a quick vision of Elias drawing her near for a long, passionate kiss. She quickly pushed the thought away. His behavior was completely gentlemanly and friendly—nothing more. This was all her own fantasy.

But when they reached the doorway to her apartment building, Elias leaned toward her. She caught her breath. She felt it. It was unmistakable—he was attracted to her; she was sure now. It was only for a moment. Warmth suffused her body. She was grateful for the darkened street, sure that her complexion would betray her feelings. Elias kissed her gently on the forehead. "I hope *you* weren't bored."

"Not at all—I'm embarrassed I was so sleepy, but I was so comfortable."

"Just think of me as your doddering maiden aunt."

"Stop!" Lucky laughed.

"Maybe we could do this again?" he suggested.

Lucky smiled in response. "I'd like that." Elias turned away, waving as he walked down the street. Lucky stood at the foot of her stairs, watching him as he shoved his hands in his pockets and finally turned the corner. She climbed the stairs and pushed open the door to the vestibule. Part of her was relieved Elias's outward behavior was friendly and noncommittal and that she hadn't made a fool of herself by expecting more, but part of her was sure there was more behind that chaste kiss. She had to admit, a big part of her yearned for more—she had been lonely for far too long.

Lucky used her key to open the front door of the apartment building. The hallway was dimly lit by a small wall sconce. She shut the door behind her, making sure the lock had caught, and turned to head up the stairs. A shadow moved. Strong fingers gripped her arm. A scream came to her lips as adrenaline coursed through her veins.

Chapter 17

"WHERE HAVE YOU been?" a voice hissed from the dark.

Lucky's heart pounded a fast rhythm. "Sophie? You scared me half to death! What are you doing here?"

"Waiting for you. One of your neighbors let me in. I want a word with you."

"Keep your voice down. I don't want to wake the whole building. My apartment's on the second floor. Let's go upstairs."

"I don't want to come up. I just want to know what you told the police that made them arrest Sage," she spat out in an accusatory tone.

Lucky stared at her blankly. "What are you talking about? We didn't tell the police anything. Nate walked in, said he was sorry, and arrested Sage. We had no warning that was about to happen. And I have no idea why. Do you?"

Sophie's shoulders sagged. She shook her head. "No. I don't. And Nate wouldn't let me see him today."

Lucky remembered the conversation she had overheard between Sage and Sophie the night she returned to the Spoonful for the cash bag. Their voices had carried clearly in the cold night air. "Sophie, tell me something. What were you and Sage arguing about the other night? Was it about this Honeywell woman?"

Sophie curled her lip. "She tried to play head games with me. She said she knew Sage a few years ago—and there was a lot about him she'd bet I didn't know. Then she made it sound like they were still in touch—implying that something was going on between them. She made me so furious. I confronted Sage about it, but he denied it up and down. But still . . ." She hesitated. The dim lighting was playing tricks. It kept Sophie's face in shadow, her eyes the only visible feature. "There was something . . . I couldn't put my finger on it—I just felt there was more he wasn't telling me."

Lucky heard a door open and close upstairs. She whispered, "Look, if you don't want to come up, you've got to keep your voice down."

"Okay, okay. I will."

"I think you're right. I think he did know her from somewhere. She came into the Spoonful one day. Sage had just come out of the kitchen, and when he saw her, he ducked back very quickly. He did recognize her. But that's all I know, believe me."

Sophie's eyes narrowed. "Are you saying you think there was something going on between them?"

"No. I don't think that at all. It was more that . . . he was afraid of her."

"You haven't answered my question. What were you doing at the jail? I saw you coming out of the station."

"I went to see him. I wanted to know if there was anyone I could contact for him or anything he needed."

"Why did you do that?"

"Sophie . . . you can't possibly think . . ." Lucky was taken aback by Sophie's tone, realizing the depth of her jealousy. "He works for us. He keeps the Spoonful running. You surely don't think I could replace him very easily, if at all. And now, with the murder, we've had no customers—no one wants to come in. It's awful for us."

"And that's your only reason? You're concerned about the Spoonful?" she replied sarcastically.

"No, it's not. Just get off it, Sophie. We care what happens to Sage. Granted I don't know him very well, but my parents thought the world of him. They really cared about you too. You know, my Mom always wrote to me every time she ran into you or heard news about you."

Sophie's eyes widened. "Oh." She took a shaky breath. "I meant what I said at the restaurant, you know. I was really torn up when I heard what happened to them."

Lucky was silent, too afraid if she opened that door she'd dissolve in tears. "Do you know if Sage has any family that should be contacted—other than Remy?"

Sophie shook her head. "Not that he's ever mentioned. I've tried to get him to talk about that stuff, but he just brushes it off."

"Jack and I have been bringing food to the station for him, and will be at least until the arraignment. If you like, I'll keep you posted and I'll tell him you're worried about him. I'm sure Nate will let you see him."

Sophie almost managed a smile. "Thanks, Lucky. I appreciate that."

"But, Sophie, listen. This Honeywell woman seems to have had quite a reputation. Can you sniff around the Resort and see what you can find out? Somebody had a motive to murder her, and if I can gather some information, maybe I can talk to Nate and keep him interested in looking further than Sage."

"You would do that for us?"

"Of course I would. I don't think he did it and I think he's been wrongly accused."

"I do too. If you really mean that, I'll give you a call soon." Sophie hesitated, then said, "I know she was fooling around with a couple of the guys at the Resort—a ski instructor and another guy. I don't know how far anything went or if it was serious. Somehow I don't think so—at least on her part. But I'll ask around and see what I can find out." Sophie pulled the front door open and then turned back. "Lucky, I'm sorry."

"For what?"

"For being so hateful for so long."

"It's gone and forgotten."

"No, I mean it." Sophie grasped her hand and whispered, "I was just so jealous of you."

"Of me?"

Sophie nodded. "You had everything I wanted—a family that cared about you. A chance to go to school—everything . . . Sage is the best thing that's ever happened to me. This is my chance and I don't want anybody to take it away."

"Sophie . . ." Lucky couldn't think what to say in response to such naked honesty. "It's all in the past. I mean that. Just find out whatever you can and let me know."

CECILY HAD SPREAD the word through town and on Saturday morning the Spoonful finally had its first customers since the discovery of the murder victim. She and Marjorie both arrived for their morning tea and croissants. Julie, the pastry chef from Bettie's Bakery, had stopped by at lunch to ask if they'd be needing any breads or rolls this week. Lucky had to tell her they wouldn't, but hopefully business would pick up soon. The truth was, they'd be in big trouble if business didn't pick up—the bills would still need to be paid. Without Sage, she didn't know how she'd ever be able to manage. For now, she and Jack and their few customers were surviving on soups that Sage had prepared ahead of time and frozen. Once those were gone, she'd have to start cooking herself, and she trembled at the thought. Even Jerold Flagg from the pharmacy had come by at lunch for a bowl of Sage's Hungarian goulash with dumplings. It gave her some slight hope they'd be able to meet their bills—at least for this month.

Jack sat at the corner table studying Hank and Barry, who were evenly matched in a chess game. He wanted to learn the game, and Hank was giving him blow-by-blow instructions and pointers as the pieces moved. Once the restaurant had cleared, Lucky poured a cup of coffee and joined them.

"Okay, Jack," Barry said. "Look at this, the rook can move all the way across the board in either direction, but only in a straight line. Like this"—he smiled—"as I take Hank's bishop." Barry leaned back in his chair gloating.

Hank groaned. "Why, you rotten so-and-so, I didn't even see that coming."

"You're asleep at the switch, you old fool. I'm beating the pants off you."

Jack laughed but quickly stopped as Hank shot a dark look in his direction. Hank turned to Barry. "Just for that, you can walk home."

"What are you talking about? Of course I'll have to walk home. They haven't even plowed my street," he grumbled. "Can you believe that?" He turned to Lucky and Jack. "I've complained to the company, but they say their contract with the town ends at the top of the hill. They plow all the way up Bear Path Lane and stop at the corner of Crestline. What's that about? I've gone to the town council and they've done nothing. How are we supposed to get our cars out?"

Lucky stopped with her coffee cup halfway to her lips. "What did you say?"

"I said, they refuse to plow my street. They keep telling me they're contracted to the town and my street is outside the town limit. If Hank wasn't willing to pick me up at the corner, I'd be snowbound. Just ridiculous!"

"No, I mean what you said before about Bear Path Lane."

"That's the one they plow and they stop when they get to the top of the hill. Why?"

"That's the road where Patricia Honeywell was staying."

"Oh yes?" Barry asked. "Which house?"

"The log cabin with the big windows at the back."

Hank nodded. "That's right. I've seen that red Jeep she used to drive around town parked in front."

Lucky asked casually, "Ever see any other cars parked there?"

Barry snickered. "I'm sure there were a few."

Hank ignored him. "Tell you the truth, I never took much interest. But, now that you mention it, I was driving home up the hill one night a few weeks ago and somebody pulled out of that driveway in a big hurry." He turned to Barry. "Remember? I told you about it the next day. Scared the life out of me. I had to slam on my brakes. I thought he was going to crash right into me."

"He?"

Hank's eyes widened. "Oh, I just meant the generic 'he.'"

"You didn't see who was driving?"

"Nah, it was dark and the lights blinded me. We both stopped and then he backed up and I passed. I had forgotten about it till you mentioned it."

"What kind of a car was it? Do you remember?"

"Well, I didn't get a license number if that's what you mean, but it was a sedan, compact size, kind of a light color, like white or silver, which is probably why it stood out in the dark."

He looked up sharply at Barry. "I know what you're thinking, but you're not gonna get away with it." He moved a piece to protect his queen. "Ya see, Jack, if I hadn't done that, his bishop could move diagonally and take my queen and that would be it—that's all she wrote." Jack nodded, studiously concentrating on the moves the men were making.

Lucky heard the phone ringing in the office. She left her coffee cup on the table and hurried down the hall to grab it in time. She was half hoping it might be Elias, calling to ask about another date. Breathless, she grabbed it on the fourth ring, just before the answering machine clicked in.

"It's me," Sophie said. "Can you come up to the Lodge tonight? There's somebody I'd like you to meet."

"Okay." Lucky knew this wasn't just a social call. It had to have something to do with her promise to help Sage.

"Eight o'clock. We'll be in the bar."

"I can make that." Lucky was sure that if any more customers showed up this afternoon, they'd be long gone before eight o'clock.

"See you then." Sophie disconnected.

Lucky replaced the receiver. Who was it Sophie wanted her to meet? Someone who had information about Honeywell? Had to be. She was heartened to think there was a chance she and Sophie could be close friends again. More importantly, she sincerely hoped Sophie's heart would not be crushed. If she could prove Sage innocent, Sophie would have a chance at the life she wanted.

Chapter 18

LUCKY COULDN'T HELP the niggling envy she felt when she surveyed the après-ski crowd at the Mountain Retreat bar. She scanned the noisy denizens. They appeared without worries, relaxed, drinking and sociable. Everyone seemed to know everyone else, yet this was a crowd of strangers to the town of Snowflake—another world existing at the top of the mountain.

The raftered ceiling was high, yet the dark woods and dim lighting created a warm ambience. A double-hearth fireplace of rustic stone dominated the center of the room, the bar stretching out behind that. Lucky skirted the fireplace and spotted Sophie at the bar. Her curly dark hair stood out against her red sweater. She was nursing a cocktail and talking to a tall, good-looking guy in a ski parka. She approached slowly, wondering if this was the reason for Sophie's call. Sophie was talking and gesturing in an animated fashion and at the same time scanning the room. She spotted Lucky and waved her over, moving down one stool so Lucky could sit between her and the man in the ski parka.

She skipped any preamble. "Lucky, this is Josh—he teaches here too. Josh—Lucky."

"Hi," Josh said, flashing a well-crafted smile.

"Tell her what you told me today," Sophie announced.

Josh's face shifted, betraying momentary confusion, suddenly realizing there was more to this meeting at the bar than he had expected. That was just like Sophie, Lucky thought. Direct, but never really open.

"Hey, come on. This isn't for public consumption." He flashed a warning look in Sophie's direction. "I asked you not to say anything."

Sophie's lips tightened. "Get off your high horse and just tell her what you told me about Patsy Honeywell."

Josh's eyes narrowed. Silent signals flashed through the air, but Sophie was determined and Josh finally seemed to realize that. He sighed and turned to Lucky. "I was seeing her—kinda off and on. She was a lot of fun. But it was nothin' serious."

"Seeing her secretly?" Lucky asked.

"Oh no. She wasn't exactly shy." He snickered into his glass.

Lucky flashed a look at Sophie, who appeared intent on her cocktail and had seemingly tuned out. "So why don't you want to talk about it?"

"I don't want to have to answer a lot of questions. I don't want the cops crawling all over me."

Sophie laughed mirthlessly. "The cops aren't even awake if you ask me."

"But wasn't she seeing other guys too?" It was very quick, but a momentary shadow flashed across Josh's face.

"I don't know," he grumbled, placing his drink on the polished bar. "To tell you the truth, she kinda dumped me. One night . . ." He grimaced. "One night I got a little drunk and showed up at her place. Maybe I was more than a little drunk, I don't know."

"What happened?"

"She opened the door but she wouldn't let me in. She was

really pissed off. I was pretty sure there was another guy with her."

"Did you see him?"

Josh shook his head. "Nah, don't know who it was. I saw a car in the driveway, another one besides hers, and I guess I got kinda mad." He looked up from his drink. Lucky thought about how young he looked, younger than she had initially thought, his youth obvious once he dropped the façade of the dashing ski bum. "I was a real jerk, I admit. I was banging on the door—I guess I knew I had had too much to drink but I couldn't stop myself."

"Do you remember what kind of a car you saw?"

Josh shrugged. "No. No idea, really."

"Try."

Josh shrugged. "I don't know. It was light colored— maybe a kinda metallic color."

Sophie sat quietly, intently watching their exchange.

"Do you remember anything else about the car?"

Josh's lips twisted slightly as he stared into his glass. "There was a sticker on the back bumper."

"What did the sticker look like? Can you remember?" Lucky had the feeling that if she kept pushing him, he'd recall something useful.

"Just a sticker—like a parking permit. It was blue and white, or white with three or four big blue numbers, and there was a word . . . like Wood something, Wood . . . I don't know. The only reason I remember that was 'cause I slipped on the ice trying to get back to my car and I grabbed onto the back bumper to get up on my feet. I told ya, I was an idiot. Didn't realize how drunk I was—otherwise I would never have gone to her house like that. I should've known I wouldn't be welcome—or there'd be another guy there. Didn't really think it through." He shrugged. "That's really all I remember."

He finished his drink in one gulp and shot Sophie a look. "Look, I don't want this to get around, and I also don't want the cops asking me any questions. I've got a good thing goin'

here. If she got herself murdered, it's no skin off my nose."
He slipped a ten-dollar bill on the bar and flashed Sophie a
lopsided smile. "Next time you ask me to have a drink with
you, remind me to say no."

Josh turned and headed for the exit to the lobby, ignoring
a wave from one of the men seated by the fireplace. Lucky
turned to Sophie. "Hope this doesn't cause you any
problems."

Sophie waved her hand in the air dismissively. "He'll get
over it. Not my fault if he jumped to the wrong conclusion
when I asked him to have a drink." She smiled impishly. "I
just wanted you to hear that story from the horse's mouth.
It's not that I think Josh bashed her head in, but I'd guess she
was seeing somebody else and maybe that was serious . . .
and maybe that somebody else got real jealous."

"Lots of maybes," Lucky replied.

Sophie waved the bartender over. "What'll you have,
Lucky?"

Lucky shook her head. She wasn't in the mood to relax.
"A coffee'd be great." The bartender nodded and moved
away.

"Apparently she had a habit of picking up two orders to
go from the Spoonful on Tuesdays. I wasn't all that observant of her order, or rather I didn't think much about it, but
Marjorie and Cecily—you remember them?"

Sophie nodded. "Oh yeah, the two sisters at the Off
Broadway." She snorted. "Not much they'd miss."

"They were . . . well . . . gossiping, I guess you'd say . . ."

"*Quelle surprise!*" Sophie remarked sarcastically.

Lucky ignored her remark and continued. "They told me
she always picked up a double order on Tuesdays but nobody
could figure out who she was meeting or getting together
with."

"Maybe she has a big appetite."

Lucky laughed. "You know, that's exactly what I said."

"And I can just imagine what those two had to say."

Lucky continued. "Whoever she was with, it must have
been rather secretive if nobody in town had an inkling."

"Damn." Sophie slammed her drink on the bar, spilling a few drops. "That's what I can't stand. Everybody's in your business. It's unbelievable."

Lucky shrugged. "There are worse things. It's annoying, but at least people look out for one another."

"I guess. But wouldn't you think somebody would have noticed who Honeywell was seeing?"

"You would think. And why stay up on Bear Path Lane and not at the Resort? Apparently she wanted her privacy, or at least that's the reason she gave Eleanor Jensen when she rented the house."

Sophie shrugged. "Who knows? Maybe somebody whose reputation would be ruined. Maybe somebody whose marriage would blow up." Sophie's eyes narrowed. "What was it the sisters said to you? Only Tuesdays?" Sophie looked thoughtful. "That definitely sounds like a guy who's married—like that's the night he tells his wife he's bowling with the boys, or some such nonsense."

"How did you get to meet Honeywell?" Lucky asked.

Sophie's lips twisted. "Patsy Honeywell—that woman was a witch! She ran a number on me about how she admired my technique and could she hire me for some privates and so on—money was no issue. The first lesson, I realize now, was a setup. She pretended to be having trouble with certain moves. The second time we got together it was obvious she didn't need any coaching. She was an expert skier. She only hired me 'cause she had some ax to grind with Sage. She really wanted to cause trouble between us. Whatever was behind it, I don't know. He wouldn't tell me, but she made it obvious she was thrilled to run into him again—like whatever was going on before could be going on now. I was furious. And she enjoyed watching me squirm. I would have been happy to do her in myself!"

"What did Sage say when you asked him?"

"He swore up and down he hated her and he'd just as soon see her dead."

Chapter 19

LUCKY FLIPPED THROUGH a three-year-old magazine about early childhood parenting. Considering the wealth of information about the care of infants, she decided that keeping a failing business going was far less complicated than caring for an infant. No wonder she never liked playing with dolls. Jack shifted uncomfortably in the vinyl chair next to hers. He was bundled up in his jacket and refused to take it off.

Rosemary, the receptionist at the Clinic, put down the phone and smiled at them. "Shouldn't be much longer. Dr. Scott will be ready for you soon." Lucky was temporarily taken aback to hear Elias referred to so formally—"Dr. Scott" had such an impressive sound.

She had questioned Jack about his medical care and learned he hadn't seen a doctor in almost ten years. He looked a little sheepish admitting that, but immediately countered with the remark that he was as strong as an ox and better off staying away from doctors. It took some convincing, but he finally agreed to have a wellness checkup when Lucky insisted. She was fortunate to be able to get him in first thing on Monday morning, usually a very busy day at the Clinic. Jack wasn't happy about any of it, and she was there with him to make sure he kept his appointment.

He shifted around in his chair and leaned over to whisper, "Lucky, my girl, none of this is necessary. I'm as healthy as the proverbial horse."

"Thought it was an ox."

"Ox then, Miss Smarty Pants," he grumbled. Rosemary looked up from her counter and smiled in their direction. Jack nodded to her.

"I know you are. I just want you to have an annual physical—have everything checked out. It's important."

"I'm not sick, Lucky—I just get confused sometimes. It's my nerves—that's all it is."

Lucky put down her magazine and reached over to squeeze his hand. "I know, Jack. Just humor me, okay? You're all the family I have now, and I want to make sure you have an annual checkup and a doctor who knows your history."

A buzzer rang on Rosemary's desk. She picked up the phone and said, "Okay, thanks." She looked over at Jack. "The nurse is on her way now." Jack, impatient, heaved a sigh and rose from his chair.

Lucky tossed the magazine back in the rack. "I'll be waiting right here for you."

A smiling woman in a pink uniform, her brown gray hair pulled back in a bun, pushed open the door and spotted Jack. "Mr. Jamieson? Hello. Please come right this way." Jack glanced back at Lucky. He looked as if he were heading to a gallows. Lucky gave him an encouraging smile.

The waiting room was empty now. Rosemary had watched their exchange with a sympathetic look. "He'll be fine. They'll take his weight and blood pressure, and draw blood for a CBC. Then he can talk to the doctor."

Lucky nodded in response. She hadn't had a chance to talk to Elias since their dinner last Friday night, and deliberately hadn't said much about Jack's "spells," as she thought of them. She didn't want to influence any opinion Elias might form. When the results were back, she'd find a private

moment when she could hopefully talk to Elias about her
fears.

Rosemary continued to stare at Lucky. "You're Lucky
Jamieson, aren't you?"

Lucky nodded and smiled in return.

"My friend Janie works for you. We went all through high
school together. She's really my best friend. She told me
about you—how you went off to college and lived in Madison. That's so great. I hope I can save enough money to do
that too. It must be so exciting to be anywhere but here."

Lucky smiled ruefully. "Sometimes. Yes. But there's no
getting away from yourself, and after a while, it's just the
same as if you never left."

"Oh, don't say that! It's all I dream about."

Lucky remembered her own yearnings when she was
younger, sure that greener pastures awaited her. She didn't
want to disillusion Rosemary at her tender age, or stomp on
her dreams. "And once you've been away, then sometimes
coming home is wonderful too."

Rosemary shrugged. "I guess. Wouldn't mind finding out."

The door on the far side of the room opened. It was
marked with a sign that said NO ENTRANCE. A plump woman
in a long beige coat with a fur collar stepped into the waiting
area. She smiled and nodded to Rosemary and walked out
through the front door. Rosemary sat up slightly straighter
in her chair and returned a tight smile.

Lucky raised an eyebrow and looked questioningly at
Rosemary. Rosemary turned to her. "That's Mrs. Starkfield,
Dr. Starkfield's wife. She stops in a lot."

Lucky spoke very quietly. "Do I detect a teensy bit of
dislike?"

Rosemary dropped her professional air and leaned closer.
"Oh, she's all right—she means well. It's just . . ." Rosemary's voice trailed off.

"Just what?"

"Actually, I feel a little sorry for her. I think she's kinda lonely. She and Dr. Starkfield never had any kids, and she tries to keep herself busy. She comes into the Clinic to help out with whatever we need. It's just—she's the boss's wife, you know. You feel like you don't want to make a mistake or say the wrong thing in front of her."

"And the other staff people don't mind?"

"No. Not at all. She and Dr. Starkfield are so cute together—he's very tall and she's so short. He adores her and we all love him. She volunteers a lot of time at St. Genesius too. She's head of the Ladies' Auxiliary. I'm sure she pretty much runs the show—has a lot to say about which minister gets hired, who's allowed to plan their wedding there, that kind of stuff. And besides, Elias is really the more senior doctor, even if he's younger. And Dr. Starkfield's real nice. We all like him a lot." Rosemary beamed.

Lucky smiled to herself, wondering if the women here had the same crush on Elias as she had always had. She picked up her magazine and managed to read two long articles, something she usually never had time to do. Finally, she heard voices approaching from the corridor. The same nurse in the pink uniform opened the door and held it as Jack returned to the waiting area. Elias followed behind him. Elias shook Jack's hand and said, "It's been a real pleasure meeting you, Mr. Jamieson."

"Call me Jack, please." He was smiling. Lucky breathed a sigh of relief.

Lucky rose and joined him as he headed for the front door. She smiled and waved to Elias.

He called out, "Lucky, give me a call when you have a minute. Let's talk about next weekend." Jack was slipping on his coat, and while his back was turned, Elias winked. Lucky realized Rosemary was staring unabashedly and felt her cheeks flaming. She did her best to avoid Rosemary's gaze.

Elias turned and reentered the corridor to the examining rooms. Lucky held the door for Jack, and as it closed behind them, she gave Rosemary a quick wave. When they had walked a few steps away from the Clinic entrance, Lucky asked, "Well, how did it go?"

"Fine, I guess. The nurse said they'd call if there was any question about the results. So I guess I'll have a clean bill of health."

"Good," Lucky replied. "That wasn't so bad, was it?"

Jack shrugged. "Those docs always make me nervous. But that young man wasn't bad at all. He a friend of yours?"

"Mmm, yes. I guess he is."

Jack stared straight ahead as they walked. "That's good. We all need friends." Lucky glanced at him quickly to see if he was teasing her, but his expression remained neutral. Jack never missed much.

As they turned the corner to Broadway, Lucky said, "Jack, I have a quick errand to run. Can I meet you at the Spoonful in a half an hour?"

"Of course, my girl. You go ahead. Janie's gonna be there—her mother's calmed down. We'll be fine."

"Thanks." She stood on tiptoes and kissed his cheek. "I'll see you in a bit."

Jack smiled and turned away, heading down the street to Broadway. Lucky stood in the bright sunlight watching him walk away. He moved slower, she noticed, his posture more stooped than she remembered. She felt a sudden pang in her chest, frightened that something could take him away. She had to make sure that didn't happen soon. Without him, what real connections would she have—not just in Snowflake, but anywhere?

She turned away and headed back to her apartment building where her car was parked. She dug her keys out of her purse and climbed in. Inside the car it was much colder. She shivered and turned on the engine, hoping it wouldn't take too long to warm up. She rummaged in the side pocket of her purse and found the slip of paper with the address she had discovered in Patricia Honeywell's datebook.

She turned back to Broadway and drove north out of the town center. Near the end of the road, she made a left before it continued to the highway. Mohawk Trail wound slowly up the hill, the homes becoming larger as she approached the top. This section of Snowflake had been built more than fifty years before, but by Snowflake standards, the neighborhood was new. It was an enclave of the wealthier residents of town, including those employed at the higher end of the corporate structure of the Resort. The house at 201 Brewster sat elevated up from the street, a two-story colonial with a brick front, its peaked roof covered in snow.

Lucky leaned over the passenger seat as she drove past, curious to get a better look. She reached the top of the hill where a small park had been carved out and then turned and drove slowly down the hill again, stopping one house before she reached number 201 on the opposite side of the street. She pulled over to the side and turned off her engine. The interior of the car was warm now, but it wouldn't last very long without the heater running. Curiosity drove her, but now that she was here, she had no idea what to do. An address in a murder victim's calendar—jotted down quickly in a margin. How had Nate overlooked Honeywell's datebook, or missed this address? What significance did it have, if any?

Perhaps Honeywell had known the residents of this home? Had they been her friends? For all anyone knew, the dead woman could have had friends—maybe even relatives—who lived in the area. That alone could be the reason she was in Snowflake. Cold started to seep through the floorboards. Lucky turned the key in the ignition and cranked the heater on full blast, shifting the dial so the rush of warm air hit her feet. What should she do? Could she simply walk up the stairs, ring the bell and ask whoever answered if they knew Patricia Honeywell? Was it possible whoever lived here had not heard of the murder? Lucky thought, *Unlikely.* And of course they might deny knowing the victim for fear they'd be entangled in a murder investigation.

Just as she had finally come to the decision to ring the bell and see who answered, the front door opened, and a woman and a young girl of perhaps ten came out. The girl was carrying a knapsack with a pink design that looked like an elongated cat. The woman wore slacks and a heavy jacket with a hood. She hurried to an SUV parked in the driveway and unlocked the doors. The young girl climbed in the passenger seat, and the woman leaned over to make sure the girl's seat belt was secure. The car backed slowly down the incline to the street and headed down the hill. Lucky put her car in gear, half wanting to follow them, but before she could, the garage door slowly rose and a white sedan pulled out on the drive. The car also backed down the steep driveway, as the garage door closed. The driver executed a turn and, following the path of the SUV, headed down the hill. On impulse, Lucky slipped the car into gear, following at a discreet distance. The white car headed down Mohawk Trail to the bottom of the hill. The SUV turned left toward the highway. The woman gave a quick toot on the horn as she made the turn. The white sedan, driven by the lone man, turned in the opposite direction, heading south on Broadway. Lucky followed several car lengths behind, passing the Spoonful and the shops on Broadway. When the driver reached Spruce, he turned right and drove up the hill toward Ridgeline. This was the route to the Snowflake Resort.

The driver didn't appear to be rushed. He moved smoothly up the hill, turning in at the stone-pillared entrance to the Resort and its attendant businesses. Driving to the very end of the main parking lot where the administrative buildings were housed, he parked in a spot near the front door. Lucky passed his car slowly, watching as he climbed out and headed for the entrance to the business offices of the Resort. These were housed in a building erected to resemble a small Swiss chalet, continuing the theme of the other buildings. He wore a long black coat over slacks and a sports jacket, a dark shirt with no tie and a plaid scarf around his neck. His hair was short and fair. He was somewhere in his midforties and carried a leather briefcase. The man appeared intently focused, a severe expression on his face as though he was about to reprimand his secretary or any other employee he found in his path.

Lucky watched until he entered the building and then backed up to read the sign above the reserved parking space—THOMAS REED—RESERVED. Lucky let her car idle behind the white sedan. Who was Thomas Reed? He lived in a large house near the top of Lexington Heights, with a wife and at least one child. And his address was in Patricia Honeywell's datebook. Was he another lover? Or was there more to the story than that? She needed to find out whatever she could about Thomas Reed.

Chapter 20

JANIE WAS HOLDING the fort at the Spoonful. She had just served soup and sandwiches to Hank and Barry, handling cook and waitress all in one. She smiled and waved at Lucky.

"Heard you met my friend Rosemary today."

Lucky smiled. "Yes. She introduced herself."

"She really likes working there but she's trying to save her money and maybe go to nursing school in a couple of years."

Lucky hung her coat on the peg that Sage always used in the kitchen. She lifted the lids of the two Crock-Pots to check that nothing was overheating or drying out. Janie followed her into the kitchen.

Lucky looked up and smiled. "I saw Mrs. Starkfield there too—Dr. Starkfield's wife."

"Oh yes." Janie moved closer. "She's nice I guess, but from what Rosemary's told me, she's always asking questions and trying to do things. I don't know if she's a control freak or thinks they're all shirkers. You know the type—one of those women who thinks she can manage her husband's office better. I don't know why she's there all the time. You'd think if she didn't have to work she'd be glad to stay away. Probably just doesn't have enough to keep her busy."

"Everyone speaks very highly of Dr. Starkfield."

"He's real nice. And he and his wife seem real close. He's always cracking jokes and making everybody laugh."

"And they like Elias too."

"Oh yeah, he's a dreamboat . . ." Janie stopped in mid-sentence, suddenly realizing that Lucky probably knew more about Elias than anyone else. She stammered, "I mean . . . I heard you were seeing him." Janie blushed.

"Oh no, not like you mean," Lucky hastened to reply. "We've just known each other a long time—we're friends."

"Uh huh," Janie answered with a neutral expression.

Lucky had no desire to fan the flames of any town gossip. She might be attracted to Elias, but that didn't mean it would be returned or that anything would ever come of it. Best to keep her feelings under wraps.

"Are you hungry, Janie? Why don't I fix us some soup and rolls for lunch, you and me and Jack? We've got a huge pot of this carrot with fresh ginger and rosemary."

"That'd be great. I am kinda hungry. And I guess it's lunchtime already."

Lucky grabbed a large tray and ladled out generous servings of Sage's soup. She quickly warmed some poppy seed rolls and laid them on a tray with a small butter dish.

Jack had been studying Hank and Barry's moves on the chessboard, but when he saw Lucky arrive with the tray, he joined her and Janie at the table. Jack shook out his napkin. "I made a list of what we have in the freezer. We should be good for a while."

"Let's just hope we get more customers soon."

Janie turned to Lucky. "I heard you went to see Sage. It's so horrible to think of him sitting in that jail. How's he doing?"

"I'm sure he's depressed, to say the least, but he didn't want to talk. I'm hoping he'll talk to Jack. And I want to make sure he gets some decent legal help. The court has to assign someone, but maybe there's a lawyer in town willing to help him. Jack or I will be bringing him food every day until . . . until they move him."

"Can't he get out on bail?"

"The arraignment's next Monday. The judge might set bail, or maybe deny it. We won't know till then. For now, he'll be in a cell at the police station."

"Poor Sage," Janie said. "Whoever would have thought . . . Meg still feels bad, still thinks it was her big mouth." She looked toward the front window, her eyes widened. "Oh no," she groaned.

The door banged open. Remy DuBois stood in the open doorway, swaying and obviously inebriated. He stomped into the restaurant leaving the door wide open behind him.

"Wha'd you do to my brother?" he shouted.

Jack rose and slammed the door behind Remy, shutting off the blast of cold air. "He's in a cell at the police station, Remy. You should go see him," he growled. "After you sober up, that is." He fixed Remy with a stern look.

"Wha'd you people tell the cops?" he shouted.

Jack and Lucky exchanged blank looks with each other. "Nothing," Lucky answered. "We have no idea what's going on. And Nate hasn't been talking to us anyway."

Remy attempted to lean casually against the counter but, missing his mark, almost fell down. He quickly caught himself, stumbling. "Yeah, sure. You're tellin' me you didn't hang him out to dry, is that it?" He was slurring his words badly.

Lucky felt a wave of frustration and anger rising in her chest. Why did everyone think she and Jack were out to railroad Sage? First Sophie and now Remy. She walked over to Remy. "No, we did no such thing, Remy. So get off it. You need to sober up and go see your brother—not come here bothering the people that are trying to help him."

Remy took a step, looking as if he were about to lunge toward Lucky. Involuntarily, she took a step back. Jack rushed over and, grabbing him by the arm, marched him to the front door. "You need to behave yourself and get straightened out—you'll be welcome here when you do that." He gave Remy a mild shove and shut the door firmly behind him. Then he turned the lock.

Remy grabbed the handle and rattled the door furiously, unable to believe it was locked against him. Swaying from side to side, he took a few steps back, reached down and grabbed a hunk of ice from the snowbank. He swung wildly and threw it at the front door, shattering one of the small panes of glass.

"You jerk!" Janie shouted.

"Damn . . ." Jack roared. "What's wrong with that kid?" He undid the lock and stormed out, slamming the door behind him. Lucky and Janie rushed over to the front window. Hank and Barry had halted their game to watch the exchange. Now that Remy was safely outside, they joined Lucky and Janie at the window.

Remy stood, his legs wide apart, trying to stay upright. He looked confused, as if just realizing what he had done. Jack approached him. Lucky couldn't hear what was being said, but she could tell Jack was lecturing him. Remy took a step backward and suddenly, like a rainstorm that ends quickly, his face collapsed, all the anger draining away. His chest was heaving and he burst into tears, falling into Jack's arms. They stood like that for a minute or so on the sidewalk. Finally Jack led Remy back inside, guiding him to a chair. He looked apologetically at Lucky. "Can you grab some coffee?" She nodded and headed for the kitchen.

"I'm sorry. I'm real sorry." Remy wiped his nose with the back of his hand. Janie looked at him disdainfully and passed him a napkin. "I don't know why I did that. It's just . . . he's my brother . . . I thought . . ."

"What did you think?" Jack asked as he sat down next to Remy.

Lucky placed a large mug of black coffee on the table. "I guess I thought you pushed the cops to arrest him. I thought you knew . . ."

"Knew what?" Lucky asked.

"About him and . . . that woman . . ." he trailed off.

Lucky and Jack stared back at him blankly. Janie sniffed

as if to say *What next?* and started gathering up dishes from the table. She carried them into the kitchen and dumped them in the sink. Hank and Barry turned back to their game, but Lucky was well aware they were hanging on every word.

"What about her?" Jack asked, not betraying that Lucky had told him Sage's history. There was no need to speak her name; thoughts of her murder were uppermost in everyone's minds.

Remy sniffed and did his best to blow his nose in the napkin Janie had passed to him. "They knew each other before."

"Before Sage came to Snowflake?"

Remy nodded. "You'll have to ask him. He made me swear I'd never tell." Remy grabbed another napkin and wiped his eyes. "I'll fix that pane of glass for you. I feel like a real jerk." Lucky caught Janie watching through the hatch. Janie rolled her eyes heavenward, as if to say, *You are a real jerk*.

"That's a deal," Jack said. "I'll put something over it for today. You come back tomorrow when you've sobered up and you can fix it then. In the meantime, drink this coffee and get it together and go see your brother. I'm sure he'd want to see you."

"I don't know about that," Remy mumbled, downing the last of his coffee. Remy stood up, still swaying. He turned to Lucky. "I'm sorry. I'll be back tomorrow to fix the glass."

When the door shut behind Remy, Hank and Barry approached Jack. "We'll be headin' out now, but we'll be back tomorrow. You let us know if you need any help with anything."

Jack thanked them and locked the door behind them, flipping over the sign to read CLOSED. Jack's face looked drained. His energy seemed to flag more often as the days passed.

"Might as well close up. Doubt anybody else will be showing up today."

Lucky said, "I can bring that food down to the police station if you're tired."

"Not a problem. I'll just put something over that pane and then head down to the station. Besides, I want to see Sage and show my support. I'm sure of one thing though."

"What's that?"

"Nate's got the wrong man."

Chapter 21

"YES, I KNOW Tom Reed." Elizabeth Dove was sitting behind a heavy oak desk in her office at the municipal building. The sky outside had turned leaden and gray. A desk lamp cast a yellow glow over the stacks of paper piled neatly around a central work space. A trailing ivy plant stood in a ceramic pot on the window ledge behind her desk, while the radiator hissed quietly underneath. Her assistant had entered a moment after Lucky arrived, handing Elizabeth a thick computer printout that looked like a budget report. Lucky could only imagine the duties Elizabeth shouldered as Mayor of Snowflake.

"Do you know anything about him?" Lucky asked.

"Well, yes. He moved here with his wife about six years ago. He's one of the original members of the LLC that owns the Resort. I couldn't tell you his official position though. What's this all about, dear?"

Lucky felt suddenly foolish. "I am so sorry to interrupt your day. I know Mondays are busy for you. We closed right after lunch and I wouldn't have bothered you, but I don't know who else I can talk to in confidence." She told Elizabeth about searching the house on Bear Path Lane and finding the Reed address jotted in the calendar. She deliberately omitted being pushed down the stairs. Elizabeth would be horribly alarmed and insist on reporting the attack to Nate immediately. That was exactly what Lucky didn't want. She wanted the freedom to poke around and talk to people, to hopefully find out what she could before Nate discovered what she was up to.

"We're members of the same party and I know he's planning to start his campaign for the state senate in a few months. I think he'll make a very good candidate, and he has a lovely family that will be very supportive."

"But what do you think of him personally?"

"You mean, do I think he was carrying on an affair with Patricia Honeywell?"

"Well, yes, that would be my next question."

"Lucky." Elizabeth smiled. "When it comes to other people's private lives, I try not to wonder. I really have no idea and I would hate to speculate. He's an attractive man. Who knows? Perhaps he was. I hate to even entertain that idea, because he'd be a complete fool if he were."

"If he were carrying on with Honeywell behind his wife's back and she became pregnant . . ."

"What?" Lucky realized she had let Elias's information slip. She mentally kicked herself. "How do you know that?"

"I can't really say. I'm sorry."

"Oh my!" Elizabeth took her reading glasses off and laid them carefully on the desk. "As I said, Tom Reed is an attractive man, bright, well educated, law degree, well-off, and all that. He's likable enough. He's also very ambitious and . . ." Elizabeth hesitated a moment. "He's developed that certain veneer that all successful politicians must have. Personally, and this is just between you and me, I sometimes distrust that. It's my prejudice, I guess. I don't particularly like him or dislike him. I just have a hard time getting a bead on someone whose stock-in-trade is that very professional patina. That's it in a nutshell. Now, that doesn't mean I think he was carrying on behind his wife's back. I certainly hope not. That doesn't bode well for the election if it should come out. And it also doesn't mean he might have fathered her child. This is all pure speculation. For all you know, that address was in that datebook because Honeywell admired the house and was interested in buying it. There could be any number of reasons she would have jotted down the Reed address."

Lucky nodded. "You're right, of course. I'm just throwing out ideas and getting your reaction."

"Do you want me to bring this to Nate's attention? Perhaps I should in any event."

"I can't stop you, of course, but if you don't mind, can you hold off a bit? I'd like a chance to see what I can learn before you do that."

"I don't like this, Lucky. I don't like this one bit—that you're involving yourself with this murder."

"I'm involved whether I like it or not just by virtue of the fact that her body was found behind our restaurant. We're now down our only chef and many, many customers. I have to do something." Lucky was annoyed that her voice sounded petulant to her ears.

"I'm wondering why Nate didn't remove that calendar or datebook or whatever it was from the house. That sounds very sloppy to me," Elizabeth offered.

"It's possible he may have glanced at it and didn't find anything remarkable in it. There wasn't much to it at all; maybe that's why it was left behind. She had made a few notations for events later on—events she'll never be attending. There was a note about the start of the lease and Eleanor Jensen's office number—that type of thing."

"And that's it?"

"Yes. Has he spoken to you about Sage's arrest?"

"No. Nor should he, really. It's not my place to second-guess the Chief of Police. I could maybe speak to him and ask him what evidence he has—in confidence—and he might tell me. But then again, he might just tell me to mind my own business."

"Oh, I forgot to mention . . . I ran into Flo Sullivan at the house. She does light cleaning for the realty office, and she told me Honeywell was frightened of someone."

"Flo Sullivan? Oh, my word, Lucky, she's the worst gossip in town. She doesn't mean any harm, but you can't believe a word that comes out of that woman's mouth. She'd spout any nonsense to get attention."

Lucky slumped back in the chair and fell silent, discouraged that all her efforts might come to nothing.

"I understand how you feel, dear. I love you like a daughter and I want you to promise me you'll be very, very careful. You don't know what you're doing, and you could stir up a dangerous hornet's nest."

Lucky heaved a frustrated sigh. "I promise you I'll be very careful, but like it or not, I have to do something. Whatever was going on in Patricia Honeywell's life got her killed. We won't get the Spoonful back on track until the real killer is found."

Chapter 22

"THANKS FOR STOPPING by. I didn't mean to scare you. I just wanted a chance to talk to you about Jack."

Lucky sat in a patient chair in Elias's office at the Clinic the following morning after Jack's appointment. She had felt a sense of dread since Elias had called her at home to say he wanted to talk to her about Jack's examination. He had particularly asked if she could stop in early before patients started to arrive.

"Have you noticed anything about his behavior or memory lately? Any cognitive problems?" he asked.

Lucky took a deep breath to quell the fear. "Yes, I have. I didn't want to mention anything until he had a complete checkup. He had an episode after we discovered the body behind the Spoonful. I'm guessing it's some form of post-traumatic stress disorder. It brought back a terrible episode from his time in the service. But he knew what was happening to him. It wasn't as if he wasn't in touch with reality."

"Anything else you've noticed?" Elias glanced at Lucky's hands. Her fingers were twisting nervously. It was obvious she was terribly worried about Jack.

"A few days ago . . . he thought his wife—my grandmother—was coming to pick him up at the Spoonful. It took a few moments before he came back to reality."

Elias nodded. "I noticed the hula girl tattoo on his arm—I asked him about it just to make conversation."

"What did he say?"

"He said, very seriously, that she was his wife—I thought he was joking, but then I realized he wasn't."

"Oh, God, Elias, what's going on with him?"

"We need to run some tests. I can set them up for him at the hospital in Lincoln Falls. There's no need to panic. I just want to rule out as many things as possible."

"Tell me the truth . . . do you think it's Alzheimer's?"

"I am not going to jump to that conclusion. The fact is there is no clinical test for that condition, but there are other tests that can diagnose problems other than Alzheimer's that could be causing his symptoms—tomography, MRI. Any number of things can cause dementia—and not just in elderly people. Many elderly people do often suffer from certain forms of dementia—mild ones, such as forgetfulness, inability to do certain tasks—and that can be caused by something as simple as decreased blood flow to the brain. One thing is important, though—he needs to stay connected. He needs to feel he's needed and wanted, and have tasks to do each day. Anything that will keep him active and busy—a job, social connections, all of that is very important."

"Like the Spoonful?"

"Yes. Exactly like the Spoonful." Any hope she once had of extricating herself from the Spoonful was out of the question. A few days before, she had felt guilty about keeping Jack hanging on her decision, but now the tables had turned. Jack needed the Spoonful if he were to continue his life with any sense of meaning. Everything had conspired to bring her back to Snowflake, to enmesh her in her parents' business and to shoulder the burden of care for her grandfather. Was that what fate was? Not a lightning bolt from the sky, but a series of small things that led to an unavoidable conclusion. There was a phrase she had once read—"turning to meet one's fate." She had turned to meet her fate. She looked at Elias and thought about his warmth and his strong hands resting on the desk. Perhaps, with luck, one's fate might not be a bad thing at all.

"Elias, you remember I asked you if Patricia Honeywell was a patient here? Have you had a chance to check your roster?"

Elias looked at her blankly across the desk. "I'm sorry. You did ask and it slipped my mind. What makes you think she might have been a patient?"

"She had a business card from the Clinic."

"Really? How do you know that?" Elias asked, a puzzled frown on his face.

Lucky was reluctant to admit to her search of the house on Bear Path Lane. "I . . . uh, it fell out of her wallet one day at the restaurant. I was at the cash register and I happened to notice." *Liar, liar, pants on fire,* she thought, hoping her face wasn't turning red.

"Lucky, look, I understand your concern for Sage, but what you're asking me to do, strictly speaking, I shouldn't."

"Anything you tell me won't go any further. And I'm sure if you did discover anything, you'd tell Nate right away, wouldn't you?"

"Of course I would." Elias heaved a sigh. "I'll have a look in the database. That should be up-to-date. But I'm sure our records clerk would have checked already, because we arranged for the autopsy. Let's see . . . let me get down to the H's." He clicked on the mouse until he reached the correct list and stared at the screen for a moment, scrolling down. "No. She's not here."

"If she just came in for something as simple as a flu shot, would she be listed in your patient records?"

"Yes, definitely. Even if she never came here again. We have to keep accurate records and histories." Elias turned away from the monitor. "Sorry, I guess this wasn't much help. What were you hoping to learn?"

"Nothing . . . I don't know . . . just information gathering.

Trying to learn anything I can about her, hoping I turn up something that helps get Sage out of jail."

Elias smiled wryly. "I wish you luck with that one. I can't imagine why he would murder her, or anyone else for that matter. But maybe there's some deep, dark story behind their relationship."

Lucky thought of Janie and Meg's witnessing Honeywell following Sage down the street and accosting him. Elias was right. There was a whole lot more to that story that she didn't know.

They heard a light knock. The office door opened and Lucky looked up to see a tall man in a white lab coat. A stethoscope dangled from his pocket. Somewhere in his midfifties, he was ruggedly handsome with dark hair graying at the temples.

"Oh, sorry, Elias, didn't realize you were with a patient."

"That's quite all right, Jon. I'd like you to meet Lucky Jamieson. She runs the By the Spoonful Soup Shop."

"Oh, really? I've heard good things about your place. I'll have to get there soon." Jon smiled and reached out to shake her hand. "Very happy to meet you." He was one of those people, she realized, with the ability to put others at their ease instantly.

"I just popped in because Abigail reminded me to ask you about the tickets."

"Oh, right. Thanks. Please put me down for two."

"Will do." Jon smiled and, with a wave in Lucky's direction, shut the door behind him.

"I'm glad he stopped in. Now that I have you alone again, would you like to attend a concert on Friday evening?"

"Here? In Snowflake?"

"There's a local choral group, and they sing sometimes with a string trio—harp, cello and violin. Jon's wife sings with them. They're really wonderful. Some are retired professionals from New York. They've formed a group and do several programs a year. I'd think you'd really enjoy it."

"I'm musically ignorant, but I'll take your word for it."

"Great." Elias smiled broadly. "I'll pick you up at seven—

it's at St. Genesius, by the way. Wonderful acoustics and a beautiful setting."

"I'll see you then."

Elias walked Lucky to the front door and unlocked it for her. Her heart lifted at the thought of another evening with him. For a moment, she had forgotten her worries about Jack. What was it about him that seemed to chase away all her cares?

Chapter 23

SAGE PICKED AT the remnants of breakfast that Bradley had passed through the hatch on a tray. He was grateful for the hot coffee, but his appetite had abandoned him. This couldn't hold a candle to the coffee at the Spoonful, but it was better than nothing—probably better than anything he'd be able to get for a good, long while. Bradley had been more than happy to explain exactly what would happen to him if the judge didn't allow bail. And since he wasn't in any position to post bail, thinking about getting out was a moot point.

He took a bite of toast and forced himself to swallow it. Looking back, maybe it was inevitable that things had turned out this way. He always swore he'd never be like his old man and make a mess of everything. Yet here he was. The old man had been a drunk who kicked at everything in his path, angry he couldn't escape from a run-down farm up in Maine. Remy took after the old man, not in cruelty but in his lack of responsibility. The nightmares still came sometimes, the old man screaming at him and Remy, telling them how worthless they were, the constant rage and beatings.

Remy was just a little kid, and when he cried, Sage would always try to comfort him. When the old man's temper grew more brutal, he wouldn't cry. He wouldn't give the old bastard the satisfaction. Nursing a silent and growing hatred for the old man, he kept his own counsel.

After their mother died, it got worse. He was drunk most every day—but never drunk enough to pass out and leave him and Remy in peace. For entertainment, he used to drag them into the barn and rip their worn shirts off. He'd pull off his belt and beat them till they bled, red welts crisscrossing their backs. He was too big to take on—even drunk. Sage did his best to protect Remy, but that only made the old man madder. When he was done, he'd lock them in the barn for the night. Sage always did his best to clean Remy's wounds, covering him with his shirt and an old blanket. They'd sleep in a pile of hay, Remy curled up on his arm like a baby. One night he made a decision. He had to get out. Remy cried but Sage promised he'd come back for him. He wouldn't forget. He told Remy to hang on until he could set something up for the both of them. He left the next day. He hiked out to the road and hitched a ride to a nearby town where he found his first job, trimming bushes for an elderly woman. When she found out he couldn't go home, she gave him a room to sleep in above her garage and some clothes that had once belonged to her husband. That was the first step in his journey to remake his life.

He worked at any odd job he could find, eventually earning enough money to take him south to New York. There, nobody knew him, nobody knew what he came from and what he was trying so hard to escape. He found a mentor, a restaurant owner where he washed dishes, who helped him get into a well-respected chef's school. There weren't a lot of avenues for a kid without an education, but Sage discovered he loved the craft of creating food. He was an artist of sorts, if one could be called an artist arranging sprigs of herbs and dribbles of chocolate. People were willing to pay good money for what he could do with a hunk of meat and some vegetables and spices. Most of all, he loved that it was a never-ending learning process, always evolving, fed by exotic foodstuffs from around the world. He nurtured himself while he fed others. He gave himself back the childhood he had been denied. More importantly, he could do that for his brother.

When the restaurant owner died, he returned to New England, but not to Maine, never Maine. He went to Boston first. As soon as he could, he sent for Remy. He berated himself for not taking Remy with him when he first left home, but that would have been impossible. It was hard enough to survive on his own through those years; it would have been impossible with a younger brother to care for. Was Remy's spirit already broken even before he took off? He'd promised Remy he'd never forget and would come back for him. He told him to have courage and survive as best he could. Maybe it had taken too long; maybe the old man had destroyed his sense of self-respect, of worth. In one way or another he'd been taking care of Remy for years, and somehow Remy never seemed to be able to stand on his own two feet. Now he'd be truly alone and on his own.

He could hear the bells of St. Genesius ringing just a few blocks away. Maybe praying would help, though he doubted it. The clanging of the bells sounded like a death knell. He held his hands over his ears and stifled a sob. He had been so careful all those years. Looking back, the false step was the job in Boston. That had been the turning point. If only he had recognized it at the time. Is that what it was all about? We struggle to escape what we come from only to end up back where we didn't want to ever be? Here he was—in a jail cell. If he had it to do over again, maybe he could have made different choices, but it was too late now. You can't turn the clock back. Everything his old man had cursed him with had come true.

He heard the outer door clang and then Bradley's footsteps. He looked up. Lucky, following the deputy, was balancing a covered tray of food. What was she doing here again? He told her not to come back. He was grateful they were willing to feed him, but Jack could have brought it just the same.

Lucky took a step back as Bradley unlocked the grated hatch and passed the tray through to Sage. "Bradley let me use the microwave in the kitchen to warm this up."

"I thought Jack would be coming," Sage said.

"I'm trying to take some of the load off him. He hasn't been feeling very well. I was at the Clinic this morning to talk to Elias."

Sage looked up quickly. "What kind of problems?"

"I'll fill you in when we know more. Right now, you're the one I'm worried about. Eat up."

Sage refused to meet her eyes as he lifted the tray. "Thanks, boss. I guess I shouldn't call you that anymore. I don't have a job now. I don't have anything anymore."

Lucky shot a look at Bradley, who took the hint and retreated. She pulled a stool over and sat down. "If you really want to know, I consider this a temporary leave of absence until they find the guilty party."

Sage looked up quickly. "I asked you not to come back here."

"Guess I don't listen very well." Lucky waited until Bradley had shut and locked the outer door. "I haven't been able to talk to Nate yet, so I don't have any information. And I haven't heard anything that would convince me—or Jack—that you've killed anyone. So maybe you can tell me why you're sitting here. What don't I know?"

Sage was silent for several minutes, but Lucky waited, not filling the silence. He finally spoke. "You'd never believe me." Something released in his chest, as if a fist uncurled from his heart. He had kept it inside for so long. Sage leaned forward, his head in his hands. "That woman . . ."

"You knew her from somewhere, didn't you?" Lucky waited.

"Boston. I used to work for her . . . and her husband. I was a live-in private chef. They had a big town house on Commonwealth, then . . ." Sage trailed off, lost in thought.

"And something happened?" Lucky prompted.

Sage nodded. "Yes. Garson—her husband—was pretty

fed up. It was obvious that marriage wasn't going to last much longer. She made a play for me. Big-time."

"What did you do?"

"Nothing. I swear. I wasn't into any games like that. I needed my job but not enough to . . . you know. It just made me sick." Sage looked imploringly at Lucky. "The other night, when Sophie and I were arguing, when we bumped into you on Broadway, it was about her—Patsy Honeywell."

"Sophie was jealous?" Lucky didn't want to let on that Sophie had already filled her in. She wanted to hear the story directly from Sage.

"Yeah, she was, I guess. More than that—maybe angry. Sophie agreed to give Patsy private lessons up on one of the tougher slopes. Funny thing was, Sophie said she didn't need instruction. She thought Patsy was a very competent skier. Anyway, Patsy must have gotten under Sophie's skin—about me—in a way that implied something had happened between us and maybe was even still going on. Sophie was pretty upset. None of it was true, but it didn't surprise me at all. I know what kind of hateful stuff she's . . . she *was* capable of."

"So when you wouldn't play along, were you fired?" It was obvious to anyone who saw him that Sage was a handsome man. Almost too good-looking, Lucky thought. She could certainly see why women would make him a target. Strangely enough, his looks belied his reserved nature.

Sage shook his head. "If only. I wasn't fired. It was far worse than that." He fell silent. Lucky didn't speak, afraid to break his mood. He lifted his head and looked through the bars of the cell. "I did a year in Walpole."

"What did you say?" Lucky struggled to understand.

"I have a prison record." Sage heaved a sigh. "I'm an ex-con."

It suddenly all made sense, why Sage had stayed at the Spoonful as long as he had, why he hadn't tried to get work at the Snowflake Resort. A company like the Resort would have run a background check. His prison record would have turned up. He'd never be hired. Never in a million years would her parents have thought of doing that. They would have liked Sage on sight and operated on trust.

"I still don't understand."

"Patsy kept trying. I did my best to be a gentleman about it and let her know in a nice way that it wasn't on, but she wouldn't give up. Finally, I had to physically push her away and tell her in no uncertain terms. It got ugly. She flew into a rage . . . she was spitting mad. I thought for sure she'd fire me then and there, or have her husband do it. It would have been a relief. So . . . I packed up most of my things and waited for the ax to fall. Looking back on it now, I should have left right away, as fast as I could get out of that house. I went to bed that night, planning to take off in the morning. Next thing I knew, the cops were waking me up and I was charged with theft."

Sage took a deep breath and looked at Lucky. "You've gotta believe me. I never did it. I never touched anything that wasn't mine in my life. When I was working in the kitchen that night, she went into my quarters and stashed a diamond necklace and a few other expensive pieces behind the cover of the heating duct. There was no way I could defend myself. She turned the whole thing around and said I did it because *she* had rejected *my* advances."

"When I came up here I thought I could finally put all that behind me. How do you think I felt when I realized she was in town for the winter? It all came crashing in on me. And then she was messing with Sophie, leading her to believe there had been something between us once and maybe there still was. I just hope Sophie believes me."

"So, because of that, Nate thinks you had a motive to murder her."

"There were times I wanted to, but believe me, I didn't do this."

"How could she have done something like that to you? That prison sentence would mark you for life."

"That's the kind of woman she was. But I know I couldn't have been her only enemy. She was vicious. It's no wonder somebody bashed her head in." Sage took a sip of his coffee and pushed the tray away. "So, that's my story. Nate ran a check on me. And you know the rest."

"Okay, so maybe you had a motive—a reason to hate her. That doesn't mean you killed her."

"Nobody's gonna believe that."

"I believe you. Besides, I have a selfish motive. I want you back at the Spoonful. And as soon as Nate finds out who really killed her, you will be."

Sage stared at her bleakly. "I appreciate that, I really do, but don't get your hopes up. Nate and his tech took a DNA swab from me. This really doesn't look good."

"If you didn't go near her, what's that going to prove?"

"That night, the night she was murdered, she followed me down the street." Lucky recalled Janie and Meg's account of watching Sage. "She . . . I don't know what she was trying to do, but she scratched me. I jumped away from her, but I wasn't quick enough." He stretched his neck to reveal a partially healed gash above his collar. "If they find anything under her nails . . . well, they'd be able to prove we fought. I wasn't thinking of that at the time; I just wanted to get away from her and I took off down the street."

Lucky realized that one contact with the murdered woman could be enough to convict him, short of any other evidence or an alibi. "Sage, you've got to keep your spirits up. There must be a solution to all this. In the meantime, Jack or I can maybe talk to a lawyer about defending you." She cringed inwardly as the words came out of her mouth. In her mind's eye, she pictured the bank statement and its dwindling total. How would she scrape together any money to be able to hire a lawyer for Sage?

"Where were you that night?"

"Home. I went straight to my place. I needed to calm down after seeing her on the street."

"Wasn't Sophie with you?"

"No. She had pulled a muscle that day and said she wanted to crash early."

"Anyone else see you that night?"

"No one. Went home. Stayed there and watched the snow."

Lucky felt a tight panic gripping her stomach. A past history—a very bad one at that. No alibi, no witnesses and a possible DNA match. No wonder Sage felt so hopeless. "Thanks for being honest with me, Sage."

He looked warily at her.

"I mean that. I don't care if you spent a year in jail. We want you back—Jack and I. I'll see you soon and Jack'll be by later to bring you dinner."

"Thanks, boss—Lucky." The corner of his mouth twitched slightly. It wasn't a smile, but at least he was talking.

BRADLEY WAS ON the phone whispering quietly into the receiver as she closed the door to the cell area. Lucky wondered why the secrecy. Nate wasn't around and surely she wouldn't care if he were making a personal call. Bradley realized she was leaning against the counter, waiting to get his attention. He straightened up and said, "Uh . . . I understand, ma'am. Chief Edgerton's out in the field right now, but I'll have him call you as soon as he returns." He quickly hung up the phone and stood. Lucky was fairly certain he was relaying every incident regarding the murder to one of his pals. Perhaps it was Bradley they could thank for the visit from WVMT, the local television station.

"Emergency?" Lucky asked.

"Uh, no. Nothing that can't wait. Just taking a message for the Chief."

"I see," she replied. "Well, I was hoping to have a chance to talk to Nate. Will he be back soon?" Lucky's eyes wandered to the counter directly behind Bradley. A large cardboard box, the size that would hold reams of paper, was sitting on the desk below the countertop. The name Honeywell was scrawled in a black marker on the outside. Bradley caught her look and turned to follow her line of sight. He moved slightly, blocking her view of the box.

"I'm not sure. I'll have him call you, how would that be?"

"That's fine, Bradley. Jack will come by later and either Jack or I—one of us—will be back tomorrow to bring more food."

"All right. Thanks," he replied.

She moved slightly to the side and pointed to the cardboard box. "What's in the box, Bradley?"

"That's evidence. You can't touch that."

"Oh." Lucky hesitated. "Is that stuff Nate found at the house on Bear Path Lane?"

"Ms. Jamieson . . . Lucky . . . you know I can't tell you anything. This is an ongoing investigation."

Lucky almost burst out laughing, certain Bradley had learned that phrase from a television script. She struggled to keep a straight face. "Well, in that case, tell Nate I came by, will you?"

"Will do."

Lucky walked to the front door. She could feel Bradley's eyes watching her. She was certain he'd be reporting her visit to anyone who would listen. If Nate caught him blabbing, he'd have his job. She pushed the door open and stepped out onto the top stair. She hesitated. Where was that box being stored? She turned back and reentered the station. Bradley had opened a lower cabinet under the counter and was maneuvering the large cardboard box into it.

"Bradley," she called out, "I think I forgot my gloves. Did I leave them on the counter?"

Bradley slammed the cabinet door and locked it with a key from a large ring of keys. "I don't think so."

Lucky reached the counter as Bradley hung the keys on a hook under the desk. "Oh, wait," she said, rummaging in her purse. "Here they are. Sorry. I'd forget my head . . . See you tomorrow." She waved and exited once more. She'd give anything to have a look inside that box, certain it contained information relevant to Patricia Honeywell's murder—undoubtedly her laptop and perhaps even her cell phone. But if the murderer had lured her to the Spoonful, or to another location by phone, then Flo Sullivan, the cleaning lady, was absolutely right. That cell phone would be in a thousand broken pieces somewhere. Maybe Nate had located the missing rental car by now. Snowflake was so small, someone must have seen it and reported it to the police.

Lost in thought, Lucky trudged slowly up the street, heading back to the Spoonful. Her amusement at Bradley's expense quickly evaporated as the reality of Sage's position hit her. As she approached the corner of Chestnut Street she heard the clanging bells of St. Genesius, one of the two churches Snowflake boasted, and the only Anglican church for miles around. She looked up to see its stone façade. Lucky's parents and most townspeople attended the old Congregational church, a square, white-steepled building erected in 1749. Plain and utilitarian, it had none of the trappings of the more elegant church. Lucky had attended services at St. Genesius twice—once for a wedding and once for a baptism. She remembered a small, quiet side chapel, open at all times. She wasn't ready to return to the Spoonful just yet. She needed a place to sit quietly and think.

She pushed open the wrought iron gate. It creaked slightly on its hinges. The path to the heavy oak door had been shoveled clear. Inside, the chapel was hushed and empty. The bells had ceased to ring. Dust motes swam in the air, and the aroma of melted candle wax mingled with the musty smell of old prayer books. Splashes of color, deep reds and blues from the stained glass windows, played across the wooden pews. Flickering candles in small red glasses stood in a metal rack in a side aisle. She slipped a dollar into a small receptacle and lit a candle, then knelt and closed her eyes. She took a deep breath, forcing a jumble of thoughts from her mind. She prayed first for her parents, then her grandfather, and finally for Sage. Whatever happened to the Spoonful, whether she could keep it running or not, Sage's life was at stake. Once the victim of a callous woman, now, with her murder, he was twice victimized.

When she was very young, she imagined the words of her prayers would float heavenward, like butterflies in a universe where prayers would always be granted. If only she had the faith of a child that things were that simple. Events of the past few days played out in her mind's eye as she stared at the flickering candle flame. Something had to be done. Prayers were all well and good, but Sage could forfeit his life, the guilty party would go free and the Spoonful would be forced into bankruptcy. Both she and Jack would be lost. Not to mention what this would do to Sophie. It was very clear what she had to do. She had to find the murderer.

Chapter 24

"WHO ARE YOU?" a sharp voice called out.

Lucky jumped involuntarily. A jolt of fear ran down her spine; she was so lost in thought, she hadn't heard anyone approach.

"What are you doing here?"

Breathless, she came to her feet and turned to face a small, plump woman in a pale blue suit. In the dim light it was difficult to make out her features. Her face was framed in soft blonde curls. She held a heavy silver candelabra in one hand and a polishing cloth in the other. Abigail Starkfield, Dr. Starkfield's wife—it was the woman she had seen at the Clinic.

"I . . . I just came in to . . ."

"How did you get in? The chapel is closed." Lucky heard a note of fear in her voice.

"The door was open . . . unlocked, I mean."

"I don't think I know you. Are you a member of this congregation?" The woman relaxed a bit, stepping closer, and spoke in a friendlier tone.

"No . . . I . . . I just stopped in to sit quietly for a moment and . . ."

"Oh. I see. Well, I'm sorry to disturb you, dear, but we're preparing for a baptism. People will be arriving shortly."

"I didn't realize." Lucky buttoned her coat around her and picked up her purse from the floor.

Mrs. Starkfield glanced at Lucky's jeans and boots. She hadn't given a thought to her dress when she decided to enter the chapel. She had to admit she wasn't properly dressed for a house of worship.

Mrs. Starkfield stepped closer and offered her hand. "I'm Abigail Starkfield, and you are . . . ?"

Lucky returned the handshake. "I'm Lucky Jamieson. My family owns . . . my parents owned the By the Spoonful Soup Shop and I run it now."

"Oh," Abigail replied, as if remembering hearing about the deaths of Lucky's parents. "Well, I am sorry, dear, and sorry I interrupted you. Normally we do these on Sundays after services, but the parents' schedules didn't permit. I hope you'll come back again."

"Yes, I will. Thank you. It's a beautiful church."

Abigail smiled in return. There was something about the shape of her face that reminded Lucky of her mother. It was gone in a flash and she pushed the thought away. "We're very proud of it," Abigail responded.

Lucky glanced down at the candelabra in Abigail's hand. Abigail caught her look and laughed. "Just polishing . . . making sure everything's ready."

Lucky nodded. "I'll be going then. It was very nice to meet you."

"You as well," Abigail said. "And I'm sorry if I gave you a fright."

Lucky smiled. "That's quite all right. No worries," she said as she shut the door softly behind her.

Outside the chapel the wind whipped her hair and bent the icy branches of the trees. She pulled on her cap and wrapped her scarf tighter. A little divine intervention wouldn't hurt at all right now, but in the meantime, she had to do everything she possibly could to solve her problems. A lot of people wanted Patricia Honeywell dead, but only one person actually committed the crime. If Nate was determined to build a case against Sage, it fell upon her to find out who else wanted Honeywell dead.

Lucky took a shortcut through the alleyway that led to the Spoonful, finally cleared since the storm. She groaned when she spotted Nate's cruiser in the tiny lot behind the restaurant. She quickened her steps, half afraid something dreadful might have happened once again, or terrified that Jack had had one of his spells. A man in coveralls with a trowel in his hand was on his knees by the Dumpster. He was carefully scraping away snow and ice from the area where Patricia Honeywell's body had been found. At least they hadn't parked in front of the restaurant, where everyone would see the cruiser. That was something. Their customers might not have returned, but the Spoonful didn't need any further advertisement of the grisly find behind their building.

Nate, standing next to the technician, and doing his best to stay warm, turned as she approached.

"What's going on, Nate?" Lucky asked.

"Got a tech on loan from the PD in Lincoln Falls. I just want to make sure there isn't any evidence buried here. I don't want any surprises when spring finally comes and the snow melts." Nate stamped his feet to stay warm. "Heard you were visiting my prisoner."

Bradley hadn't wasted any time. Lucky nodded. "Yes. We're also providing food for him." She tried not to let a note of resentment creep into her voice over the fact that Nate had arrested the best chef Snowflake had ever seen. If she hoped to do anything to get Sage out of jail and the Spoonful back on track, it would be better not to make an adversary of Nate.

"Hey, how 'bout some coffee?" Lucky asked. "You must be freezing."

The technician looked up hopefully at her suggestion,

and Nate blew on his hands to keep them warm. "Uh . . . thanks, Lucky. We'd really appreciate that."

"I'll be right back—unless you'd like to come inside?"

"Nah, we better keep going. We should be done soon."

Lucky ducked through the back door of the Spoonful and headed for the kitchen. "Hi, Jack," she called.

"Hi, yourself." He smiled widely and approached the kitchen hatch.

"I just offered Nate and his guy some coffee. They look like they're freezing out there."

"Good idea."

Lucky poured coffee into two heavy-duty paper cups, placed them in a cardboard tray with cream containers and sugar and headed out to the parking lot. She rested the container on the hood of the cruiser and watched Nate dump two sugars and cream into his cup. The technician continued to dig through ice around the Dumpster. Lucky stuck her hands in her pockets and casually asked, "Is there something specific you're looking for?"

Nate grumbled. "Nope. Just covering my bases. We don't want to miss anything."

"Are you looking for her other earring?" Lucky hazarded.

"How do you . . . what makes you think that?" Nate shot her a look that would have made anyone cringe. Lucky would have shriveled up as well, except she realized this was the best chance she had to talk to Nate and hopefully get him to open up to her. She said a silent prayer that Nate never ever found out she had searched the house on Bear Path Lane.

"I remember seeing the body. There was one earring dangling from her . . . right ear, I think. But I didn't see one on her other ear."

"Lucky, you know I can't talk to you about this. I don't want my case blabbed all over town."

"You think I would do that? Give me some credit, Nate." If only Nate knew what a gossip Bradley was, she thought.

Nate sipped his coffee and watched the technician chipping away at the ice.

"Did you find a cell phone on her by any chance?" Lucky persisted.

"Lucky." Nate turned to her, his eyes drilling holes into her head. "I'm not gonna repeat myself."

"Okay, okay." Lucky fell silent but finally couldn't resist one more question.

"Have you found her rental car yet?"

Nate didn't respond.

Exasperated, Lucky pushed on. "Come on, Nate. Give us a break . . . please."

Nate heaved a sigh. "We found it. It was up the road that leads to Lexington Heights."

Lucky's ears went up. "So maybe the murderer dumped the body here and left the car someplace else?" she asked hopefully. If that were the case, then the Spoonful would be relieved of the distinction of being the scene of the crime.

Nate's face was closed. He assumed what Lucky thought of as a cop's inscrutable expression.

"Nate, what possible motive could Sage have had?"

"You'll have to ask him. It's not something I can talk about."

She couldn't know for sure but suspected Nate had arrested Sage on the basis of his past with Honeywell. She wasn't about to tell him she already knew about that past. Discretion was the best course.

"Jack doesn't believe Sage is guilty, by the way." She knew she was annoying Nate, but hoped he carried a bit of guilt about the effect on their business and wouldn't blow his top.

"That's commendable. I have the greatest respect for your grandfather. I've always looked up to him. You know that. And I know Sage's worked for your family for several years, but . . ."

"But what?"

"Nice guys commit murder too."

"You're not convinced she was killed here, are you?

And"—she indicated the technician—"this might confirm it."

The man in the coveralls stood and turned to Nate but, spotting Lucky still standing there, was unsure if he should speak. He shook his head negatively at Nate. "Nothing."

"Okay. Let's pack it up, then." He turned to Lucky. "We'll be out of your way now."

Lucky climbed the steps to the back door of the Spoonful. "Just for the record, Nate, I trust Jack's opinion. I think you're making a terrible mistake."

Nate didn't even honor her remark with a look. He got behind the wheel of the cruiser and waited while the technician packed his tools, stepped out of his coveralls and tossed them in the trunk. He grabbed the coffee that was probably cold by now and climbed into the passenger seat. As soon as his seat belt was fastened, Nate drove off without a backward look.

Lucky watched the police car until it turned out of the alley onto Broadway. Shivering, she hurried inside, hung her jacket in the closet and kicked off her snow boots. Something delicious was warming in the kitchen. She slipped on a pair of loafers and headed down the hall. She lifted the lid of the Crock-Pot and peeked at the contents. Jack had warmed a container of Sage's pea and barley soup with bacon. A loaf of bakery bread was heating in the oven. Jack sat with Hank and Barry at a corner table, watching their chess game intently once again. He looked up when he heard her footsteps in the kitchen. He rose from the chair slowly and approached the hatch to the kitchen. Lucky could tell his back was hurting.

"You feeling okay, Jack?" she asked.

"I'm fine. It's just these old bones. This sitting around isn't good for me. Much better if I'm busy and moving around. How's our boy doing?"

Lucky smiled ruefully. "Seems depressed— understandable. I brought him the food but he wasn't very interested in eating."

"Did he have anything to say?"

Lucky shook her head slightly, indicating Hank and Barry at their corner table. "Quite a lot, actually, but I'll tell you later." She whispered, "When we're alone."

Jack nodded. "I knew there was something. I could tell that day—the day Nate took him. He didn't even put up an argument or look surprised."

"You'd think he was guilty, wouldn't you?"

"If you didn't know him, yes. But we know him. Anybody that cares that much about food . . . well, I just don't buy it. I just can't figure why Nate was in such an all-fired hurry to arrest him."

"Have you eaten yet?"

Jack shook his head. "Been too busy trying to learn chess. Thought I'd wait for you."

"Why don't I dish out some bowls for all of us?" She smiled. "Might as well offer some free soup to Hank and Barry—at least they've been loyal customers."

Jack nodded. "I'll set a table for us."

Lucky grabbed a large round tray and ladled the soup into four hefty bowls. She fixed a basket of sliced warm bread and added a small butter dish to the tray.

"Hey, Lucky—we can pay," Barry said as he moved to the larger table. "No need for charity here."

"That's all right—maybe next time. Today is just a thank-you for showing up." She glanced over at Jack, busy tearing off a slice of bread and spreading butter on it. Lucky thanked her stars that Jack was still here. She couldn't imagine what it would feel like to be totally alone in the world. She felt a rush of sympathy for Remy. He must be terrified that Sage could be locked up for life. Remy wasn't standing on very solid ground to begin with, and Sage was the only person he had in the world.

She looked around the table. Holding her soup spoon aloft, she said, "To Sage."

The toast was echoed around the table. "May he return quickly to the Spoonful!"

"Amen," Barry added.

Hank said, "I heard you're feeding him down at the jail. How's he holding up?"

Lucky shook her head. "Not good. Not good at all. It wouldn't hurt if you stopped in just to say hello and tell him you're on his side. Might lift his spirits."

"That's a very good idea. Everyone in this town is whispering and tiptoeing around. That poor guy must feel like a leper. I know how I'd feel if I were in his shoes. I'd be chewing at the bars and screaming."

"The scariest thing is he seems resigned. I guess that's what bothered me so much today."

"Resigned?" Barry echoed. "Like he doesn't believe he has a way to defend himself, or he doesn't think anyone would believe him?"

"Both, I suppose."

Barry shook his head. "I just don't get it. He was quiet, kept to himself, never caused anybody any bother. I'd see him around town with that cute girlfriend of his and he seemed real happy. He wasn't one to run around with strange women like that Honeywell character."

"No, he wasn't," Lucky answered. If she ever let it slip what the history between Sage and the murder victim was, she could imagine how tongues in the town would wag. She wasn't free to tell anyone what Sage had confided to her, but she wished she could. Maybe if people knew what had been done to him, they'd have a bit more sympathy.

Barry broke off a hunk of bread. "Saw Nate out back," he offered, hoping someone would fill in the rest.

"Yes," Lucky sighed. "With a technician."

"What were they digging around back there for?"

"Nate's not going to tell me, but I'm sure he wants to figure out if she was killed there, or just dumped there. Personally, I hope it's the latter."

Hank said, "Be a whole lot better for the Spoonful if that were the case."

"I agree," Barry said, dipping his bread into the last of his soup. "I think it's just terrible that more local people aren't coming around. They should be ashamed of themselves. They'd be the first to complain about corporate take-over in the town, believe you me. If they don't get a move on they won't have a local place to stop in to and then you'd hear them whining." Barry turned to Hank. "Maybe we should have a word with all the people we know and encourage them to come back."

"Sure. I agree you'd hear a lot of bellyaching if the Spoonful went under. Tourists—what do they know—but the real people here, they should be ashamed of themselves. I think I'll make some phone calls this very afternoon." Hank stood and slipped on his jacket.

Barry rose from his chair. "Thanks for lunch—Jack, Lucky. We'll be back tomorrow and we insist on paying, so no more nonsense about free food."

Once they had gone, Lucky carried the dishes into the kitchen, while Jack rinsed them and loaded them into the dishwasher. When they had finished, Jack pulled up a stool and sat at the counter. "So tell me how it went."

Lucky repeated a condensed version of Sage's story to Jack. When she had finished, Jack whistled. "I knew it."

"What do you mean?"

"I knew he had done time."

Lucky's eyes widened. "How did you know?"

"Lucky, my girl, I've been around all kinds of men most of my life. I never said anything about it to your parents, but I could tell. It was the way he walked."

"His walk?"

"Uh-huh," Jack responded. "You can tell. Takes a lot to break the habit of shuffling and looking down at the floor. Said 'jail time' to me."

"And you never asked him about it? Or said anything to Mom and Dad?"

"No—no need. I kept an eye on him for a bit, just to be sure, but I finally decided he was okay in my book and I didn't worry about it anymore. Besides, look how lucky we were to get a chef like him."

Lucky smiled and reached up to rub his rough cheek. "You are full of surprises, Jack, you know that?"

Jack smiled in return. "Marjorie and Cecily were here this morning too—while you were down at the police station. I don't want you to worry. Everyone'll start coming back. When Nate figures out he's arrested the wrong man, things'll be normal again."

They heard the front door open and close. Jack looked out through the hatch. He turned back to Lucky and whispered, "Speak of the devil, it's Nate."

Lucky's eyebrows shot up.

"Anybody here?" Nate called out.

"Come on in," Jack replied. "Be right with you." Jack left the kitchen and joined Nate at the counter.

"Just decided to stop back for some food. You folks open?"

"Just barely," Jack replied. "What'll you have?"

"Got any of that chili today?"

"Coming right up," Lucky called out. She filled the order and passed the bowl through the hatch.

She overheard Nate. "Wanted to stop by and see you, Jack. Maybe have a private word."

Lucky decided to remain silent. Nate's father had died young, and Jack, an old friend of his father, had always made an effort to keep an eye out for Nate. It was Jack who had encouraged him to go into law enforcement.

The phone in the office started to ring. Lucky hurried down the corridor and pushed open the office door. She grabbed the receiver off the hook.

"Can you get up here in the next hour?" It was Sophie's voice—without preamble.

"Uh . . . sure . . . okay. Just need to make sure Jack's all set here."

"Good. There's somebody else I want you to talk to."

"Where should we meet?"

"I've got a private in a few minutes. I can't be there, but go to the Ski Shop and ask for Chance. He knows you're coming. He's a friend."

"All right," she replied hesitantly. Lucky wondered why all this unsolicited information was being offered to her and not to the police. Was Sophie setting her up with people who were willing to lie? Maybe she had a change of heart where Lucky was concerned, but she also had an agenda to make sure Sage was out of jail. She shrugged the feeling off. Sophie might have her faults and petty jealousies, but Lucky couldn't conceive of her being able to coerce others into giving false information. After all, Lucky could very well go straight to the police with the information she had gathered. And in truth that would be the exact right thing to do.

"Ask for Chance. He'll only be in the shop for another hour."

Lucky sighed. "Okay. But Sophie, this is just gossip. I'm not sure it'll do Sage any good at all."

"It's a lot more than gossip. You'll see. Honeywell was a very busy lady—and certainly not that much of a lady." Sophie snickered and hung up the phone.

Lucky heard murmured voices from the front room as she slipped on her jacket and boots. She stuck her head around the corner. "Jack, I'm going out for a bit. I'll check back later."

Nate had stopped in midsentence.

"See you later." Jack waved to her.

Sophie's call had been good timing. She had a feeling Nate would tell Jack things he wouldn't say in front of her. Perhaps, she hoped, he was having second thoughts about arresting Sage.

Chapter 25

CHANCE WAS A tall, wiry man. His biceps bulged under his sweater, and his dark hair was pulled back in a ponytail. Lucky wandered around the shop pretending interest in the merchandise while Chance waited on two customers, a couple, obviously from the city and anxious to buy the latest equipment and accessories. She listened to his line of patter as he led his patrons from one expensive item to another. After ten minutes of encouraging sales talk, he rang up their purchases and, with a last dazzling smile, walked them to the door.

He had sidled up to her before she realized it. "Hi. I'm Chance. Can I help you with anything?" His smile implied he could help her with many things that weren't available at the Ski Shop. A shaft of sunlight played across his features. Crinkle lines around his eyes and a few streaks of gray gave the lie to the youthful appearance he had first presented.

Lucky smiled in return. "Sophie asked me to come see you. She said you had some information about Patricia Honeywell."

His smile melted away, replaced by a coldly cautious glint in his eye. "And you're Lucky, right?"

She nodded.

"I told her I'd talk to you, but nobody else. She twisted my arm. I don't even know how she knew about me and Patsy." He looked thoughtful for a moment. "Oh, I get it. Josh. That's how. Jeez, that kid needs to learn to keep his mouth shut. I don't know this guy they've arrested. Never met him, but I guess he means something to Sophie."

"He means something to me too. He works for us."

"Oh yeah? Where's that?"

"At the By the Spoonful Soup Shop. He's our chef."

"Really? Hey, I've heard about your place—heard good things, but never been there."

"It's a great place," Lucky replied proudly, surprised at her own reaction, "but it won't be for long if Sage isn't released."

"Okay." He sat down on a display bench and faced her, all business now. "What do you want to know?"

"You were seeing her?"

He shrugged. "Yeah. Every so often. Nothing regular. Nothing serious. But I wasn't the only one."

"Do you know who else she might have been seeing?"

"Well, that kid Josh had a fling—I know that, but I doubt we were the only ones she dated."

"Anybody serious?"

He stared off into the middle distance. "To tell you the truth, if I had to guess, I always had the impression that me and Josh were just for show. She really didn't have a great deal of interest in either one of us."

"What makes you say that?"

"Always had the feeling we were trotted out to make somebody jealous. You know, almost like high school stuff. A girl pretends to like another guy to get the guy she really wants to make a move."

"Somebody who couldn't make a decision? Or wasn't free to make a decision?"

"Yeah. Like maybe some married guy—or a married guy

with bucks. Although I doubt money was a motive. She had plenty herself. And I know there were a couple of Mr. Honeywells in her past." He laughed ruefully.

"Any idea who she might have been trying to make jealous?"

Chance shrugged. "Who knows? I didn't really care. I kidded her once about it, but she wasn't talking. Whoever it was, he must have been important to her. She was real secretive. I figured it had to be somebody local."

"Why do you say that?"

"Why else would she be in Snowflake? Don't get me wrong. I love this place, but she could've *wintered . . .*"— Chance spoke the word with a roll of his eyes and a shrug of his shoulders—". . . anywhere. She had real money—she could've been skiing in Gstaad for crissakes. Why here?"

"Look," he continued, "I'm only talkin' to you on Sophie's say-so. You go to the cops with any of this, and I'll deny I ever knew her. I don't want those people sniffing around, asking questions, maybe screwin' up my business. I've got a good deal here. I get to ski free all winter and I do a good business. I don't want to land in jail."

Lucky thought ruefully that Sage, who hadn't been involved with Patricia Honeywell, was sitting in jail at this very moment. Who said life was fair? Either Chance was a very good liar or he had no particular feeling for the dead woman. Josh was relatively young and innocent. He had been hurt because he didn't know Honeywell was just playing with him.

"So you think there was something or someone in Snowflake she wanted."

"Why else would somebody like her come here and not stay in a posh suite at the Resort. Why stay in town?"

"Is there anything else you can recall? Something she might have said or done that didn't seem important at the time?"

Chance shrugged. "I saw her having dinner one night at the restaurant with one of the big guns from the front office."

"Really! Who?"

"Guy named Reed. But I don't think they had anything goin' on."

"Why not?"

"Mmm." Chance thought a moment. "Looked like they had their heads together, but seemed more like business. I only spotted them from a distance anyway, and neither one of 'em looked too happy. I wasn't going to go anywhere near them."

"Anything else—or anybody else you can think of?"

Chance shook his head. "Nah. Don't think so. Don't forget, I didn't see her very often. I never called her—she always called me when she was bored."

"Okay." Lucky buttoned her jacket, preparing to leave. "If you think of anything—anything at all, would you give me a call?"

The dazzling smile returned. "Sure will. Here, jot down your number." He strode to the counter and returned with a pad of paper. She scribbled her full name and gave him the number of the Spoonful. "It'll either be me who answers or my grandfather Jack."

Chance looked at the number she had written down. "Much rather talk to you than your grandfather." He smiled once again, his eyes casually raking over her. She pulled her collar up and headed for the door. He couldn't know, but she was immune to his charms. Way too slick—not the kind of guy that would interest her.

"Thanks, Chance." At the door, she turned back. "I mean that. I appreciate your talking to me."

He held up a hand, silently, as she stepped out into the cold.

"YOU COULD HAVE been really hurt and lain there for days before anyone found you. And how do you know it wasn't the murderer in that house—whoever pushed you down the stairs?" Jack shoved his sandwich away and rubbed his forehead as if to remove the image of his granddaughter tumbling down a flight of stairs. Lucky had made sure they were settled in with some food before she told Jack of her adventure in the house on Bear Path Lane.

"What did Nate have to say?"

"Don't change the subject."

"Has he had second thoughts?"

Jack's lips tightened. "He spoke to me in confidence."

Lucky wailed, "Jack, please!"

"Lucky, my girl. I promised him I wouldn't repeat anything. I just can't. Let's just say the investigation isn't over but he's still convinced he's got the right man."

"Oh." Lucky groaned. "That doesn't sound good."

Outside, the wind had picked up, blowing dry snow like fairy dust across the windows of the restaurant. The weather reports promised a warming trend that hadn't materialized as yet. The neon sign glowed bravely in the frost-covered window. The Spoonful was open for business even if no one came.

"You're trying to distract me. And it won't work," Jack grumbled. "I hate to think who was in that house. I should have been with you. I know I'm failing in a lot of ways, but I'm still strong. If you're gonna do things like that, promise me you'll let me know and I'll come with you."

He had given her the opening she was waiting for. "Actually, there is something you can help me with."

"Say the word. I'm ready."

"Whoever was in that house was desperately searching for something. When I first went into the bedroom, it was a little messy, the bed wasn't made and a few things were lying around. But when Flo and I came upstairs . . ."

"Who did you say? Flo? Flo Sullivan was there?" Jack had a panicked look on his face.

"I forgot to tell you that part. Flo found me. She's been working for Eleanor Jensen, cleaning the rental houses. When I came to, she was kneeling over me and she helped me upstairs."

"Oh," Jack grumbled. "Well . . . in that case."

"She asked for you too," Lucky offered with a straight face, doing her best to gauge Jack's reaction.

"I hope you told her I died three weeks ago!"

She smiled sweetly at her grandfather and struggled not to burst out laughing. "She asked me if you were still as handsome as ever."

"Oh, dear Lord, keep that woman away from me. When she worked here, I could barely get away from her. She kept trying to corner me in the storage closet. I know what she's doing—she's husband hunting, but I am *not* available. I told her that. I . . ."

"Jack. It's all right. Don't worry. I'm sure she's moved on by now." Jack was working himself up into a snit.

"Hmph. I doubt it. But anyway . . . I'm sorry I interrupted. Finish your story."

"Well, when we came back upstairs and looked in the bedroom, it was completely torn up. Jewelry on the floor, drawers pulled out and turned upside down, even the mattress and the box spring had been pulled off the bed. Stuff dumped all over the place. Somebody was in a big hurry to find something they believed was still there."

Frown lines settled on Jack's face. "You think he was already in the house and you might have interrupted him?"

"Possibly. Or he had a key or got in through a window and I didn't hear anything. The house is pretty big. Doesn't look it from the outside, but it has bedrooms on the lower level too. Maybe he didn't know the police had already been there. Or maybe he was just so desperate, he had to take that chance. It's possible that whatever it was he was searching for, he had reason to hope the police hadn't found it."

"Lucky, we don't know anything other than it was someone who knew her, or knew who she was, but not necessarily someone who was familiar with the house and what was in it."

"True. There's a whole range of possibilities. But my bet would be someone was already there when I arrived." She shuddered suddenly at the thought that someone could have been watching her, dogging her footsteps as she rummaged through the bedroom, lying in wait until they had a chance to put her out of commission. She remembered the impulse she had had to call out when she first opened the door. Was there something in the atmosphere that was telling her she wasn't alone? Her senses should have been more alert.

"There were things that should have been there and weren't, like her laptop and cell phone. Eleanor told me Nate had already been to the house, so he probably took them. Or maybe they were in her car. By the way, Nate's found the car but he's not gonna tell me what he found in it."

"I'd like to get my hands on whoever it was who did that to you. And you"—Jack pointed a finger at her—"you were very reckless to go there alone. For all you know, you walked right into the path of a murderer. And we may never know what they were looking for." Jack pulled his plate closer and, wrapping his big hands around the roast beef sandwich, took a large bite.

"That's just it. That's what I want your help for. When I was at the police station, I saw a cardboard storage box with the name 'Honeywell' written on it. I'm sure whatever is in that box is what Nate took from the house the first time he went through it. He left her clothing and cosmetics and things there to be packed up later. But he must have been looking for some clue about her history, her current life . . . something . . . to figure out who killed her. I want to look through that box."

"Terrific, my girl. Just how do you plan to do that? Ask Nate nicely and smile pretty? And then he'll just let you rummage through to satisfy your curiosity?" Jack replied with a smile.

"Very funny. No, that's not exactly what I was thinking."

"Okay, I'm all ears."

Lucky took a deep breath, marshalling her thoughts. "What if . . . what if Nate is out somewhere in town, which he is a lot, and Bradley's on his own down at the station.

What if we figured out some way to lure Bradley out of the station just for five or ten minutes? That's all the time I would need, I think."

"And what if the box isn't there anymore? What if that evidence tech has taken it, or . . . you can't find it? And that's assuming we could get Bradley out of the station."

"I saw Bradley shove the box into a big cabinet under the counter. He locked the cabinet door with a key."

"And where are the keys kept?"

"On a key ring on a hook under the front desk."

"Hmmm." Jack stroked his chin thoughtfully. "I don't know. I don't like the thought of interfering with Nate like that."

"If we can pull it off, he'll never know. What harm can it do? The techs have already looked at everything. I'm not going to remove anything. I just want to see what's in that box."

Finally Jack looked up with a glint in his eye. "All right. I like it. But you have to promise you won't remove anything—that's evidence after all, Lucky. I guess you could be charged with evidence tampering, or obstructing an investigation—something like that. I don't know . . ." Jack trailed off, thinking about the prospect some more.

"Any evidence that a lab would look at would have to be in a container of some sort. I don't know what I could find. I don't know that I'd find anything at all, but we have to do something before Sage gets railroaded. Maybe her cell phone is there. I could check her most recent calls. It might lead to someone in Snowflake that we don't know about yet."

"Well"—Jack wiped his mouth with a napkin—"I have an idea that might work. It would only give you maybe ten minutes. Do you think that's enough time?"

Lucky nodded. "It'll have to be."

Jack chuckled. "Reminds me of that time in Okinawa when we had to break into the supply room. Did I ever tell you about that time?"

"Yes, Jack, you did," Lucky replied patiently.

"Well, there I go, just like an old geezer. Telling the same stories over and over. Let's head out then. It's just gone two bells—there's no time like the present. I'll call the station and ask for Nate. If he's not there, we'll head down in my car. You just follow my lead."

Chapter 26

JACK DROVE TO the other end of town and then headed up Green Street as though driving back to the Spoonful. This street was almost as wide as Broadway, two lanes with room for parking on either side and lined with high snowbanks. Directly in front of the police station, a path had been shoveled from the sidewalk to the street. This was their second pass down Green. Lucky wasn't sure why Jack was circling this second time, but she knew him well enough not to ask.

"Seat belt on, my girl?" he asked.

Lucky nodded.

"Just hold on now." Jack slowed to a crawl. He checked in the rearview mirror. There were no cars behind them. He pulled up just past the cleared path that led through the snowbank and came to a full stop. He glanced over at Lucky to double-check that her seat belt was fastened, then put the car in reverse and revved the engine, slamming backward into the snowbank in front of the station.

Lucky's eyes widened. She glanced over at Jack, just to make sure he had intended to do what he just did.

Jack smiled and turned to her. "Uh-oh. Now look what

I've done. I believe we're stuck." He gave her a broad wink. He put the car in drive and, keeping his foot on the brake, revved the engine. He shook his head. "I guess we're stuck, my girl. Do you think Bradley's inside and could give us a hand?"

Lucky smiled broadly. "Well, Jack, I'm sure he is. I'll just go inside and ask." She unhooked her seat belt and climbed out, clambering over the icy snowbank. She rushed up the stairs and pushed open the front door. Bradley was at the counter, engaged in another whispered telephone conversation. She eyed him suspiciously. It reinforced her belief that Bradley was responsible for the television crew turning up on their doorstep so soon after the murder. When he saw Lucky, he cleared his throat, and in an overly officious tone, said, "We can't give any comment on that. I'll let the Chief know you've called." He replaced the receiver hurriedly.

Lucky adopted her most anxious expression. "Bradley, my grandfather's outside. Do you think you could give him a hand? His foot slipped on the pedal and we're stuck in the snowbank."

Bradley pursed his lips. "I'm sorry. I can't leave the desk. Nate's not here."

"He just needs your help for a minute. Just a little push and I'm sure he can get the car unstuck. He's late for a doctor's appointment," Lucky added for extra measure. Then she whispered conspiratorially, "I had a hard enough time getting him to agree to see the doctor and I don't want him to miss it."

"What if someone calls?"

"Tell you what, I'll stay right here and grab the phone if it rings."

"What if Nate calls. I'll never hear the end of it if he thinks I left the station."

"You're not leaving the station unattended. You're just outside the glass doors. If anything happens, I'll come get you."

Bradley turned over the possibilities in his mind, trying to imagine the consequences of Nate catching him absent without leave. Lucky watched the mental struggle flit across his face.

She waited a moment, and then finally said, "Please, Bradley." Outside, the gunning of Jack's engine was becoming louder and more insistent as he pretended to try to extricate his car from the snowbank.

"All right," Bradley finally said. "I've got a bag of sand somewhere in the back; that might help."

"You're a doll!" Lucky exclaimed. "I'll be right here. Don't worry."

Bradley lifted up the hatch separating the counter from the main room and headed down the corridor to the storage closet. He returned a few moments later, grunting as he carried the bag of sand out the front door to Jack's car. Lucky watched him awkwardly climb the snowbank, struggling to hold on to the bag and deposit it on the street.

Lucky walked closer to the glass doors and watched them carefully. Jack pantomimed getting into the driver's seat and indicated that Bradley should give him a push. A thrill ran up her spine. There was very little time. She rushed behind the counter and retrieved the key ring from the hook. Dismayed, she stared at the key ring. There had to be at least twenty keys, but which one opened the large cabinet? She searched her memory for the one Bradley had used when he locked the cabinet, but nothing came to mind.

Frantically, she pushed the larger keys to the end of the ring. She guessed those might lock the front and back doors of the station, the cells and the door to the cell area. Her fingers quickly flipped through the smaller ones. They were too small—probably made for mailboxes or small lockers. Finally, she isolated six keys that looked as if one of them might possibly be the right one. She glanced quickly at the outer door again. Jack was intermittently revving his engine, causing the car to appear to move an inch or so and then slide back. He was doing an excellent job of being stuck. Bradley was at the left rear bumper, pushing with all his strength every time Jack gunned the engine. She hoped he didn't throw his back out or develop a hernia—then she would feel guilty.

She moved quickly to the side counter and, kneeling on the floor, tried the first key. Too large. Fumbling, she tried the next three keys, the last one almost jamming in the lock. Frustrated and panicking, she took a deep breath to calm her nerves. Bradley's voice was louder; he was moving nearer to the outside door. She peeked up over the counter. Bradley had one hand on the door handle as if ready to come inside.

Lucky swore under her breath and quickly stood by the telephone. Bradley pushed the door open and called out.

"Anybody call, Lucky?"

She quickly moved her arm, holding the key ring behind her. Her heart was beating rapidly. "No." She managed to smile at Bradley. "Very quiet. How's Jack's car?"

Bradley shook his head and returned to the street.

Lucky wished there were time to visit with Sage, but she didn't dare waste a moment. She moved back to the cabinet and knelt in front of the lock. Only two more keys to try. One of them had to fit. Her hands were shaking and she fumbled the keys. The second one fit the lock perfectly. She noted it had a small covering of orange rubber at the top. Why hadn't she tried that one first?

She tucked the keys in her pocket and hauled the box out halfway, resting it on the floor. There was no time to lift it onto the counter and have a more leisurely look. She raised the top. It was the kind of cardboard box made to hold records and didn't contain very much at all. She rummaged through quickly. At the bottom was the laptop that had been missing from the computer case. Several plastic bags held different items. In one was a bottle of men's aftershave. Either someone left this behind or Honeywell had bought it for her various guests. A sheaf of papers was bundled in a see-through plastic envelope. She pushed the packet of papers out of the way in hopes of finding a cell phone. There wasn't one.

She slipped open the top of the plastic envelope, pulled

the papers out and quickly leafed through them. There was
a rental agreement for the cabin on Bear Path Lane and
several sheets of paper clipped together with records of car
rental and insurance. At the very bottom of the stack was a
stiff blue folder, the kind of thing schoolkids use to keep
papers in, the flap fastened with a round paper hook and
string. She quickly undid the string and slid out several
pieces of bond paper. The top sheets were stapled together
and represented an agreement of some sort between a limited liability company and a corporation called Snowflake
Enterprises, Inc. Under that, on heavy bond paper, was a
document entitled PROMISSORY NOTE. The language read,
"FOR VALUE RECEIVED, I, the undersigned, promise to
pay to the order of Commonwealth Equities, Inc., the sum
of Five Million, One Hundred Thousand Dollars
($5,100,000.00) with interest on any unpaid balance . . ."
Lucky skipped the rest of the legal language and scanned to
the bottom. "The principal and any unpaid interest must be
paid in full by March 8 . . ." February 28 . . ." There were
two signatures at the bottom. One was Tom Reed, the other
on behalf of Commonwealth Equities, Inc. She whistled
softly to herself. Tom Reed owed someone an awful lot of
money. Was it just coincidence that the due date of the promissory note was a couple of weeks after Patricia Honeywell's
death? Chance, at the Ski Shop, had felt Honeywell and Reed
were discussing business when he saw them together. Perhaps he was correct. But what was the thread that connected
Commonwealth Equities with Patricia Honeywell?

The hairs on the back of her neck stood up. It was too
quiet outside. Jack wasn't revving his engine any longer. She
had broken out in a cold sweat. With trembling fingers, she
replaced the promissory note and agreement, slid it back into
its stiff folder and refastened it with the small loop of string.
She tossed it back in the box, shoved the box onto the lower
shelf and slammed the cabinet door. She glanced at the outer
door. Bradley held the bag of sand in his arms and was about
to push the door open. She heard Jack call out to him and
engage him in a short conversation. Bradley turned back

toward Jack to respond. Lucky's glance returned to the cabinet. The key was still in the lock. She turned the key and quickly pulled it out of the lock. She skated to the front counter, hanging the keys on the hook under the desk. She had just managed to plop into Bradley's seat when he finally pushed the door open. A blast of cold air hit her face.

"Any luck?" she asked.

"No. Jack wants you to call a tow truck."

"Oh, too bad. I think the number's in the glove box. I'll be right back." Lucky hurried to the front door and pushed it open. Jack was standing on the street by the driver's door.

"Hang on, Lucky," he called. "I'm gonna give it one more try." He winked at her and climbed back into the driver's seat. Lucky waited. She heard the engine rev and saw Jack's car jump forward a couple of feet. She smiled. He had done a great job of waylaying Bradley.

She pushed the door to the station open and leaned inside. "Hey, Bradley. Jack finally did it. We won't need that tow truck after all. Thanks for your help though."

Bradley was turning slowly around inside the counter as though looking for something. Lucky had a moment of doubt—had she inadvertently moved something? Was it something that would give her away? If Bradley figured out what she had been doing and told Nate, it could get very ugly. She hated to think of the ramifications.

Bradley finally turned to her and waved. "Not a problem." He looked at her more carefully. "You're sure nobody called?"

"Nope. Not one call, Bradley."

"Okay. Bye."

Lucky rushed down the stairs and out to the street, climbing into the passenger seat. She flopped back and breathed a sigh of relief. Jack drove slowly down the street, finally turning to her. "Find anything?"

"Sure did." Lucky took a deeper breath. "A very good motive for murder. If I can connect the dots."

Chapter 27

LUCKY PEERED OVER Elizabeth's shoulder as Elizabeth deftly accessed the Vermont Secretary of State website.

"When did you come across this company's name? And how does this relate to the murder?"

"I found the name about an hour ago. And I'm not really sure how it's connected."

"Where did this information come from?"

"It's probably better if I don't tell you. Just trust me," Lucky replied.

Elizabeth raised her eyebrows and turned back to her computer monitor. She typed "Commonwealth Equities" in the search area, and a moment later, the reply flashed on the screen: "No records found."

"Well!" Elizabeth exclaimed. "Wherever this company is, it's not in Vermont. Frankly, my first thought was Massachusetts—because of the Commonwealth name. Let's try there."

Lucky held her breath until a list of companies popped up on the screen. "There it is," she exclaimed. Elizabeth double clicked on the entry and read out loud, "Edmund

Garson is the Agent for Service of Process, with a Boston address. Sometimes they list the corporate officers, but not always." Elizabeth sighed. "This doesn't tell us much."

"Did you say Garson?"

"Yes. Why? Does that mean something to you?"

"I've heard that name before. But where?" Lucky cast her mind back and suddenly remembered her conversation with Sage at the police station. "Sage . . ." she trailed off.

"What about him?"

"If I'm not mistaken, he . . . well, he has a history with Patricia Honeywell. I'm not really free to talk about it, but I could swear he mentioned the name Garson. Yes. That's it!" she exclaimed. "I'm sure that's what he said. Her husband's name was Garson."

"You know, I have a friend at this office in Massachusetts. Corporate officers have to be listed in their records, even if they don't list them on the website. We could send an e-mail, but perhaps a phone call would be quicker."

"I really appreciate your doing this, Elizabeth."

"No trouble at all." She checked the clock on her desk and flipped through her Rolodex, smiling when she found the listing she was searching for. She dialed the number and picked up the receiver as it rang. "Hi. Eloise? Yes, it's me. How are you?" Elizabeth smiled and nodded as she listened to the response at the other end of the phone line. "I have a favor to ask, though. Hope you don't mind. We have a situation here—I'll explain more when we chat next time—but I'm wondering if you could give me the names of the corporate officers of a Massachusetts company." Elizabeth nodded and paused. "Sure," she replied.

Elizabeth covered up the receiver and turned to Lucky. "She's got me on hold. She's checking."

"How nice to have a friend in high places."

"Yes, isn't it? We met at a New England seminar a few years ago and we chat every now and then—we both love to crochet and we got to talking about patterns and then, well, just struck up a friendship." Elizabeth took her hand off the receiver. "Yes, Eloise. I'm here. Yes, I have a pen."

Elizabeth cradled the phone to her ear and started writing on a pad of paper on the desk. "That's great," she said when she had finished. "I'll explain more next time. Right now, I really can't say much. Thanks again." Elizabeth hung up the phone.

She turned to Lucky with a wide smile. "Well, Edmund Garson is the President. And . . . Patricia Honeywell Garson is the Chief Financial Officer."

"So this Edmund Garson must be her ex-husband."

"Or she could be a widow. We don't know, but obviously, she had a right to collect on that promissory note."

Lucky gathered her thoughts. "Elizabeth, that's a direct link from Honeywell to Tom Reed."

"Correct. There's a link. But we don't really know the relationship. Let's assume Tom Reed owed Garson and/or Honeywell that sum of money. For all we know, he's perfectly capable of repaying that loan on time. We also don't know their relationship—Tom Reed, for all we know, could be a close friend or a relative and that's why her company made the loan to him. It doesn't mean he murdered her because he couldn't pay up on time. And even with her death, it doesn't alleviate his obligation to her or this corporation. I'm just playing devil's advocate here."

"But it would buy him time—maybe even several months."

"True. But what worries me is that *if* Reed is hiding something, and that's an *if*, and it comes out at some later date, it would really hurt our party in the campaign. Perhaps I need to have a private chat with him, just to make sure there's no future scandal that could blow up in all our faces. Depending on what he tells me, I probably won't be able to share it with you."

"I understand, Elizabeth. I can't thank you enough for at least listening to me."

"You've got my ear anytime you need it. But I worry about you, sticking your nose in all of this. Please be careful."

* * *

MEG HAD CALLED that morning to see if she was needed and Lucky reluctantly told her not to bother. She apologized for the lack of work and said she wished she could offer more, but Meg seemed to take it in stride. Lucky knew both girls had occasional work at the Resort, which assuaged her guilt somewhat. There was no point in paying an unnecessary employee, especially now that the bank account was on the verge of running into the red.

Lucky flipped over the sign on the front door and lit up the neon sign in the window. Jack had recruited Remy to wash dishes and keep the kitchen clean, and surprisingly, he was doing quite a good job of it. Right now, he was on a ladder scrubbing down the higher storage shelves, something that hadn't been done for a long time. Remy, still feeling guilty about turning up at the Spoonful three sheets to the wind and breaking the glass in the front door, had volunteered for the assignment, free of charge.

She and Jack had put their heads together and decided to do their best to re-create their version of some of Sage's recipes. Sage had never referred to a cookbook, and as far as Lucky could see, never wrote anything down. Was it possible he cooked every recipe from memory, even allowing for the occasional changes or embellishments?

Jack had dug an old cookbook with a cover designed to look like a checkered tablecloth out of the bookshelf in the office. Since they really had no customers to speak of, Jack wanted to use the time to practice. What he didn't say was that his attempts might be permanent if Sage was convicted.

"I have a surprise for you."

"For me?" Jack raised one eyebrow.

"Close your eyes." Lucky smiled.

Jack looked surprised but did as he was told. Lucky reached under the counter and lifted up the CD player. She placed the disc of big band music on top of the player.

"Okay. Open your eyes."

Jack stared at the player in front of him. "Whoa! Where did you get this?"

"At Mom's house. I forgot it was there, and I found the CD at the pharmacy. I thought it would come in handy here."

Jack picked up the disc and studied the song list. "I remember some of these. But you'll have to show me how to use that thing."

"It's really easy." Lucky plugged the player in and ripped the covering off the CD case. "Just press this button right here. The top pops up, then press the disc down like this," she said, illustrating. "Then close the top and hit the play button, right here."

Jack nodded. "I can do that. Although I may need my glasses to see the little symbols." A second later, a saxophone solo swelled at the start of the first song and filled the restaurant with a mellow sound.

"Beautiful," Jack replied. His eyes took on a far-off look. "We should have had music playing here a long time ago. I don't know why we didn't think of it before."

Remy called from the kitchen. "Wow. That sounds great—nice to have music while you work."

Lucky leaned on the counter, leafing through the pages of the cookbook. "What do you want to try first?"

"You pick. I'm game for anything."

Lucky studied the recipes, trying to choose something she was in the mood for and also something for which they had the ingredients. "Here's a recipe for potato leek soup with watercress. Do we have any watercress?"

"Nope. But we can use parsley or maybe some chives on top."

"Come on in the kitchen. Let's get started. I need to start the dishwasher too. Should have done it last night. But I'll peel the potatoes and you can be the soup master for today."

Jack pulled a pot out from the cabinet and dribbled a few drops of walnut oil in the pan. "I think we should experiment. This might be too strong a flavor, but it might work." He added the leeks and shallots that Lucky had chopped to the oil and let them soften. When Lucky had finished peeling and chopping the potatoes and a few sticks of celery, Jack added those to the pot with water and chicken stock.

"No onions?" he asked. "Never heard of making soup without onions."

"Well, leeks and shallots are their first cousins, so I'm sure it's fine," she answered.

"Here we go, my girl." Jack stirred the mixture with a wooden spoon. A slight nutty fragrance assailed her nostrils as the broth simmered. Jack turned down the gas and covered the pot. "Smells good, so far. Sage would be proud of us."

"Maybe I can get him to write down some of his recipes when I see him next. That is, if he doesn't consider them his intellectual property."

Jack laughed. "Tell him we won't feed him until he . . ." Jack stopped in midsentence. The dishwasher was making deep grinding noises.

Lucky bit back her reply when she heard the noise. Jack dropped his spoon and moved closer to the dishwasher, cocking one ear to listen to the sound it was making. Suddenly the dishwasher came to a grinding halt and the kitchen was silent.

Remy had stopped scrubbing and climbed down the ladder. "That doesn't sound good."

Lucky groaned. "We don't need this now." She heard the phone ringing in the office. "Hang on, Jack. I better grab this." She hurried down the corridor to the office and caught the phone on the third ring. It was the Spoonful's landlord, Norman Rank.

"Hello, Lucky. I just wanted to remind you, it's the first today. I hope you'll be getting your check to me before the end of the day."

Lucky felt her face grow hot. She knew it was the first of the month, but with all that had happened, it had slipped her mind to stop by Mr. Rank's house with her check. How could she forget? If she hadn't been so busy sniffing around Patricia Honeywell's life, she would have been taking better care of her own. She recovered quickly. "Of course, I'll be

there within the hour. I hadn't forgotten." She added, "I'm
heading to the bank first to make deposits, and then I'll come
see you."

Norman Rank cleared his throat. "I heard about the trouble down there. I hope it hasn't affected business." Lucky
could visualize his fussy demeanor without having to see
the expression on his face. "You know, your parents always
stopped by with their rent check before it was due."

She gritted her teeth at the judgmental remark rather than
respond in anger. His implication being, of course, that she
was unqualified or incompetent in some fashion to take over
and run the business successfully.

"Yes, I'm sure they did." *And since your rent check is due
today, you'll receive it right on time,* she thought, but bit
back the words. "See you very soon."

As soon as she hung up, she pulled the ledger out of the
drawer. Their account was almost completely drained, and
they were short of the rent by several hundred dollars. A
feeling of exhaustion came over her. The only way she could
pay the rent and all the rest of the bills this month would be
to transfer the last of her earnings from her former job into
the restaurant's account. Had her parents had this much
trouble? Her impression had always been that the restaurant
was booming and her parents had no financial difficulties,
even though she knew they worked very hard. It must have
been tough for them nonetheless.

She took a deep, shaky breath. Now the dishwasher had
given up the ghost. Even if, by some miracle, Sage were
released, would their business return to normal? Maybe
there was a cloud over the Spoonful that nothing could dis-
pel. Maybe it was her. Maybe she was the jinx. She made a
notation in the ledger for the amount she would transfer and
then deducted the rent, writing a check payable to Norman
Rank who owned most of the commercial spaces in town,
inherited from one of Snowflake's original families. She
thought if she ever achieved any financial success, she'd buy
the building herself and never have to pay rent again.

She returned to the kitchen to find Jack half lying on the

floor and the dishwasher pulled out from the wall. The soup still simmered on the stove. He had spread newspapers on the floor and was busy removing the back covering of the machine. Remy knelt by the toolbox and searched for a screwdriver.

"Is it fixable?"

Jack peered up at her. "Possibly. Think it blew its transmission. But if I can't figure it out, we'll have to call someone. Any money left in the account?"

"Sure." Lucky decided she wouldn't tell Jack just how low they were. He didn't need to worry. "We'll be okay. I'm heading over to Norman's to pay the rent. I almost forgot today's the first, and . . ." An idea had formed in her head. "I have another errand to run but I'll be back later."

"You go ahead. Remy and I can hold the fort."

Chapter 28

ONCE LUCKY HAD transferred the last of her funds into the restaurant account and driven to Norman Rank's house to drop off the rent check, she returned to her apartment to change her clothes. She dressed in her black skirt and boots and long coat. She wanted to look her best if she had any hope of gaining access to the corporate offices of the Resort. She drove up the hill toward the Snowflake Resort. When she reached the top, she entered through the drive marked by stone pillars. She headed for the building that Tom Reed had entered just two days ago, passing by the spot where he had parked his car. There it was—a silver Saab. Nice looking, undoubtedly with all the bells and whistles. Was this the car Josh had seen at the house on Bear Path Lane? She hit the brakes and stared at the bumper. No blue and white sticker; not even a residue of glue where a sticker might have been. She scanned the parking area, but all the spaces were marked RESERVED. She'd have to park in the next lot and walk back.

She wasn't at all sure what she planned to do here. She couldn't very well go to Nate and tell him she had searched his evidence box. She also couldn't tell him she had rummaged through the house on Bear Path Lane where she had found Reed's home address. Reed owed Honeywell or her corporation a great deal of money, and perhaps he was in a position to repay that money on the due date, but perhaps he was not. Perhaps, and she realized this was all speculation, he had borrowed from the corporation in order to invest in the limited partnership that owned and ran the Resort. If so, that investment earned him a share of the profits, and a very nice living for himself and his family. If he couldn't repay the money on time, Honeywell could have brought a lawsuit against him, uncovering his shaky finances. Surely he had a hefty share of the profits here, but was it enough to pay back $5 million on demand? And then there were his political aspirations. It wouldn't help his campaign to be sued for nonpayment of a promissory note while he was running for the state senate.

She wasn't sure what she was going to say to Reed, but she knew she wanted to meet him, no matter what wheels she might set in motion. She had been accused of opening her mouth and putting her foot in it often enough, and she knew it was a fair assessment, but the time had come to upset a few applecarts. Tom Reed wasn't above suspicion. After all, she justified, she was doing what Nate should be doing. Reed might have an office at the top of the mountain, but he and his family still had to get along in Snowflake.

She pushed through the door and entered a reception area. A slender young girl with very long red nails sat at the console. She was reading a fashion magazine and reluctantly pulled herself away from an ad for the latest colors in lip gloss.

"Can I help you?" She looked up, eyes rather glassy, as though bored and waiting for her day to end.

"I'd like to speak to Mr. Reed."

"Do you have an appointment?"

"No. I just had a minute and wanted to stop by. We're old . . . we have a friend in common. I'm sure he'd like to speak with me."

"Your name?" she asked.

"Lucky Jamieson." Lucky smiled back at her with what she hoped was a confident smile.

The girl's lips twitched ever so slightly as if to say, *I doubt it*, but she reached for her telephone and hit an intercom button, repeating Lucky's message.

The girl nodded and finally put down the phone. "Step through that archway and turn to the right. Mr. Reed's office is the third on the left."

"Thank you." Lucky turned and headed farther into the building. As she rounded the corner, she spotted the man she had followed standing in the corridor looking out for her. He smiled smoothly as she approached. The kind of smile a used car salesman first gives you when you walk on the lot, as if to say, *I'm your best friend and you're going to be so happy with the deal I'm about to offer you.*

He held out his hand as she neared him. "Ms. Jamieson, is it? Please step inside."

"Thank you."

He held the door open and followed her into a large modern office.

"Please—have a seat. Now, how can I help you?" His eyes gave her a quick perusal, wondering if she were selling something, or if there were something he could sell to her. "We might have a friend in common, did you say?" Never one to pass up a business opportunity.

"Friend might not be the best way to put it."

"Oh?" he replied, rearranging the pens on top of his desk.

"But I believe we both have a connection of sorts with Patricia Honeywell." Was it her imagination or did his facial muscles tighten slightly?

He hesitated a moment too long. Lucky could see the wheels spinning behind his eyes—eyes that had grown rather hard in the last few seconds.

"Patricia Honeywell, did you say? Hmm." His breath drew out as if trying to remember who that might be. "And what would your connection to Ms. Honeywell be?"

"It's because of her that my business is in a bit of trouble, to put it mildly. Her body was found behind our restaurant and our chef has been arrested for murder."

"Oh," he said, surprised. "Oh," he repeated. "Well, that's too bad. I'm just not . . . I'm not sure what this could have to do with me. I don't quite remember her, that is if I ever knew her."

She crossed her fingers and dove in. "I doubt you could have forgotten the large sum you owed her—or still owe her estate."

There was no doubt about it now; his complexion paled. "How did you . . . Who are you?" he demanded.

"Exactly who I've told you. I just wanted to meet you in person and talk to you."

"Why? What do you want?" The eyes had turned a steely gray and his jaw was clenched.

"I don't wish you any harm. I only want the guilty party punished."

"And you think?" he blustered. "Are you implying that *I* had something to do with a murder? How dare you!" he exclaimed. "Didn't you just say your . . . what was it . . . cook was arrested for her murder? Why are you here—in my office?"

"Chef. 'Chef' was the word I used. He may have been arrested, but I doubt he did it. I think somebody else— somebody with a very strong motive—killed her. I just wanted to talk to you about the money you owed her."

"Well, fine. You've done just that. And for your information, *if*, and that's *if*, I owed her any money, then I would still owe that money to whoever represents her estate. And I think, young lady," his voice became a harsh whisper, "you need to get the hell out of my office and this building right now."

Lucky slipped out of the chair and put her hand on the doorknob. She turned back, trying her best not to let her voice tremble. "I just have one more question."

"What?" Reed snarled.

"Was there more to your relationship than just business?" she asked quietly.

He placed his hand on the phone. "I'm calling security right now."

"No need. I'm leaving." She slipped through the door and hurried down the corridor, past the girl still reading the fashion magazine. Once out in the cold air of the parking lot, she took a deep breath and let it out slowly. Tom Reed could very well have been the person who tore up the house on Bear Path Lane and shoved her down the stairs. He was guilty of something. She just wasn't sure if it was murder.

Lucky trudged back to her car. She noted that all the lots at the Resort had been plowed and swept clean—better even than the streets of the town. Reed had a very good reason to want Honeywell dead. Five million was a lot to come up with if he was hurting financially. His house, as nice as it was, couldn't possibly generate that kind of a loan. Had he needed that cash to buy into the partnership and assure his position? With Honeywell dead, there'd be no need for him to meet the demand date of the promissory note. As he said, he would still owe the cash to her estate, but her death would buy him time. Honeywell must have had an attorney in Boston, and that attorney would have the information to track down Tom Reed. She would have been able to sue Reed personally, but would she have been able to cause financial difficulties for him at the Resort? Had Tom Reed torn up the bedroom on Bear Path Lane searching for the promissory note? It could take weeks, perhaps months, for an attorney to sort out her affairs and for someone to come knocking, asking for repayment. Was her attorney, whoever he or she might be, alerted to the fact, and ready to pounce? Or had she contacted a local attorney, licensed to practice law in this state?

Lucky reached her car and shoved the key in the lock. She needed to get back to the Spoonful. After her promise to Jack, she felt a bit guilty not giving him a heads-up about her plan to confront Reed, but she knew he'd never approve.

A footstep crunched in the snow behind her. She whirled to find Chance, smiling, and standing a bit too close for comfort. She felt a shiver of fear. She was some distance from the office building and it was growing dark. No one knew she was here.

"Hey there!" Chance smiled a slow, suggestive smile. "We meet again."

Lucky gulped, trying to recover from her initial scare. She backed up against the door of her car to move away from him. She finally managed a smile. "Just visiting."

"Really? Here?" Chance looked around, obviously aware that the only near building housed the administration offices.

"I could ask you the same question."

Chance smiled even more lazily. "Well, since you ask, I have a date with that cute little receptionist in there," he said, pointing to the main entrance. "Very handy to have friends in administration—especially ones that keep you posted on the gossip." He shoved his hands in his pockets. "Have you had any luck unearthing more dirt on our Ms. Honeywell?"

"Not really," Lucky replied.

"Oh. I thought maybe that's why you were visiting the offices of the big guns—Tom Reed to be more specific." He raised one eyebrow and leaned lazily against the door of her car. Lucky didn't respond to the taunt. "What was the name of your restaurant again? I'll have to make sure I stop in next time I'm down in the town."

"By the Spoonful. We run a soup shop—soup and other things."

"Where is it? On Broadway?"

Lucky nodded. His nearness was making her uncomfortable. And after all, she thought with a chill, he had been involved with Honeywell too. For all she knew, Chance had lied through his teeth and had a very good motive to kill, maybe even better than Tom Reed. She turned her key in the lock and said, "Excuse me," forcing Chance to move away and allow her to open her car door. She climbed in, but before she could close it, Chance laid his hand on the door-jamb and leaned closer. There was a glint in his eye that Lucky thought could turn nasty in a split second.

"I'll definitely stop by real soon." He smiled, watching

carefully for her response. She felt like a small mammal transfixed by a snake.

"That would be great," she replied neutrally, reaching out to pull the door shut against his advances. *Did this work on most women,* she wondered?

Chance lifted his hand, but before she could shut her car door, he said, "Oh, actually I almost forgot. There was something I meant to tell you."

"And what was that?" His casual attitude was irritating her no end.

"Well, one time Patsy twisted her leg—skiing. I saw her that night and it seemed it was bothering her. I offered to get her an appointment up here with one of the ortho docs, but she just laughed and said not to bother. Said she got all her medical treatments for free. Just struck me as strange— thought you might be interested, that's all."

"What did she mean by that?"

"Who knows? Maybe she had somethin' going with one of the docs up here. The Resort offers everything. There are three on staff, two orthopedic guys and one trauma doc."

Lucky remembered the card from the Snowflake Clinic she had found in Honeywell's datebook and the brochure she had picked up from the Snowflake Clinic. She turned and rummaged in her purse. She handed the folded brochure to Chance.

"Did you ever see her with any of these people?" The cover showed a smiling group shot of the entire Clinic staff: Elias and Jon Starkfield, their assistant and nurse, the records clerk and Rosemary and Melissa, the two receptionists.

Chance took it from her outstretched hand and studied it briefly. He shook his head. "Nope. Never seen any of these people, much less any of them with Patsy." He handed it back to Lucky. "Like I said, I didn't see her that often. Only when she called." He smiled again. "Sorry—not much help, I know."

"Thanks anyway."

Chance backed away and Lucky pulled her car door shut.

She drove slowly toward the gate and saw Chance in the rearview mirror watching her. He turned finally and headed for the administration building just as she reached the access road. Would Chance have passed on his information if he hadn't accidentally run into her? Was their meeting an accident? She shivered. Had he somehow been keeping tabs on her? Ridiculous! She pushed the thought away.

As she drove, she replayed her conversation with Tom Reed. He had had an extreme reaction. Of course, in all fairness to him she had alternately accused him of infidelity and possibly murder. Maybe he was perfectly justified in his reaction, but there was something not quite right there, nonetheless.

And what exactly had Chance said? *Said she got all her medical treatments for free.* Was she seeing a doctor? Someone at the Resort where three doctors were on staff? Someone at the hospital in Lincoln Falls where many more doctors must have parking permits? Perhaps that's what Josh saw the night he slipped on the ice, or was it someone closer to home? Someone in Snowflake? Chance thought Honeywell had a reason to be here—to be close to someone in Snowflake. A married man? Otherwise why would a woman who thought nothing of carrying on multiple affairs be secretive? There were only two doctors in Snowflake, and one was married. She thought of Elias but quickly pushed the thought away. It just couldn't be possible.

Could Jon Starkfield not be the down-to-earth, likable man and devoted husband he appeared to be? Was that an act? His wife seemed a very charming woman, but that didn't stop a lot of men from straying. Why would someone like him—a respected man in his fifties—carry on, especially with a woman like Patricia Honeywell, a socialite with money who knew no boundaries? There was only one person she should talk to and that was Elias—surely he would know Starkfield well enough to know if his partner were capable of such a thing.

When she reached Broadway, she drove past the restaurant. It was closed. Jack must have decided to close up and go home. Hopefully one or two customers might have strayed in during the afternoon. There had to be someone within a ten-mile radius who hadn't heard of the murder and didn't suspect the Spoonful of harboring a murderer. It was frightening how quickly years of good reputation could be washed away by one dreadful act.

Chapter 29

LUCKY HEATED WATER in the kettle to brew a cup of tea. She turned a kitchen chair toward the window and sat, staring out into the dark—a darkness carpeted by white snow. The old Victory Garden took up most of the square block area behind her apartment building. Its entrance was on Spruce Street to her left. A tall wooden fence separated the Garden from its neighbors and marked its entire perimeter. Maple, Elm and Spruce and the alleyway parallel to Broadway were the streets that formed the square block enclosing the Garden. To her right was the parking lot behind the Clinic with access only to Maple Street. From her perch she could see the top of the Spoonful, but the back fence of the Victory Garden blocked her view of the alleyway behind it.

She mulled over Chance's remark once again. Jon Starkfield could fit the bill—local and married. She sipped her tea and thought about him and his wife. Jon and Abigail Starkfield—two opposite personalities—Jon, charming and distinguished and warm, and Abigail, pleasant but buttoned-up and conservative. Perhaps marriage was like that—people balancing each other out. She thought about her

parents, her Dad only slightly stricter than her Mom, but
both of them open and friendly people, always ready to
extend a helping hand to anyone who needed it. They were,
in that respect, two peas in a pod, but perhaps some mar-
riages weren't like that at all. People married the people they
needed to be with, a spendthrift and a frugal person, an
outgoing spouse and an introverted one.

There were superficial similarities between Patricia Honeywell and Abigail Starkfield. Abigail must have been very
pretty in her youth. The years had marked her, but Lucky
could imagine her as a young woman, blonde curls framing
her face, her figure slim. Patricia Honeywell, whatever one
might think of her morality, had been very well liked by
men. That could be especially tempting for a man who may
have become bored with his wife of many years. Was Jon
Starkfield a serial adulterer, or was his involvement—
assuming he was the secret lover, Lucky reminded herself—
an impulsive act, a mistake he later regretted? Perhaps once
involved he couldn't or wouldn't extricate himself.

The promised warming trend had arrived and layers of
ice were melting. A large chunk fell from the roof of the
building and flew by Lucky's kitchen window, landing with
a thunk in a snowdrift in the garden below. Lucky leaned
forward in her chair to look out. She slid the window open
a few inches and placed some nuts on the windowsill, sure
the squirrels would find them in the morning.

The garden behind her building shared a fence with the
Victory Garden. In the center of that fence was a gate into
the Garden, empty and covered with snow now that the town
was in the depths of winter.

She pushed her window open and leaned out, careful not
to go too far in case another chunk of ice fell from the roof.
She craned her neck to get a better view. The Snowflake
Clinic next door boasted a small parking lot that could
accommodate perhaps eight cars at most. A chain link gate
in that fence opened into the Garden. On the Broadway side,
she knew, a wooden gate led from the Garden to the alleyway that ran behind the Spoonful.

What if Patricia Honeywell were carrying on a secret affair with Jon Starkfield? What if she hadn't been killed at the Spoonful, but at the Clinic? Was she threatening to expose an affair and destroy his marriage? Was she pregnant with Starkfield's child? If that were the case, that Honeywell threatened Jon Starkfield, could he have killed her? There were a lot of "ifs," but the pregnancy and a secret lover implied a great deal of passion. Could that passion have led to murder?

Lucky cast her mind back to the discovery of the body by the Dumpster. She closed her eyes and tried to recall every detail of that shocking moment as Sage stood next to her. She remembered the tuft of hair sticking out of the ice and the light catching a sparkling earring dangling from one ear—the right ear. She was sure Nate had been searching for that other earring and hoping to find enough blood to prove she had been killed there. If that earring wasn't behind the Spoonful, then it could have been knocked off during a struggle. And if there had been a struggle, that earring would be at the place where Patricia Honeywell was killed.

Lucky stared at the large square of snow in the center of her block—no one would be in the Victory Garden now. In spring, when the snow had melted, local residents, mostly retirees who were lucky enough to be allotted a small garden, would be clearing their plots of land, getting the earth ready for summer vegetables. No one would venture through the melting snow and mud now. It was possible those gates were never locked. If there had been an after-hours assignation and she had been killed at the Clinic or in the parking lot behind the Clinic, could Starkfield have dragged her body through the gate and across the Victory Garden to the alleyway behind the Spoonful?

Lucky finished the last sip of tea and slipped on her boots and jacket. It was time to do some digging. She left her building and passed by the Clinic on her way around the corner to Broadway. She reached the entrance to the narrow alleyway that led to the back of the Spoonful and halted. She had the distinct feeling she was being watched. She turned quickly and scanned the street. Had she imagined a shadow in the doorway on the other side of Broadway? Her heart was pounding. She waited and continued to watch the shadows but nothing moved. Her nerves were playing tricks on her. She took a deep breath and headed down the alley. She unlocked the back door and flicked on the hallway light. Another small door in the corridor led to a narrow storage closet. She rummaged in the dark until she felt the wooden handle of a spade that Jack used to break up ice. Carrying it with her, she turned off the overhead light and relocked the door. Holding a small flashlight, she examined the wooden gate that led into the Garden. She pushed as hard as she could on the gate but it wouldn't budge. It had to be locked or barred from the other side.

Frustrated, she hurried out to Broadway, hoping she'd not be noticed carrying a shovel. She slowed down as she passed the doorway on the opposite side of the street. It was empty. Her eyes must be playing tricks on her. She continued on her way and met no one. She turned the corner on Maple and walked down the narrow drive that led to the parking lot of the Snowflake Clinic. A small night-light glowed from the lab in the rear of the building, but the lot was empty of cars. The gate into the Garden here was secured with only a simple hasp—no lock. Quickly, she flipped it open. It made a loud squeak on its hinges. She pushed the gate with difficulty, hampered by the heavy, wet snow. She squeezed through the gate and, walking at an angle across the Garden, reached the wooden gate behind the Spoonful. This one was barred by a wooden slat. She lifted the slat and struggled to pull the gate inward. Using her shovel, she scooped snow out of the way until the gate moved freely. Before the storm hit there had been very little snow on the ground. It would have been much easier then. She pulled the gate completely open and stared across the alleyway to the exact spot where Patricia Honeywell's body had been found.

She didn't need her flashlight here. Moonlight reflecting off the softening snow lit up the entire Garden. Lucky saw the holes her footprints had left, a clear track from the Clinic to the gate behind the Spoonful. On the night of the murder three feet of snow would have fallen on top of any prints left behind. There might have even been a trail of blood, impossible to find now.

Someone could have easily—or not so easily—but someone with a certain amount of strength could have dragged a body from the back of the Clinic through the Garden to the rear of the Spoonful in an effort to draw attention away from the Clinic. How much could a body weigh? Perhaps the slim woman had weighed anywhere from 110 to 130 pounds. Lucky was sure she herself would have been able to drag such a weight that distance. Even easier if the body had been placed on a blanket or tarp. The dangerous part would have been the risk of being seen, but that night everyone was hunkered down, drawing their drapes and awaiting the storm. Dressed in dark clothing on a deeply overcast night, no one glancing out a window would have noticed anything at all. The storm started around nine o'clock and lasted for several hours. It would have been possible to easily move the body within the first two hours. After that, snow and wind might have made things more difficult for the murderer. Any footprints or blood trail would have been covered quickly. If the victim had only been unconscious, had she been left to die in the cold? Lucky shivered. Who could have done such a thing?

Lucky closed the gate and did her best to return to the Clinic gate by stepping in the same prints she had left moments ago. If there was evidence buried under the melting snow, could it be retrieved? Or would most of it melt away? Most importantly, she would have to go to Nate with her thoughts—if only he would listen to her.

She closed the chain link gate behind her and flipped the hasp over the pole, hoping no one would notice her footprints the following day. If Starkfield were the murderer, he might wonder who had trudged through the area behind the Clinic and left telltale prints.

Lucky stood by the gate, shovel in hand, staring at the back door of the Clinic. If the murder occurred here, what

was Honeywell doing? Waiting for Jon Starkfield? Would he
have asked her to meet him here after hours? Did he kill her
inside the Clinic? Or did he meet her here in the parking lot?
Was she taken by surprise?

How would a man kill a lover he wanted to get rid of?
Especially if that man were a doctor? Would he strangle her?
Would he inject her with poison? Did she die from her head
wound? Lucky shivered, suddenly frightened to be standing
alone in a dark parking lot.

The Clinic had closed early because of the snowstorm. If
she had been waiting here for Starkfield and he didn't arrive,
would she drive away? Unless she were sure he was inside
the Clinic. If he hadn't joined her within a few minutes,
would she have gone to the back door of the Clinic and
knocked—sure that the staff was safely out of the way?
Whoever struck her could have been hiding behind a car or
the small Dumpster. Two piles of frozen snow were heaped
next to the doorway. Lucky thought back to the day of the
discovery of the body—in her mind's eye she saw the blood
on the left side of the head, an earring dangling from the
right ear; the missing one would have been on her left ear.
If she had been standing at the back door to be let in, and
was struck on the left side of her head, the impact could have
sent her reeling to the right. Did she hit the wall of the
entryway?

Lucky scanned the doorway with her flashlight. Much of
the snow had been shoveled away and some had melted. If
Honeywell had been struck here, and, she admitted to herself, it was a long shot, perhaps there were bloodstains still
visible. Lucky scanned the windows of her apartment building next door and the backs of the houses on Elm Street.
When she was sure no curious neighbor had spotted her, she
started chipping away at the snow and ice piled on the side
of the doorway. If she found bloodstains or the missing earring, she was sure it would be enough to go to Nate and
convince him to continue his investigation.

Holding the small flashlight in her mouth as she worked,

she whittled away at the frozen pile at the side of the doorway, scooping it down the stairs. It was slow going, and in the dark she wondered if her eyes were playing tricks on her. She couldn't be sure of seeing anything with such a small light, but perhaps she'd find the missing earring. After three quarters of an hour, she had managed to clear the ice and snow from the entryway. She was sweating profusely under her sweater and jacket but still terrified of making noise that would attract attention. If anyone looked out a back window on Elm Street and spotted her, they'd think she was trying to break into the Clinic.

When all the snow and ice had been cleared away, she scanned the wall and doorstep carefully with her small flashlight. Nothing. No bloodstains, no missing earring, nothing. She sat down heavily on the cold concrete step and mopped her brow. Nothing to prove that Patricia Honeywell was murdered here. Any evidence had most likely been taken away by the plow that had cleared the lot.

A footstep crunched in the snow. She leaped to her feet and grabbed the shovel. Adrenaline coursed through her veins. "Who's there?" she called out. She scanned the lot quickly. Empty. There was only one way out and that was the narrow driveway that led out to Maple. Someone was in that drive. She was sure of it.

She had to get out to the street. She'd be trapped here. She shoved the flashlight in her pocket and gripped the shovel with both hands, holding it at waist level pointed away from her. She quickly stepped around the corner of the building. A dark figure stood at the end of the drive pressed up against the building.

"Hey," she yelled at the top of her lungs. She started running toward the dark figure, and as she came closer, he turned and ran. There was something familiar about the figure, but she didn't stop to think about it. She ran to the sidewalk, still holding on to her shovel, ready to use it as a weapon if need be. By the time she reached the street, the dark figure had turned the corner on Spruce and disap-

peared. She halted at the entrance to her building to catch
her breath. He was moving too fast. She couldn't possibly
catch up. But she had a good idea who had been stalking her.
She'd bet her last dollar it was Remy. Had he been watching
her the whole time she had been digging through the snow?
She shivered and climbed the stairs to her building.

Chapter 30

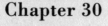

LUCKY DRESSED HURRIEDLY the following morning, her arms stiff from chopping ice outside the Clinic the night before. She had a little time to herself since she and Jack wouldn't open the Spoonful until eleven o'clock. She wasn't at all sure why they were bothering to open at all. They might just as well hang a quarantine sign on their door to warn people away.

She hurried out of her building and went next door to the Clinic, hoping Elias was on duty. She needed to talk to someone, preferably him, about her suspicions. Inside, several people were awaiting their appointments. One woman was doing her best to hang on to a squirming boy while rocking a carriage with a crying infant. Rosemary was manning the front reception desk.

"Hi, Rosemary, I wonder if I could speak to Dr. Scott. I'm sure he's busy, but I can wait if he has a few minutes for me."

"Oh, he's not on today. He's doing rounds over at Lincoln Falls. Dr. Starkfield is here, if he can help you. Is it about your grandfather?"

Lucky hesitated. "Uh, yes and no," she said, unwilling to admit that her visit to Elias had nothing to do with Jack. "I'm on my way to the Spoonful and . . . I think I lost an earring. I was just wondering if someone had found it."

"I haven't. But I'll check with the other receptionist. She might know if anyone's turned anything in. Did you want Dr. Scott to give you a call anyway?"

"No need. It can wait. I'll call him tomorrow. Just had a quick question about something."

Rosemary looked dubiously at her. Lucky was sure her excuse sounded flat. Then Rosemary smiled, realizing Lucky's motive was probably romantic. Lucky felt even more uncomfortable. "Should I let him know you were asking for him?" she asked with a knowing smile.

"It's all right. I was just passing by and thought I might catch him for a second."

Rosemary continued to smile broadly. "He's at the hospital in Lincoln Falls today, but he'll be back to town tomorrow."

The door to the inner rooms opened, and Abigail Starkfield stepped into the reception area behind Rosemary. She smiled at Lucky and said, "Oh, hello. We meet again. Can I help you?"

"Thanks, no. I was just asking Rosemary if Dr. Scott was on duty today."

"He's not available today, but I'm sure we can squeeze you in."

"There's no need. I just wanted a word with him. He examined my grandfather the other day." Lucky noticed Rosemary's slight smile.

"Elias mentioned you'll be attending our concert tomorrow night." Abigail smiled broadly. "I hope you like our little presentation. We have some wonderful singers."

"I'm looking forward to it."

"I'll tell Elias you were here, and I'll see you at St. Genesius."

With a last glance at Rosemary, Lucky beat a hasty retreat. Rosemary undoubtedly thought she was suffering from lovesickness. She wished it were that simple. She turned and headed around the corner to the Spoonful. She wanted very badly to talk to Elias about her theory. A body could have easily been dragged through the Victory Garden and left behind the Spoonful. Her theory, of course, was based on the assumption that Starkfield was Abigail's lover and killer. She admitted to herself it was a wild leap, considering it was based on a claim by a man she didn't know in the slightest. For all she knew, Chance could have fabricated the entire story, although it did have a ring of truth. Seeing Abigail at the Clinic was a sobering moment. She was confronted with the reality of what her theory could mean. If she were correct, that Starkfield was Honeywell's lover, it would be devastating to a woman like Abigail. How much more devastating would it be if Starkfield were a killer. Maybe it was best Elias wasn't available. It would give her the day to mull over her suspicions. Time enough to talk to him tomorrow evening.

LUCKY TRUDGED AROUND the corner to the Spoonful and entered by the front door. Sophie had arrived early and was seated at a table with Jack, sipping coffee. Lucky slipped off her coat and joined them. The restaurant was otherwise empty. Hank and Barry had yet to arrive, and it was too early for Marjorie and Cecily. Lucky heard the sound of running water in the kitchen.

She looked over at Jack. "Remy's here early," she remarked.

Jack nodded. "It's good for him to have something to do. His nerves are on edge."

"Mine too," Sophie joined in. "It's like we're all waiting for the other shoe to drop." Sophie heaved a sigh. "I spoke to Nate this morning. He thinks he'll be taking Sage to Bournmouth either tomorrow or Saturday."

Lucky reached across the table and squeezed Sophie's hand. Jack shook his head. "I wish this had gone another way."

"Me too." Sophie blinked back tears.

Lucky had no response. A sense of gloom had settled over their table. "More coffee anyone? I know I need a cup."

"Nah," Jack replied. "I'm fine."

"Sophie?"

Sophie shook her head negatively and stared blankly out the window. Lucky rose and slipped into the kitchen. Remy was bent over the dishwasher and jumped when he felt her presence.

"Remy, why were you following me last night?" she asked, resisting the urge to be accusatory.

"Me?" His face drained of color. "I don't know what you're talking about."

"Oh, come on, Remy. I saw you. I chased you. Don't lie to me."

Remy's shoulders slumped. "I'm sorry. I didn't mean to scare you. I was coming out of the Pub and I saw you walking down the street with the shovel. I was curious. And then I was worried about you. You shouldn't have been back there all alone."

Lucky stared at him for a long minute. His explanation sounded reasonable enough. "Then why did you run away?"

"Embarrassed, I guess. I couldn't figure out what you were doing, but I didn't want you to think I was spying on you." He shrugged his shoulders. "What were you doing back there anyway?"

Lucky was tempted to explain, but caught herself. "It's a long story, but it doesn't matter anymore. I'll tell you someday."

She hoped that Remy was as innocent as he claimed to be and he had no ulterior motive in following her.

Chapter 31

ELIAS HELD THE door open as they entered the church. High above the heavy bells jangled, announcing the start of the concert. Small sprays of flowers and evergreens tied with ribbon were fastened to the ends of each pew. The musicians had arranged their instruments—a harp, cello and violin— in front of the steps that led to the altar. Lucky watched in fascination as they tuned and prepared for the concert. Elias led her to a pew toward the front on the right side. She scooted in and slipped her coat from her shoulders.

Elias handed her a program. "I think you'll be pleasantly surprised." Barring the day earlier that week when Abigail had surprised her in the side chapel, it had been a few years since Lucky had seen the interior of St. Genesius. The nave was well lit. Exposed beams crossed above their heads from either side, meeting in the middle. The windows were all stained glass set in Gothic arches. The noise level increased as people wandered in, found seating and conversed with their neighbors in adjoining pews. Most of the attendees were friends and relatives of the singers, but the choral group had gained in popularity, and Elias had mentioned that much of their audience traveled from other towns to hear their programs.

Finally the lights dimmed as in a theatre. The singers entered from the side of the altar in single file and stood in prearranged sections on the steps above the musicians. Their conductor stood in the aisle and raised his baton, and the first notes swelled through the church. Lucky referred to her program. There were four numbers, an intermission and then four more songs. One was a Bellini piece, another a Mendelssohn selection in German. Lucky regretted knowing so little of classical music. As she listened, she noticed the different voices were scattered, not isolated in sections, lending a depth and resonance to the sound.

Lucky saw Abigail standing in the second row between two women. After the third piece, Abigail moved to the front carrying her sheet music. She placed the pages on a stand and sang a solo accompanied only by the harpist. The words were French. The notes were haunting. Lucky glanced down at her program. It was a Fauré piece called "Après un rêve." Her schoolgirl French was rusty, but she could still decipher some of the phrases. *You called me and I left the earth to run away to the light.*

Abigail's voice was lovely. The notes swelled and lingered, weaving an achingly lovely story. Lucky imagined how much her mother would have enjoyed this. She closed her eyes and let sound wash over her, memories of her mother flashing before her eyes. She felt, like the song, as if she could leave her body behind and rise to the rafters transported by this music. The end of the program came all too soon. Lucky turned to Elias and whispered, "They're fantastic."

He smiled and nodded. "Aren't they? Some are retired professionals, some are amateurs, but they're all highly trained." He stood and helped her slip her coat on. "There are refreshments in the lobby. Let's get something hot to drink."

They navigated the aisle as people gathered their things and left their seats. Lucky was instantly alert when she saw

Tom Reed and his wife on the far side of the church. She hoped he hadn't seen her, or that if he had, he wouldn't say anything unpleasant. She cringed when she remembered how blunt she had been in his office. She hadn't really wanted to take that tack, but reviewing it in her mind, what other choice had she had, other than to come right out and ask her questions? He had a right to take offense at her prying, but all the same, his reaction was extreme.

Elias looked at her. "Anything wrong?"

She snapped out of her thoughts and turned to him, smiling. "No. Not at all. Sorry, just lost in thought."

The front entry area was cold, chilled by blasts as many left or lingered in the doorway. The noise level rose as friends greeted one another. A group of people were gathered around a table where CDs from earlier performances were being sold. A few of the singers had joined friends and were chatting by the pastry tray.

"Elias! Glad you could make it." Jon Starkfield exited from the church and placed a hand on Elias's shoulder.

Elias smiled and turned to Lucky. "Jon—you remember Lucky Jamieson."

"Yes, of course I do. Did you enjoy the performance?"

"Very much," she responded. "I was impressed. Your wife has an amazing voice."

"Yes, she does. She works very hard for these performances—they all do. But I know she'll appreciate your compliment. Would you excuse me? I see some friends across the room." Smiling, he moved quickly around a group and joined two men who were preparing to leave.

Elias maneuvered her toward the coffee urn and filled two cups with coffee. "Sugar and cream?"

"A little cream, please."

He passed her a paper cup with a napkin wrapped around it. "Careful. It's hot."

Lucky scanned the crowd, but other than the Reeds, still on the other side of the room, she didn't see anyone she recognized. "Do you come to these concerts often?"

"I have only been one other time." He took a sip of coffee.

"But I was so impressed with their work. You can imagine how many hours of rehearsal this takes. They do maybe four or five performances a year, and I thought you'd like to hear them."

"Well worth it. Thank you."

"Elias!" a woman's voice called out. Lucky spotted Abigail Starkfield moving through the crowd, still dressed in her black velvet gown and jacket. "So glad you could make it." She stood on tiptoe and kissed Elias on the cheek.

"Wouldn't miss it for the world." Elias responded with a wide smile. "Abigail, I don't think you've met . . ."

"Oh, but I have." Abigail offered her hand. "Hello, Lucky. Did you enjoy our program?" Abigail smiled brightly. Once again Lucky found something reminiscent of her mother in Abigail's face.

"I most certainly did. It was amazing. I particularly loved your solo."

"Oh, you're too kind, but thank you anyway. I've never turned professional, like some members of our group, but I do my best to keep up." She turned to Elias. "You and Lucky will have to stop by for dinner soon. We have one more program to do here at the end of next week and then I'm free for a while."

One of the other singers, a dark-haired woman with wire rim glasses, moved closer to Abigail. "Sorry to interrupt, but I wanted to check with someone—do we really have two more rehearsals, one tomorrow and one next week?"

Abigail nodded. "Yes, sorry, dear. Two more, then we're done." The woman nodded to Lucky and Elias and scooted away.

Abigail turned back to them. "Our rehearsal schedule's been so tight. We worked as long as we could the night of the blizzard and then rescheduled rehearsals till everyone could travel, so we're trying to make up for lost time. But when I'm done with the next program, I'll give you a call."

Elias answered, "I'd love to come for dinner soon."

Abigail smiled at Lucky. "And please bring this lovely

young woman. You can let me know what night would be convenient." Lucky wasn't sure what impression Abigail had of their relationship. She spoke as if she assumed they were a couple, but Lucky herself wasn't exactly certain what form the relationship was taking. Maybe Abigail was simply being cordial. She was obviously very fond of Elias—perhaps she thought of him as a younger version of her husband, or even as a son.

Elias turned to her. "Hope you didn't feel as if you were being put on the spot. But, whenever this dinner materializes, maybe you would like to come with me."

Lucky decided not to try to second-guess what others thought of her and Elias. "I'd love to. It was very kind of her to offer."

"That's Abigail. A heart of gold. They're both very lucky people to have each other. And I think she's as happy here as he is."

Lucky cringed at Elias's comment. Hopefully he was correct, but nonetheless, she still intended to broach the subject of Starkfield's possible involvement in the murder.

They tossed their paper cups in a wastebasket behind the temporary serving counter and headed for the exit. She saw Tom Reed's head lift up over the crowd. He had spotted her. She looked directly at him, and he glared at her in return but made no move to approach. They stepped outside and Lucky breathed a sigh of relief. Reed had certainly remembered her, but she was sure he wouldn't want to discuss his financial situation in such a setting. And he certainly wouldn't want any hint of involvement with Patricia Honeywell to create gossip. No, probably the last thing Tom Reed would do would be to approach her.

"I hope you don't mind that we didn't drive. It's colder than I thought it would be tonight. I guess our warming trend is over."

Lucky wrapped her scarf more closely around her neck and slipped on her gloves. "Not at all. I love to walk at night." Their boots crunched in unison as they headed along

Chestnut Street toward the center of town. "Actually, it's funny. I stopped here a few days ago."

"You did?"

"Yes. I had just come from seeing Sage at the jail and I needed a place to . . . I just needed a quiet spot for a while before I went back to the Spoonful. I met Abigail that day. She was a little brusque at first, but I guess she was busy and they were preparing for a baptism."

"Really? That doesn't sound like her at all. I know she's very involved with this church. She heads up the Ladies' Auxiliary or something like that, so she does a lot of volunteer work here. Maybe she was just pressured."

"I guess you're right. I wasn't dressed very well, just jeans, so maybe that turned her off."

Elias chuckled. "She can be a bit of a stickler for propriety." They had reached the corner of Broadway. "How 'bout a drink? It's not very late. We could stop at the Pub if it's quiet, or we could pick up my car and drive up to one of the places at the Resort?"

Lucky was enjoying the intimacy of their walk. She was afraid the Pub might be noisy this time of night, but she didn't particularly relish the idea of going to the Resort either. For a second, she considered inviting him back to her apartment, but it was still full of boxes and she hadn't much to offer him. Would it sound too much like an invitation to spend the night? She was sure he was attracted to her, but she still didn't feel she had a clear signal from him.

"The Pub sounds fine. I'd like that."

The Snowflake Pub was casual, with round tables and booths and seating around a fireplace. It was warm and comfortable, although occasionally a rowdy bunch would arrive and spoil the ambience.

Elias held the door open for her and they entered to find very few patrons. Two people were at stools at the long bar, a couple sat across from each other in a booth and no one was by the fire. Lucky headed straight for two empty chairs near the hearth. The waitress arrived a moment later to take their orders. She smiled suggestively at Elias as if she knew him. Lucky asked for a hot mulled wine and Elias ordered an ale. The waitress jotted down their orders and smiled at Elias again. Lucky felt a frisson of jealousy, wondering if he had taken other women here. She couldn't resist. "Do you come here often?"

He turned to her in surprise. "Me? Not at all. I think I've been here twice, if that. Both times, it was for someone's birthday at the Clinic." He chuckled. "I'm a very boring guy. I'm either working, studying the latest research papers or fixing up my house. No time to play. A dull boy." He grinned.

Lucky didn't think he was a dull boy at all. She was taken aback by the jolt of jealousy she had felt and was secretly relieved he didn't know the waitress.

"Hey, speaking of a change of pace, if you're free next weekend, may I take you to dinner? I promise not to inflict my cooking upon you."

"I was not *afflicted* by your cooking." She laughed. "And yes, that would be wonderful."

"I promise you a real restaurant—five-star this time."

The waitress returned with their drinks, and Elias slipped some bills onto her tray, telling her to keep the change.

Lucky took a sip of her wine, fragrant with cloves and cinnamon.

"You mentioned visiting Sage at the jail." He looked at her questioningly.

"We've been taking care of his meals until his arraignment on Monday morning."

"And the Spoonful? Has business picked up any?"

"No." She shook her head. "Other than a few regulars and some tourists who hadn't been here long enough to hear the gossip—nothing. This woman . . . this thing . . . I don't know what to say. I don't know how long we can hang on and still pay the bills."

Elias put a warm hand on her arm. "If you need a loan to keep going, please let me know. The Spoonful's an institution. I'd hate to see it fold. And my feeling is that winter tourists will have very short memories. It's only locals that will keep the gossip alive."

"Oh, Elias, I really appreciate that. But I couldn't possibly take money from you. I just wouldn't feel right about that. What needs to happen is for Sage's name to be cleared. Frankly, I don't think she was murdered at the restaurant at all."

"You're still convinced Sage is innocent?"

"I am. And this woman . . . well, from what I've learned, she was carrying on with a few people, but I think—no, I know—she must have been a real threat, otherwise she'd still be alive. And I'd be willing to bet her pregnancy had something to do with it."

Elias grimaced. "Lucky, whatever you do, please don't mention that to anyone. It will come out eventually, but I really shouldn't have let that slip."

"Don't worry. I haven't and I won't." She remembered that she *had* slipped and told Elizabeth, but she could completely trust that Elizabeth wouldn't tell a soul. "But if Honeywell was using the pregnancy to blow up someone's marriage, then that's a pretty good motive."

Elias shrugged. "Hopefully Nate will figure it all out. And I hope for your sake you're right about Sage."

Lucky swished the dark liquid around in her glass. "Elias, how well do you know your partner?"

"Jon? He's a great guy. I've known him for several years and watched him practice. He's a very good doctor, and well loved at the Clinic." Elias's face became more serious. "You're not asking me about him because you're suspicious of him, are you?"

"Not particularly of him. I'm just asking." Lucky told him about speaking to Chance at the Ski Shop and his remark that Honeywell had free medical treatment.

Elias stared at the fire and took a sip of his beer. "I don't want to rain on your parade, but you don't know this guy from Adam. How did you meet him?"

"Sophie—you might know her—we grew up together

here, in Snowflake. Sophie's been seeing Sage and she's completely broken up about his arrest."

"But couldn't she just trot anyone out to say just about anything? If her feelings are as you say, she'd do anything to undermine Nate's case against Sage."

"That may be true, but I don't see what reason this guy had to lie. He spoke to me only because Sophie asked him to. Otherwise, I never could have gotten any information out of him."

"I don't know . . ." Elias looked doubtful. He was quiet for several minutes. Finally, he turned to her. "I know you believe Sage is innocent, but you can't really know for sure. I know you want him back at the Spoonful and everything to return to normal, but you should let the police do their job, and stay out of it."

Lucky bristled. "I don't agree, Elias. I think Nate jumped the gun arresting Sage and I don't think he's guilty. I really don't. Yes, I have selfish reasons for wanting him out of jail, but mostly I just want the guilty person to be where Sage is. Because if he isn't guilty, then a murderer is among us." She was immediately regretful that her tone had been so vehement.

Elias sat back in his chair. "And you're thinking that Jon might have been involved with this woman?"

"It's possible, isn't it?"

Elias's face took on a stony expression. "No, it's not. I can't believe that. I know him pretty well and I can't imagine his getting involved in something like that. Particularly with a woman like that."

"A woman like what?" If Elias's life was as cloistered as he said, how would he know anything about Patricia Honeywell?

"I hear the gossip around town. It's pretty hard to avoid. But Lucky, you're asking a lot of questions. Questions that could hurt a man that I have the greatest respect for, and I consider Abigail a friend as well. You know how rumors get started, and rumors can kill someone's reputation in a town this size."

Lucky felt chastised. Elias was right. "I'm not meaning to hurt anyone. I just want the guilty person arrested and I want the reputation of the Spoonful restored. I don't know why you find that so hard to understand—my parents worked their whole life to create that goodwill and that reputation."

Elias's face softened. "I know they did. And I sympathize with what you and Jack are going through. Just please be careful who you talk to. If you're right and there is a murderer at large, you could be his next target."

Chapter 32

LUCKY WAS STILL reviewing her—what should she call it—her "argument" with Elias of the night before. It wasn't really an argument, but somehow things had not turned out well. He was silent walking back to her apartment. He was a perfect gentleman, but she suspected he was upset with her. She blushed when she remembered how accusatory she must have sounded, how obnoxious it was to ask Elias about his partner. But when she remembered how he had responded, she felt the anger rising again.

She swiped at the counter and arranged forks and spoons and knives in their holders for the third time. She felt like a child who had been chastised, like a woman who wasn't entitled to her thoughts and opinions. As if she had no right to be asking questions—just pat the little woman on the head and she'll be quiet. His reaction had infuriated her. It made her all the more angry when she remembered how she had fantasized the night might end—with a passionate kiss or something that made it obvious to her where Elias stood. He kept asking her out, but their time together was always very chaste—almost ambivalent. She wasn't sure she was ready to go any further, but she did want to know if he had feelings for her or if he was just being friendly and passing time because he had nothing else to do.

Marjorie and Cecily had come and gone, Hank and Barry hadn't arrived as yet and still there were no customers. Jack had learned that Sage was being moved to the facility in Bournmouth today. His arraignment would take place on Monday. Lucky stared at the neon sign in the window, vivid against a darkening sky. Another snowstorm coming in.

The bell above the door jingled. Lucky looked up hopefully as she felt the blast of cold air. Sophie stood in the doorway. She stared at Lucky, glanced at Jack and her gaze swept the restaurant. "You weren't kidding about business being down, huh?"

"Nope. Want some coffee? It's on the house."

"Love some." Sophie marched across to the counter and heaved herself onto a stool with a sigh. "Have you heard?"

"About Sage?"

"They moved him this morning."

Lucky placed a hot cup of coffee in front of Sophie and poured one for herself. "I'm so sorry, Sophie."

Sophie nodded. Her face twisted and then the tears started. Her breath came in ragged gasps. Lucky moved around the counter and sat next to her, putting an arm around her shoulders while she cried.

"It just all seems so hopeless," she mumbled, angrily swiping at her nose. Lucky passed her a napkin.

"It's never hopeless. Don't give up on Sage."

"I'm not giving up on Sage. That isn't what I meant. I just meant . . . this whole mess." She blew her nose noisily. "Have you found anything out?"

Lucky glanced over at Jack, seated with his newspaper by the front window. He caught her eye and returned discreetly to his reading. "Yes and no. But Chance told me something interesting. I think she was seeing somebody who . . ." Lucky hesitated, unwilling to betray Elias's confidence that Honeywell had been pregnant. And unwilling to share her suspicions about Jon Starkfield.

"Who what?" Sophie demanded.

"My suspicion is that she was seeing someone who wasn't free—someone most likely married and possibly she was threatening him."

"Well, duh . . . do you know who?"

Lucky shook her head. "I've talked to everyone I can think of. I keep running into dead ends. But I'm not giving up. Look around you. We're going to be in bankruptcy if this isn't cleared up. What's Jack going to do? What am I going to do? Here I've inherited a successful business and before I can turn around, it's ruined. I'm just as desperate as you."

Sophie nodded. "I'm sorry. None of this is your fault. I don't mean to sound like I'm attacking you."

"Did he tell you they've taken a swab from him—for DNA?"

"No." Sophie had a frightened look in her eye. "What good would that do, if he hadn't been with her?"

Lucky thought carefully how to frame her words. "The girls—Janie and Meg—the night of the storm. The night Honeywell was killed . . ."

"Spit it out, Lucky." The color had drained from Sophie's face.

"They saw Honeywell in her car. She pulled over and jumped out and accosted Sage on the street. He was just walking home. According to the girls, he didn't touch her; he held up his hands as if to say, *Leave me alone.* But it looked to them as if she took a swipe at him. I asked him about it and he confirmed it. There's a scratch on his neck. He jumped back and walked away very fast. I don't mean to upset you anymore, but what if . . ."

"You're saying what if some of his skin was under her fingernails and they can prove it," Sophie finished. "Damn," she muttered. "If only he had been at my place that night. He'd have a perfect alibi."

Lucky had heard the explanation from Sage but was curious to have Sophie confirm it. "Why weren't you together?"

Sophie looked at her quickly. "The storm. I was stuck at work late and then I had an early morning bunny class—

indoors at the Resort. You know, for people who are just learning techniques before they go out on the slopes. I was afraid if I went home, I might not be able to get back the next morning, so I just stayed there."

Lucky kept her expression neutral. She had told Sage she pulled a muscle and wanted to fall into bed. Why had Sophie just given her a long-winded explanation of her appointments? It was possible that both explanations were true and maybe Sophie didn't want Sage knowing she was spending the night at the Lodge. One of them wasn't telling the whole truth, and that just might be Sophie.

A needling fear arose in Lucky's mind. What if Sophie weren't as innocent as she appeared? What if . . . what if she knew a lot more than she was saying? What if she were somehow involved in Honeywell's murder—even as an accessory after the fact—but never imagining that Sage would be a suspect? She wondered if Sophie was using her to reveal something she couldn't herself reveal.

"Sophie—are you sure you've told me everything you know about this?"

Sophie's eyes opened wide. At first she was silent, unable to respond. Lucky could see the wheels turning behind her eyes, then a flash of irritation. "What . . . ?"

"There's something else. I don't want to get into all the details, but I found out Honeywell had been getting some threatening phone calls—warning her to get out of town."

Sophie's eyes widened and two red spots appeared on her cheeks. "How did you . . ."

Lucky looked at her quizzically. "Sophie . . ."

The bell over the door rang. Sophie turned quickly to see who had arrived. It was Rosemary from the Clinic. She shut the door behind her and held a hand up in greeting. Sophie turned back to the counter without a word, shooting an irritated look at Lucky. Quickly, she wiped her eyes. Lucky waved at Rosemary, indicating she should join them at the counter.

Rosemary pulled off her cap and unwound her scarf, glancing at Sophie. "I hope I'm not interrupting anything?"

Sophie waved her hand. "Not at all. Join us, please. We're just commiserating together."

"Where is everyone?" Rosemary looked around the restaurant.

"Staying far away, obviously. Are you here for lunch? If so, you're very welcome—we have two choices of soup and three choices of sandwich today," Lucky replied.

"I'm on my lunch break. I don't have long, but soup and half a sandwich sounds great."

"How about our chicken artichoke soup with tarragon and white wine and an avocado, tomato and sprout sandwich?"

Rosemary smiled and nodded.

"Okay," Lucky said. "Just take a minute." She retreated to the kitchen and dished out a generous bowl of soup and quickly prepared the half sandwich, returning to the counter and placing the dishes in front of Rosemary. "Hope you like this. We don't have a lot ready these days."

"This'll be wonderful. Thanks." Rosemary pulled off her gloves and stirred the hot soup. "I really came over for a chance to talk to you away from the Clinic."

Lucky's ears went up, and Sophie swiveled on her stool to stare curiously at Rosemary.

Rosemary took a large bite of her sandwich. Still chewing, she said, "You remember you told me you thought you lost an earring? And I said I hadn't seen one?"

Lucky nodded in response.

"Well, I asked Melissa, the other receptionist. She said a patient had gone out to the parking lot and then came back. The woman had found an earring by the steps to our back door."

"What did it look like?"

"Don't *you* know?" Rosemary looked at her in confusion.

Lucky was stumped for words for a moment. "Oh yes, I remember now. It was dangly with rhinestones."

Rosemary wrinkled her brow. "You're kidding, right?"

"No. Why?"

"Well, Melissa said this earring looked very expensive,

like diamonds. That's why she remembered. She put it in the box we leave in the drawer for lost items, and she asked everyone else—our nurse, the lab woman who comes in sometimes and the records clerk—and they all said it didn't belong to them."

"Is it there now?" Lucky asked, excitement rising in her chest.

Rosemary took a last bite of her sandwich and wiped her mouth delicately with a napkin. She dipped her spoon into the soup and sipped the hot liquid carefully. "This is delicious. Thanks, Lucky. Did you make this?"

"No. It's one of Sage's he had prepared ahead of time." Impatient, Lucky asked again, "Is the earring still there, at the Clinic?"

"Well, that's the strange thing. Melissa said she put it in the drawer, but now it's gone, so somebody took it. Now why would somebody steal one earring, even if it is valuable?"

Lucky felt her hopes dashed. She was willing to bet that earring matched the one found on Patricia Honeywell's body. It could prove she wasn't killed behind the Spoonful. It would go a long way toward clearing the restaurant and hopefully Sage. It might also point in the right direction to her killer. The more she thought about it, the more it seemed likely that Honeywell could have been killed at the Clinic.

Sophie turned a questioning look on Lucky. Lucky shot her a quick glance to be silent. "Well, that couldn't be mine. Believe me, I don't own any diamonds. I'm sure whoever it belongs to got it back."

Rosemary quickly finished her soup. "I hope so. I just wanted to tell you myself, and not say anything around the Clinic. Tell you the truth, I was just afraid somebody might have stolen it. And I didn't want to get blamed for it."

"I won't breathe a word, believe me."

"Thanks, Lucky. This was a treat. What do I owe you?"

"It's on the house." Lucky smiled.

"Are you kidding?"

"Nope. But you have to come back again and bring some more customers with you, okay?"

Rosemary laughed. "I'll do my best. People are being so silly about this whole thing."

Lucky thought "silly" was hardly an adjective to describe the terror a murder conjured up, but she was glad Rosemary at least had that attitude. Lucky wondered if the information Elias had given her was accurate—that Honeywell wasn't a patient at the Clinic. As far as the computer records went, it was true, but what if she had been a patient and her name had slipped between the cracks. Perhaps work had piled up and the records clerk hadn't gotten around to entering the information. Or perhaps someone at the Clinic had deleted her name from the database.

"You've never seen this Honeywell woman at the Clinic, have you?"

Rosemary was winding her scarf around her neck. She hesitated. "I've never seen her there. Why do you ask?"

"No special reason. Just curious. If she was staying in the town, she might have needed to see a doctor for some reason."

"Anything's possible, but I'm sure I've never seen her there. I think I'd remember someone who wasn't local." Rosemary headed for the front door. Lucky moved quickly around the counter and followed her. She opened the door for Rosemary and then stepped outside with her, holding the door closed with her hand.

"Rosemary—one other thing." Rosemary raised her eyebrows. "What kind of a car does Jon Starkfield drive?"

"You're full of questions today, aren't you?" When Lucky didn't respond, she continued, "A black Volvo—he and Abigail have identical cars." Rosemary waited to see if Lucky would explain her curiosity. "What's going on, Lucky? Why are you asking about Dr. Starkfield's car? Is there something you know that you're not saying?"

"It's nothing, really. I saw a car for sale up in Lexington Heights, and I thought it might be his, but the car wasn't black. I must have mixed things up."

Rosemary's curiosity seemed to be satisfied by Lucky's answer. It was a weak answer, but better that excuse than have Rosemary picking away at her for asking questions, or even worse, spreading gossip at the Clinic. Rosemary headed down the street and Lucky returned to the counter.

"Okay." Sophie grabbed her arm as she tried to pick up a dish from the counter. "What was all that about an earring?"

Lucky was hesitant to confide in Sophie. Other than wanting to clear Sage's name, she wasn't totally sure Sophie didn't have another layer to her agenda. She hesitated but finally decided she couldn't see what harm it could do—as long as Sophie kept her mouth shut. She leaned over the counter and spoke quietly. "Don't you dare breathe a word of anything I tell you. It's really all speculation anyway, and I don't want Nate or anybody else coming down on me."

Sophie shook her head negatively. "I won't. Just tell me."

"I don't think Honeywell was killed here. She could have been attacked in the lot behind the Clinic."

"Where did you get that?"

Lucky glanced over at Jack. Jack was the person she trusted most in the world, but she wasn't ready to tell him her suspicions until she had something concrete. "I ran into Chance the other day. He remembered something— something he didn't think anything of the first time I talked to him."

"Yes?" Sophie asked expectantly.

"He said Honeywell hurt her leg skiing one day, and he offered to check if one of the doctors at the Resort could see her. She said not to bother, she'd be fine. Then she said she got all her medical treatment for free anyway."

"And you're thinking she was seeing one of the doctors at the Clinic."

"I was looking out the kitchen window from my apartment and realized that, other than the alleyway behind here, the only thing that separates the parking lot behind the Clinic from the alleyway is the Victory Garden, and there are gates on each side of the fence around the Garden."

"And the murderer could have dragged her body from the Clinic to the alleyway and dumped her here."

Lucky nodded.

"Assuming you're right, that her body was dumped here

to draw attention from the real murder scene, it's just as possible she was killed in her car and someone drove it here and dumped the body. Or her body was loaded into somebody's car and the alleyway was as good a place as any to leave her. It doesn't prove she was killed at the Clinic."

"When they found her . . ." Lucky took a deep breath. "I saw the body, Sophie. And there was an earring dangling from her ear—only one earring. Nate and his technician have gone over that area with a fine-tooth comb and it hasn't turned up."

"So Rosemary's just confirmed that an earring was found. But you have no way of knowing if it matches the one you saw on Honeywell's ear."

"In a nutshell, yes. That's why I was hoping it was still in the lost-and-found box at the Clinic."

"I see."

"The other night—I dug around in the snow and the frozen ice to see what I could find."

"Anything?"

"No. But if the earring found at the Clinic was Honeywell's and it's gone missing, then somebody stole it, and that somebody must work at the Clinic."

Sophie gasped. "You could be right. Maybe she had something going with that older doctor. And what about that cute younger one—what's his name?"

"You mean Elias Scott," Lucky answered, watching Sophie carefully, wondering if she was aware of any gossip that they were seeing each other, but Sophie's face betrayed no sign of it. "Still doesn't prove anything. She could have been a patient at the Clinic. Could have met someone else there at night—I don't know. But please, Sophie, don't repeat this. Keep it under your hat. It's just a wild guess and I can't prove it and I don't want to ruin anybody's reputation with gossip. Please."

"Damn. I wish we could have gotten our hands on that earring." Sophie stood, slipping on her jacket. "I better get going. I've got to get up to the Resort. I'll call you soon. You call me if you hear anything else, okay?"

"Wait a minute. Not so fast."

Sophie halted in her tracks and turned slowly back to Lucky, a guilty grin on her face. She didn't say a word.

"What did you do?"

"What are you talking about?"

"You know very well what I'm talking about. I saw your face when I told you Honeywell was getting threatening calls."

"So? She deserved it." Sophie shrugged a shoulder. "I got one of the guys in the office to call a few times."

"Sophie!"

"Teach her to mess with my head." Sophie smiled, turned on her heel and waved good-bye over her shoulder.

Lucky watched Sophie's retreating back. One mystery solved, at any rate. And hopefully she hadn't just committed a big mistake in telling Sophie about the earring and her suspicions about the Clinic. Sage may not have an alibi for the night of the murder, but it really hadn't occurred to her that Sophie might not have one either. If no one could confirm that she stayed at the Resort all night because of the storm, Sophie could be under suspicion as well.

Chapter 33

JUST BEFORE NOON, two customers came in—a middle-aged couple. Lucky was sure they were winter tourists and also sure they must have just arrived in town and hadn't heard the local gossip. They looked around questioningly. "Are you open?" the man asked.

"Yes, we are. Please have a seat." Lucky led them to a table near the window where passersby could see new customers. Every little bit helped, she thought. "Our menu's a little limited today." *Our chef's in jail.* "But we have a very nice chicken and artichoke soup and a potato leek. For sandwiches, we have turkey with dried cranberries, grilled cheese with bacon and an avocado, tomato and sprout sandwich."

The new customers ordered two bowls of the potato leek with halves of turkey and cranberry sandwiches. Lucky returned to the kitchen and quickly made up their order. She glanced out through the hatch, where Jack sat at a table reading the newspaper, and caught his wink.

Lucky wondered if it was worth attempting to talk to Nate about the earring that had been found at the Clinic. She doubted it, but she felt it was something she had to do, even if Nate became angry. That is, if he wasn't annoyed with her enough as it was.

LUCKY SAT ON a hard wooden bench in the outer waiting room and watched Bradley peck at the typewriter behind the counter. Nate was due back any moment, or so she was told. She was impatient, but there was nothing for it but to wait. Now that she had summoned up her courage, she didn't want to back down. But she didn't dare mention to Nate any knowledge of the datebook, the fact she had searched the house on Bear Path Lane or that she knew there was a connection between Tom Reed and Honeywell. She wasn't supposed to know any of this, and she wasn't about to let on to Nate that she did. Considering that she had promised several people she would keep her mouth shut, she wasn't sure what she could reveal. She wasn't supposed to know Honeywell was pregnant nor that the murdered woman claimed to get her medical treatment for free. Her lips were sewed shut. If she revealed anything at all she was sure Nate would accuse her of interfering in his investigation—not that there was an ongoing investigation that she could see.

She heard a door slam in the rear of the building, opposite the side where the cells were. Heavy footsteps came down the corridor toward the front desk. She jumped up and approached the counter so Nate could not ignore her presence. He pushed through the swinging counter door and slipped off his jacket, hanging it on a chair by a rear desk. He looked up and spotted Lucky. His expression was not exactly welcoming, but she forged ahead.

"Hi, Nate."

He heaved a sigh, preparing himself for more questions. "What can I do for you, Lucky? Sage isn't here now."

"I know. I heard. It's something else. Can I talk to you privately?" She noticed that Bradley's ears went up.

Silently, Nate held out a hand and indicated his small office. He waited until she entered and then shut the door behind them. He sat heavily in the large chair behind his desk. He still hadn't said a word.

Lucky took a deep breath and started in. "Nate, even if you're not willing to confirm it, I don't think that Honeywell was killed behind the Spoonful."

Nate's eyelids flickered a tiny bit. Lucky continued, "I think she could have been killed behind the Snowflake Clinic and her body dragged through the Victory Garden to the alleyway behind the Spoonful before the storm started."

Nate stared at her for a long minute. Finally, he said, "Do you have any evidence to prove this theory?"

"Well, sort of." She glanced at Nate. "I know she only had one earring on when she was found. And I don't think you've found the other one." She was feeling braver now that she had begun. "I asked the receptionist at the Clinic if they had a lost and found and if anyone there had found an earring. Rose-mary said there was nothing in their drawer where they keep lost items, but she'd ask around. The other receptionist said that a patient *had* found an earring by the rear door and turned it in. She put it in the lost-and-found drawer."

"And where is this earring now?"

"That's just it. The other receptionist and Rosemary couldn't find it. It was gone, but the girl swears she put it in the drawer." As soon as the words were out of her mouth, she realized how silly this would sound to Nate.

Nate sat silently staring at her. He blinked his eyes once and said, "So because an earring was found behind the Clinic, you've jumped to the conclusion that this was the murder victim's missing earring."

"Nate, I saw the earring on her ear that morning. The description of the earring that was found was very similar."

"How was it described?"

"Long, dangling, perhaps diamonds."

"Lucky," he started patiently, as if speaking to a child, "maybe . . . just maybe it was her earring. She could have lost it anywhere at any time. She could have several pairs of earrings that are similar. It doesn't prove a damn thing, and now, of course, it's disappeared."

"Exactly. That's just it. It hasn't disappeared. Someone at the Clinic stole it. They didn't want it found. It's too much of a coincidence."

"It's rather moot, don't you think? Since it's now gone? And, let me guess, you have an idea who might have stolen this earring."

Lucky ignored the last sarcastic remark. "Will you at least talk to the other receptionist and show her the one that was on the body and see if she can confirm it?"

Nate didn't respond. Finally, he grabbed a pad of paper. "Okay, what's her name?"

"It's Rosemary who told me about it. Melissa is the other receptionist."

"What's her last name?"

"I don't know."

"Great. That's just great. You don't even know her name. She can't find the earring she says somebody, I'm sure she can't remember who, turned in, and now that earring's disappeared. That's all just great. As if I don't have enough to do," he grumbled.

"I think you should talk to Dr. Starkfield."

Nate looked up at her quickly. "And why is that?"

"I think he might have been involved with Honeywell."

"You think? And do you have anything to prove his supposed involvement with the murder victim?"

"No." Lucky had promised not to betray Chance's confidence, and even if she did, she was sure Nate would dismiss it.

He raised his voice. "Are you really expecting me to question a respected member of our community on the basis of your wild imaginings? No way in hell! Now, is there anything else you'd like to contribute to my investigation today?"

Lucky shook her head. "No. I'll be on my way."

"You do that."

She rose from the chair and managed not to slam a door on the way out. Bradley sat at the counter, a smarmy look on his face, as though satisfied she had experienced the wrong side of Nate's disposition for once.

ELIZABETH'S DESK WAS organized with neatly stacked piles of municipal documents, minutes of town council meetings, and recommendations from the Teachers' Association and the School Board. She carefully transferred a pile of documents to the side of her desk and gave her full attention to Lucky.

"I know you're frustrated, dear, but Nate has a point. If the earring were available, then it could be matched to the victim. It could also mean that she had been at the Clinic earlier, lost the earring, but didn't realize it at first. It's not a clear-cut path that points a finger at the Clinic as the location of her murder."

"I realize that. It's just that the more time elapses, the more likely it is that any investigation will grow cold."

Elizabeth sighed and leaned back in her chair, gazing at Lucky over the top of her reading glasses.

"I am so sorry to bother you when you're busy, but I just had to talk to someone—preferably you."

"I always have time for you, dear. Don't worry about that. I often come in on Saturday. It's quieter and I can get so much more work done. You're right to be concerned about Sage. But turn this around and look at it from Nate's point of view. He had motive . . ."

"What motive? She was no threat to him anymore. He had served his time and created a new life."

"The prosecution could argue that it was all too much for him, long pent-up rage just exploded. You know how attorneys can go on." Elizabeth slipped her glasses off and laid them carefully to the side. Her white hair glowed under the desk lamp. "To continue . . . perhaps he had motivation; if not a motive, he had opportunity; he had no alibi and her body was found conveniently near an area that he was familiar with. And we're still awaiting the lab results—DNA and all that."

"All the more reason to suspect a setup. If I were Sage and I killed Patricia Honeywell, the last place I would leave the body would be at the Dumpster behind the Spoonful. I'd be pointing a finger at myself."

"Do we know for sure she wasn't killed there?"

"I think that's what Nate and his technician were digging for, evidence of blood or a struggle or something that would place the crime there, and I can't get him to talk to me about it, but I'm positive they didn't find what they were hoping to find. The police have found her car, and I don't know if there's evidence of anything in the car. I don't know anything at all. I'm grasping at straws."

"I understand your frustration, but don't go making mountains out of molehills. For all we know, she was killed by a jealous ski instructor."

"What do you mean by that?" A chill ran up Lucky's spine. She thought of Sophie's jealousy. Could she be determined enough to kill a potential rival and then clever enough to ask Lucky to help her clear Sage?

"One of the men from the Lodge. What did you think I meant?"

"Oh." Relief flooded through her.

"What are you thinking of doing now? You have a very stubborn look on your face." Elizabeth studied her carefully. "I hope you're not thinking of going anywhere near Jon Starkfield. If one ounce of what you suspect is true, you could be putting yourself in danger."

"I'm sorry, Elizabeth. But if Nate isn't willing to question him, so be it. There's nothing stopping me."

Lucky hurried down the street, so lost in a jumble of thoughts, she had gone two blocks before she remembered to button her jacket. She shivered and fastened the buttons with chilled fingers. The person she most wanted to talk to was Elias. She hoped he wasn't still upset that she had questioned him about Jon Starkfield, but that was before she knew about the earring being found at the Clinic. If memory served her, he only worked a half day at the Clinic on Saturdays, and his house was just a block away. She might be able to catch him.

She reached the large white Victorian on Hampstead and stood staring at the house for a moment. No sooner had she started up the walkway when she heard a car engine start. She retraced her steps and, glancing down the drive that led to the garages, saw that a garage door was open. Elias was on his way out. Bad timing. She had rushed over, anxious to talk to him, but she should have called first.

Elias's hand rose up to adjust his rearview mirror. He had spotted her standing on the sidewalk. She was sure he'd think she was obsessing about this murder, but he was the only person she felt she could talk to about her suspicions of Jon Starkfield.

The silver sedan reversed slowly down the drive, careful to avoid the snowbanks on either side. Lucky froze. A white sticker with blue numbers that read Woodside Medical was visible on his rear bumper. The same sticker that Josh had seen outside Patricia Honeywell's cabin. It wasn't Jon Starkfield who was offering free medical care—it was Dr. Elias Scott.

Chapter 34

"Lucky. Hey—what a surprise!" Elias lowered his window and leaned out. "Were you coming to see me?"

Lucky's heart was racing. The blood drained from her face. For once, she wasn't blushing, but she couldn't get her lips to move.

"Are you okay? You look like you've seen a ghost."

"I . . . I just came by . . ." she stammered, unable to form words. The implication that Elias had been one of Honeywell's lovers overwhelmed her.

Elias waited patiently, letting his engine run and staring at her with a concerned expression. "Are you sure you're all right?"

"Um . . . yes," she managed to say. "I just wanted to let you know I can't make it next weekend. Sorry."

"Oh. Well, I'm happy to take a rain check if you're busy."

Lucky turned and started walking away before Elias could ask any more questions.

"Lucky!" he called after her. "Wait up."

She kept walking. She heard Elias's engine turn off. His car door slammed as he hurried to catch up to her. She felt like bursting into tears. The thought of Elias making love to Patricia Honeywell made her sick to her stomach. She couldn't possibly talk to him and pretend nothing was wrong.

She turned and held up a hand. "Sorry. I can't. I'm very late." As she turned away from Elias, his confused expression tore at her heart. She hurried down the sidewalk, almost breaking into a run in her haste to get away from him.

She slammed through the door of her apartment building. She didn't dare go to the Spoonful in the state she was in. She reached the kitchen and sat down heavily in the kitchen chair, the same chair from which she had stared out the window at the Victory Garden just three nights ago. She could barely contain her fear and her anger, not sure which emotion was uppermost. She burst into loud sobs, her chest heaving. *What an incredible fool I've been,* she thought. Suspicious of Jon Starkfield and all the time it must have been Elias. She had blindly taken his word that Honeywell had never been a patient at the Clinic. Perhaps he could have deleted the records at the Clinic himself. Had Elias murdered his lover? She was pregnant and threatened to ruin his reputation in town. Had he murdered her and cold-bloodedly attended the autopsy? She had fantasized about Elias since she was young and now hoped he was actually interested in her. Worse, she couldn't let him know her suspicions. She might not be safe herself.

She heard a loud knock on her apartment door. Terrified, she leaped to her feet. Stifling her tears, she crept down the hallway.

"Lucky!" It was Elias. He had followed her here. "Lucky—talk to me. Please open the door."

She shivered in fear. How could she tell him she knew he had been Honeywell's lover? She had to cover her true feelings. She crept closer to the door. "Elias, please go away. I'm fine."

"I'll go away if you tell me what's wrong. Please, Lucky, talk to me."

Lucky put the chain over the front door and cracked it

open. Elias looked concerned and confused. Perhaps he was a consummate actor. He glanced at the chain. "I'm not intending to force my way in, Lucky. I was just worried about you."

"I'm sorry. I didn't mean to cause you any concern. I've just been upset about Jack." It was the only lie she could think of on short notice.

Elias nodded. "Okay. I understand. Has anything happened to upset you? Has Jack had another episode?"

Lucky nodded. "I can't talk about it right now. Please. Please leave me alone."

"Would you like me to stop off and see him? I'm just on my way over to Lincoln Falls to see a patient, but it wouldn't be any trouble."

"No—that's okay. But thank you anyway. I'll talk to you later."

Elias stood for a moment, unsure whether to leave or to try to elicit more information. Lucky shut the door, unwilling to let him get close again. She waited a few minutes and finally heard his footsteps descending to the front door. She breathed a sigh of relief.

Hands shaking, she washed her face in the bathroom sink and put a cold cloth on her swollen eyes—how could she have been so blind? How could she not have been suspicious of Elias's interest in her? Perhaps he made a career of seducing women—seducing and killing them.

She had to get to the Spoonful. Jack would be worrying about her. She had to pull it together and pretend that nothing was wrong. The last thing in the world she wanted to do was make Jack worry.

She opened the apartment door and walked softly to the hallway window that overlooked the street. She peered out in both directions. Elias was nowhere to be seen. Hopefully, he had walked back to his car. She didn't want to run into him when she was in this state. He would see that she had been crying—as if how she looked mattered at all now. At best she had been falling for one of Honeywell's lovers, or at worst, a murderer.

She went back inside her apartment, checked her face in the mirror and slipped her coat on again. Walking quickly to the end of her street, she turned onto Broadway. When she arrived at the Spoonful she was surprised to see two more new customers—winter visitors.

"Lucky, my girl. Everything all right?" Jack looked closely at her face.

"I'm fine, Jack." She gave him a big hug as he stood by the cash register.

"You don't look all right."

"Just coming down with a cold—that's all. Nothing to worry about," Lucky replied. Movement in the kitchen caught her eye. She looked at Jack questioningly. "Who's back there?"

Jack smiled. "Remy. Turns out he knows how to cook. He's not his big brother, but he'll do in the meantime."

"What do you know?" Lucky smiled back, deliberately pushing thoughts of Elias out of her head. She would have to talk to someone, but she didn't know who she could trust. Her heart was breaking at the thought that Elias had been involved with Patricia Honeywell. Her schoolgirl fears seemed ridiculous in light of the fact that his car had been parked at the cabin on Bear Path Lane. The thought of his attending the autopsy on Honeywell was even more revolting.

Hank and Barry were at their corner table—back to playing Connect Four. "How are the chess lessons going, Jack?" she asked.

"Getting there. I've figured out how all the pieces move. Now I just have to think a few steps ahead, but I'm getting it slowly."

The door opened, letting in a blast of cold air. Marjorie and Cecily called out in unison.

Jack raised a hand in greeting. Lucky did her best to smile. "What can I get you?"

"Oh, just two teas, please.We've already had our breakfast. We're opening later today. We had to drive over to Lincoln Falls to pick up a few things."

"Coming right up."

Marjorie's eyes strayed to the kitchen. She gasped. "Is Sage back?"

Lucky smiled. "No. I wish. Remy's helping us out for now. Not that we really need any help, but Jack thought it would be good for him to stop by and have something else to do. He's pretty upset, as you can imagine."

"Oh yes," Cecily replied. "I can imagine. Just terrible."

Lucky brewed the tea in a pot behind the counter then carried it out to them.

"How is that nice young doctor these days? Is he stopping by this afternoon?" Marjorie looked up quizzically as she took her first sip of tea.

"Uh, no. Not today." Lucky turned away, hoping her heart wasn't on her sleeve.

"That's too bad. We thought perhaps there was . . ." Cecily trailed off. Lucky caught Marjorie giving a nudge to her sister's elbow.

Lucky did her best to smile naturally, but she was sure it looked more like a grimace. "Not at all. We're just friends." *At least we were.*

The sisters exchanged a look but said nothing. An uncomfortable silence settled over the counter.

Lucky heard the phone ringing in the office. She hurried down the hall to grab it in time, relieved that she had escaped the sisters' scrutiny.

"Why, hello! Is this Lucky?"

"Yes it is." Lucky didn't recognize the woman's voice.

"This is Abigail Starkfield." Lucky heard chatter and background noise through the receiver. "We've just finished our rehearsal for today, and I was wondering . . . well, I know this is very short notice, but we've decided we'd like to celebrate a little and have a late lunch together. Do you think you could accommodate us in a few minutes?"

"Oh." Lucky was speechless. She quickly wracked her brain, trying to remember how many people made up Abigail's choral group, not to mention their musicians as well.

Her second panicked thought was how much food was on hand and was it enough to feed lunch to a large group.

"If you're crowded right now, dear, don't go to any bother. We can find someplace else—perhaps up at the Resort. I just thought I'd try the Spoonful first."

"Uh. No. Please. That would be wonderful. It won't be a problem." She rubbed her forehead, praying she could manage. "We'll see you in a bit." She hung up the phone and ran into the kitchen.

"Remy!" Remy jumped involuntarily, dropping a saucepan on the floor with a great clatter.

"Lucky . . . you're gonna give me a heart attack."

"Remy, we're going to have about . . . thirty or so people in a few minutes. Can you start making . . . what do we have? Start making up some turkey and dried cranberry sandwiches and some roast beefs with that deli mustard. I'll be back in a minute and do some grilled cheeses with bacon. I think we have enough soup already warmed for everyone." She shot a look at Remy, who appeared as if he were about to faint.

"I've never done any sandwiches. Jack just showed me how to use the Crock-Pots."

"Don't worry, it's easy," she called out, pulling loaves of bread onto the counter. "Use the rye for the roast beef, lots of mustard with pickles, and . . . let's see, use the sourdough for the turkey and dried cranberries. They'll have to be happy with just a few choices."

Lucky moved quickly over to Jack's table and whispered in his ear. He looked up and smiled. "Told you so," he said. "Good thing I got that dishwasher fixed up. I'm on deck now, don't worry." He headed down the hall and slipped on one of the aprons from the shelf. "I'll help Remy in the kitchen. You'll be all right on your own out here?"

"Yes, I'll take the orders and deliver the trays." *Why couldn't Janie or Meg show up now?* she thought.

True to her word, Abigail arrived shortly thereafter. She was with a group of five. "Here we are!" she called out. "The rest will be here in a few minutes."

They settled in at one of the larger round tables. Lucky explained the menu, and everyone seemed quite happy with the choices. She took orders for three bowls of potato leek and two bowls of the butternut squash soup with bleu cheese. Four people ordered whole sandwiches. Jack arrived with place mats, napkins and silverware and quickly laid the tables. No sooner had he done that than the door flew open again, ushering in more cold air and another twenty or so singers and musicians. Lucky recognized the woman who had played the harp at the concert.

Marjorie and Cecily swiveled on their stools, watching the activity. Jack turned on the CD player, and the room filled with the sound of a forties' swing number. Everyone was laughing and talking, and two of the men stood and sang along with the CD player to the amusement of the entire room.

Cecily touched Lucky's arm shyly as she rushed past. Lucky turned to her. "Isn't this wonderful? Just like old times. How nice of them to come here."

"It surely is. I wonder . . ."

"Do you think that nice young doctor might have told them about the troubles you've been having?" Marjorie asked.

Lucky's face froze. Of course. Why else would Abigail suddenly decide to march the entire choral group over to the Spoonful. Conflicting emotions flashed across her face. For a few minutes she was elated that they had customers again and the restaurant would be full of happy, hungry people. Elias! If only she had never gone to his house earlier. If only she never knew about the blue and white sticker on the silver sedan. Drunk as Josh may have been that night, he described it very well. It was a parking permit for the Woodside Hospital in Lincoln Falls, a permit for a reserved doctor's space.

"Is anything wrong, dear?" Cecily asked.

Lucky snapped out of her reverie. "No. Nothing. Sorry, my mind just wandered."

"Well, you better get busy if you want to keep all these customers happy."

Lucky nodded and grabbed four orders from the hatch. She could see Jack guiding Remy as they both put sandwiches together. Lucky filled a tray with glasses of water and deftly placed them before each customer. She raced back to the kitchen and repeated the action with steaming cups of coffee and tea. She did her best to push thoughts of Elias out of her mind. She didn't think Elias had actually arranged this to happen today. It was more likely that Abigail had asked about her, and Elias had explained the difficulties the Spoonful was having.

When everyone had finished their soup and sandwiches, Lucky made the rounds and refilled coffee cups. Several people stood chatting together as they paid their bills at the cash register. Finally only Abigail and four others, a man and three women, were still seated. Lucky approached and asked them if there was anything else they might like.

Abigail spoke first. "That was delicious. I'm so glad we came here. We'll be back again whenever you have room."

"It was very kind of you to think of the Spoonful."

"Not at all. This is a charming place. I'm only sorry I wasn't familiar with it before, but I will definitely come back and I'm sure the rest will agree. Don't you?" she asked, turning to her friends at the table. They nodded their assent and chimed in with compliments.

Somewhere in the confusion, Marjorie and Cecily had slipped away. Lucky walked Abigail and the last of the singers to the door and waved good-bye. She closed the door behind them and plopped down in a nearby chair. "Well, Jack, that was a real workout. I can't remember when I last moved that fast."

Jack smiled from behind the cash register. "We're out of shape, my girl. We're out of shape." Jack beamed.

"Hey, Remy! How you holding up?" Jack shouted into the kitchen.

Remy's head popped up in the hatch. "I hope those sandwiches were okay."

"They were great," Lucky called over her shoulder.

"There are some extras here. What should I do with them?"

"Bring 'em out on a tray. We need a break," Jack hollered back.

A few minutes later, Remy carried a dish heaped with sandwiches to one of the larger tables.

Lucky sat and flipped open her napkin. "Remy, aren't you eating anything?"

Remy stood awkwardly next to the table. "I . . . uh . . . Is it okay?"

"Of course, it is," Jack replied. "Come on, you worked for your lunch today."

Lucky glanced sideways at Remy. Where she had once thought he seemed shady, she realized now his ambiguous behavior was insecurity. She knew nothing of his and Sage's early life, but she suspected Remy had spent most of his life reacting like a whipped dog. She smiled at him. "Remy, you were terrific today. I can't thank you enough. I don't think Jack and I could have handled that big rush ourselves."

Blood rushed to Remy's cheeks. She was sure he wasn't used to any compliments. "It's me who should be thanking you—especially after what I did. I feel pretty stupid."

"It's all forgotten, Remy. Eat up and enjoy," Jack replied. "Can you pass me that mustard?"

Lucky and Jack exchanged a smile as Remy turned back to his food. For a moment Lucky forgot all about Elias and the shock she had felt when she saw his car. She would eventually confide in Jack, but she couldn't do it now in front of Remy, as she was sure she'd burst into tears.

Chapter 35

"I DON'T KNOW how I got through the day yesterday." The parchment lampshade in Elizabeth's living room cast sepia-toned light over the room. A log sputtered and crackled in the fireplace. Elizabeth's cat, a fluffy gray male, was curled in a ball on the hearth rug. Lucky felt her muscles relax for the first time since she'd seen Elias's car. If she weren't still so upset, she could have curled up like the cat and slept for three days. She sank back into the soft cushions of the couch, her face strained, while Elizabeth sat in an old-fashioned rocker, crocheting and listening.

"Run this by me again. I'm not sure I have the story straight." Elizabeth placed her yarn on her lap, giving Lucky her full attention.

"It all started with Josh—the ski instructor up at the Lodge. He had been seeing Honeywell. One night . . . well, I guess he took it more seriously than she did, and he got pretty drunk. He went to the house on Bear Path Lane and suspected she was with another man. She wouldn't let him in, and he saw another car parked in the drive. Honeywell

sent him away. He was a mess and lost his footing and he
slipped on the ice. I asked him about the other car. He only
remembered that it was light colored. He grabbed the car's
bumper to get back on his feet and saw a white and blue
sticker with numbers on it—just like the sticker on Elias's
car. It's a doctor's parking permit for Woodside Hospital.
And then Hank told me . . ."

Elizabeth shook her head. "What does Hank Northcross
have to do with this story?"

"He lives farther up the hill past Bear Path Lane. He
remembered a silver sedan pulling out of her driveway one
night. He remembered because it almost hit him."

"And this . . . Josh . . . he said the car he saw was a silver
sedan?"

"Well, no. Now that I think about it. He said he didn't
remember except that it was light colored. Oh, Elizabeth, it
must have been Elias who was seeing her, and all this time
I suspected Jon Starkfield." Lucky snuffled behind her damp
tissue.

Elizabeth passed her a fresh tissue. "Okay, now listen to
me. I'll buy that the blue and white sticker is a parking permit for Woodside. That makes perfect sense, but a lot of
people could have silver sedans, and Josh didn't specifically
say it was silver, now, did he?"

"No."

"And there *are* doctors working for the Resort?"

"Well, yes," Lucky replied.

"So . . . assuming she was seeing a doctor who had a
parking permit for Woodside Hospital, why would you con-
clude it was Elias, and not one of the doctors from the
Resort? After all, she was skiing there every day. And you
said she wasn't a patient at the Clinic."

"I'm not sure I can even believe that. I took Elias's word
for that."

Elizabeth sighed patiently. "Well, assuming she wasn't a
patient, and the girl at the Clinic can back up what Elias told
you, it's far more likely that her so-called free medical care

would be coming from a doctor at the Resort. Your logic just doesn't hold together, dear. Sorry."

Elizabeth picked up the bundle of yarn in her lap and leaned closer to the lamplight. "Lucky, I want you to listen to me. You've been in a state of shock over your parents, worried about Jack, worried about the business and now Sage's arrest and the murder. You've had a lot on your plate. Before you jump to the conclusion that Elias was Honeywell's lover . . ."

"But what if he was her murderer? What if he was the father of her child? That's what's been making me so sick. The thought that he was her lover, and then possibly her murderer and that he actually attended the autopsy. It's so horrifying."

"Let me finish, dear. Before you jump to all those conclusions, why don't you find out where he was the night of the murder? Then if you can, and he has an alibi, you'll at least know he's not a killer. Frankly, I can't imagine a man like him being attracted to someone like this Honeywell character anyway."

"You can't?" Lucky asked hopefully.

"I've lived a long time and I'm very good at judging people. I can't see it. I'm not saying I can't be wrong, but Elias strikes me as a very empathetic person. This Honeywell woman—I'd noticed her around town—well, she was a lot of things, but frankly the first thought that occurred to me when I saw her was 'cold' and maybe a little too flashy, if you know what I mean."

Lucky nervously tore a tissue into shreds. "Maybe I overreacted. Elias followed me home and tried to find out what was wrong. I hope I'm wrong. I just don't know how I can find out where he was that night."

"What about your friend at the Clinic—the receptionist? What's her name—Rosemary? Maybe you can find some discreet way of asking her who was on call that night?"

Lucky took a deep breath. "You're right. I know you're right. I'm such an idiot. I overreacted and made a total fool of myself."

"Now—drink your tea. And sleep on all this. Would you like to stay here tonight? That's a very comfortable sofa and I have an extra bedroom."

"Thank you. I think I should probably walk home. I've bothered you enough."

"We have some other things to talk about."

Lucky looked up. "We do?"

"I have to ask for your solemn promise that you will never repeat this conversation. I need your silence now. My reputation is at stake here too, don't forget."

"Elizabeth, I would never do anything to hurt you."

"I know you wouldn't, and because of that I'm trusting you. There are other lives involved here, and this will have to be handled very discreetly."

Elizabeth took a deep breath. "I talked with Tom Reed. I told him that information had come to me that he had a connection with Patricia Honeywell. I also told him that I was duty bound to report this to Nate, but before I did, I needed him to be completely honest with me. He was rather defensive and upset, and demanded to know what information I had and where I had obtained it. I stonewalled him. I told him no one wants any unpleasant surprises in the upcoming campaign. And it would be best if he came clean with me right away. If he told me what his connection with Honeywell was . . . I didn't say I had seen a promissory note, by the way, since neither you nor I had any business sticking our noses into Nate's investigation—but if he would be straight with me, then I'd do what I could in the way of damage control, but I certainly wouldn't do anything unethical or illegal. And I'm sure if that fellow at the Resort had seen them together, other people had too."

"What did he have to say for himself?"

"He swore he wasn't having an affair with her. Thank heavens, because if that came out, he could kiss his political career good-bye."

"And?"

"You were right. It took some doing, but eventually he broke down. He needed funds to invest in the partnership. He wasn't wealthy enough to do it on his own. The loan was coming due. He would have been able to pay almost half of it to her by the deadline, but he had asked her for an extension on the rest of the monies. She refused."

Lucky listened raptly. "A few million dollars makes a good motive."

"Yes, it does. Except killing her would make no sense."

"What was she planning to do if he didn't pay the full amount?"

Elizabeth pursed her lips. "She threatened to take him to court. And make sure that the case received a lot of attention."

"Would that mean he could lose the election?"

"Possibly. No one wants to vote for someone that can't meet their financial obligations. He was between a rock and a hard place. If she had sued, he would have been able to drag the suit out for months. Her death buys him the time he was asking for—without the repercussions of public embarrassment."

"So her murder gives him what he wanted without any jeopardy to his campaign."

"Yes. It's an unpleasant thought. I told him to go straight to Nate, to discuss the issue. That way he'd look like an upstanding citizen that was trying to do the right thing, and he'd still have time to tap other resources to repay the note. After all, Nate or the prosecutor would eventually put it together. If he spoke up first, it would look far better for him."

"Do you think he could have killed her?"

"No, I don't. I contacted Nate and told him that Reed had voluntarily spoken to me, and that I had advised him to go straight to Nate," Elizabeth continued. "Nate checked the Reeds' whereabouts on the night of Honeywell's murder. Both he and his wife were out of town at a fund-raiser and were stranded in the storm. They have hotel receipts to prove it. He couldn't possibly have returned to Snowflake and committed a murder."

"So, we're back to square one."

"That we are. My advice to you is to find out where Elias was that night and do what you can to make amends."

Chapter 36

LUCKY HAD TOSSED and turned most of the night. She had finally fallen into a fitful sleep but woke up with a half-remembered nightmare about trying to reach the Spoonful in a blizzard. Every time she glimpsed the neon sign, a snowdrift blocked her path. The more she struggled, the harder it was to walk through the snow that pulled on her feet like quicksand.

Would things have been better if she had never started asking questions about Honeywell and sticking her nose where it didn't belong? But how could she not have done what she'd done? The Spoonful was barely able to make its rent, and Sage was in jail for murder. It wasn't just she and Jack who were at risk; the life of a man who had been wrongfully accused once before was on the line. Now she needed to find out where Elias was the night of the murder. And she'd have to do it without letting him know. She had no idea how she'd be able to do that, and if he had no alibi, her dilemma still wouldn't be solved. If he did have an alibi, and found out that she had been checking up on him, he'd be angry, more than angry. On top of all that, he still might have been Honeywell's lover and the father of her child.

She cast her mind back to her conversation with Elizabeth the night before. Elizabeth was right. She was a complete idiot. But then, she had reason to suspect Elias. How else could she explain the parking permit with blue numbers? On the other hand, Josh had admitted he was drunk; he could have made a mistake. Even so, Elizabeth was right about one thing. Lucky had let her own overwrought imagination run away with her. Her advice was good advice. Get to the bottom of it and stay rational.

She slipped into the office and dialed the number of the Clinic.

"Snowflake Clinic." Lucky breathed a sigh of relief when she heard Rosemary's voice.

"Hi, Rosemary. It's Lucky Jamieson."

"Oh, hey, Lucky, how are you?"

"I'm good, thanks. I have a favor to ask." Lucky screwed up her courage.

"Sure, what is it?"

"Could you stop by the Spoonful on your lunch break? There's something I'd like to ask you about."

"Okay. Sounds great. Love to see you."

"Lunch is on me again."

Rosemary laughed. "Best offer I've had all day. I'll see you very soon then."

Lucky nervously wiped off the rear counter, moving each item, mopping, then replacing salt shakers, napkin holders and cups and saucers. She noticed that one of the linen napkins was out of line. She grabbed the pile and started refolding them for lack of anything better to do. Lucky thought she would scream in frustration if Rosemary didn't arrive soon. She glanced at the clock several times, but it seemed the hands refused to move. Jack sat quietly reading his newspaper and finally looked up at her.

"Lucky, my girl. You seem nervous as a cat. Everything all right?"

"Sure, Jack." She forced herself to smile. "Just straightening up."

Jack nodded, with a dubious look on his face. "Well, let me know if you need any help moving salt shakers," he replied sarcastically. Lucky knew she hadn't fooled him at all.

Finally Rosemary approached their door. The bell rang as she rushed in. Her lunch was already on the counter, a meatloaf sandwich and a bowl of potato leek soup.

"Hi, Lucky. Hi, Jack," she called out.

"Hello there," Jack responded.

"Lucky, thanks so much, but I can pay."

"No need. Just wanted the chance to talk to you." Lucky looked over at Jack, who made a display of shaking out the newspaper and ignoring them.

Rosemary slipped off her coat and threw it over the stool next to her. She grabbed the ketchup bottle and, opening her half sandwich, poured a large dollop over the meatloaf. She covered it with bread and took a huge bite. "Mmmm. This is so good. What did you want to ask me, Lucky?"

"You remember the night of the big storm. What time did the Clinic close that night?"

Rosemary looked thoughtful for a moment. "Well . . . I guess it was around five o'clock. Normally, we'd have stayed open till eight o'clock."

Lucky reorganized the silverware once again, doing her best to appear casual. "So I guess Elias was on call that night."

"Actually, yes. I remember because I tried to reach him and he didn't answer."

Lucky's heart skipped a beat. "What? What do you mean?"

"Just that. I couldn't reach him. I was the last to leave. I was locking up and I saw that the lab hadn't picked up the blood draws—probably because of the storm—and I was worried that maybe some of the tests were urgent. I didn't know what I should do."

"And he never returned your call?"

"Well, he might have. I wouldn't know. I left so I could

get home before the storm hit. I finally just put the tray in the refrigerator till the lab could pick it up next day. Turned out it was no problem. I spoke to him the following day and he said that was fine. No harm done. Why are you asking?"

So intent on hoping Elias was where he should have been that night, at home, and available by phone, she hadn't worked out a good excuse for her prying. She finally settled on something close to the truth. "I was just hoping that someone might have been around the Clinic that night—in the parking lot maybe—and might have seen any activity in the alleyway behind the Spoonful." She leaned her elbows on the counter. "I'll tell you what I think. I don't think that woman was killed here. I think she was left here. I guess I was just hoping some observant person might have been around."

"Well, you can see part of the alleyway from the Clinic parking lot, but not the entire thing. Not the part behind the restaurant because of the fence. In any case, nobody was around that night to see anything. We had closed up shop."

Lucky managed to maintain a calm expression even though her thoughts were racing wildly. Elias was on call that night, but he didn't respond to Rosemary's message. Or if he did, it wasn't within the half hour it would have taken her to close up and lock the doors. Why didn't he call back to see what she needed? Where was he that night?

LUCKY WATCHED JACK through the glass partition as the technician helped him stretch out on the table. She could see but not hear her explain to him exactly what would happen during the test. Jack, inside the bare tiled room, smiled at Lucky through the glass window. The technician hurried out of the room, passed Lucky and took her seat in front of the computer monitor. Jack waved a hand as he was moved slowly under the MRI machinery.

Lucky looked anxiously at the technician. "Are you sure this is safe for him?"

The woman flashed a professional smile. "Absolutely. We

always warn patients to be still and warn them about the noise the equipment makes, so they won't be frightened."

Lucky persisted. "If it's perfectly safe, why do you have to leave the room and shut the door?"

"I have to keep track on the computer. I can't be in both places," she replied patiently, intent on her computer screen.

"Can you tell me again how exactly this works?"

The technician swiveled in her chair to face Lucky. To her credit, she displayed no annoyance. "To put it in simple terms, the procedure excites the hydrogen atoms in the body and that's how we'll be able to get a layer by layer picture of your grandfather's skull and brain."

Lucky shivered. Exciting the body's hydrogen atoms. And what if the hydrogen atoms didn't want to be un-excited? This was as crazy as teleportation.

"This is completely noninvasive. There's really no need to worry."

Lucky took a deep breath and stood patiently at the glass window, even though she knew Jack couldn't see outside the machinery that enclosed his head.

Several minutes later, the technician spoke. "That's it. We're done. Everything's ready to go to our radiologist."

"How does it look?" She was almost too afraid to ask.

"That's for the radiologist to decide." She smiled. "If it's any comfort, I saw no anomalies. My only concern is that the radiologist gets a perfectly done test." She hurried into the room and helped Jack up. He was smiling and no worse for the wear. He shifted off the table and the technician led him through the door.

"That wasn't so bad, now, was it, Mr. Jamieson?" She smiled up at him.

"No. Not at all. Didn't like all those noises and clicks, but nothing hurt."

Lucky held the door open for Jack as they returned to the radiology waiting room. "Have a seat, Jack. I'm just going to check with the nurse to see if there's anything else we need to do here."

The phone call had come in the day before from an

appointment clerk at Woodside Hospital in Lincoln Heights.
The clerk had explained that tests had been ordered for her
grandfather. Would it be possible to have him come in the
following afternoon? Lucky had agreed, anxious to do whatever was necessary to help Jack, but both disheartened and
relieved that Elias hadn't called himself to tell her he had
arranged for the tests. She knew she should call him and
thank him, but under the circumstances, she couldn't bring
herself to do so, especially since her questions about his
possible—Lucky clung to Elizabeth's cool logic—
involvement with Patricia Honeywell still went unanswered.
Even so, she couldn't help but wonder if she might run into
him in the maze of corridors at the hospital.

She sat at the small cubicle across the desk from the
nurse. "I just wanted to make sure you had my grandfather's
insurance information. I think he's seen everyone he needs
to see here before we drive home."

"Let's see." The woman turned to her computer monitor.
"Your grandfather lives at 42 Birch Street, Snowflake. Is that
correct?" Lucky nodded. "Looks like he's all set. You'll get
all his results within the week, I'm sure. Who's your attending? Oh, I see, it's Dr. Scott." She smiled across the desk.
"You're very lucky to have him. Wish he kept his practice
here; he'd be my doctor."

Lucky looked up in surprise. "Why is that?"

"Not many like him. He's old-school." The nurse laughed
at Lucky's perplexed expression. "I mean he's young, of
course, but very thorough and involved with his patients.
Doesn't let anything slide. Why, he followed one of his
patients and her husband over here himself—the night of the
big blizzard. She was in labor, very close, and he wanted to
make sure nothing happened before her husband could get
her here. Not many like that anymore, believe me. None that
I can think of."

Lucky was thunderstruck. The night of the storm. The
night Elias didn't respond to Rosemary's call. "That's amazing," was all she could mumble.

The nurse chuckled. "Not so great for him. He had to

sleep on a cot in the doctor's lounge. He was right to follow them over though. That baby came real quick. If they had been delayed on the road, that baby would have been born halfway between Snowflake and Lincoln Falls. Worse—if their car had broken down, that little one might not have survived."

Lucky managed to mumble thanks and return to where Jack was seated.

"Are we finally done? I don't want to be poked and prodded anymore. I want to get home."

"Home it is, Jack." Lucky smiled for the first time, relief finally sinking in with the knowledge that Elias, whatever his involvement, couldn't possibly have murdered Patricia Honeywell.

Chapter 37

"JACK, ALL THE tests were negative. There are no signs of a stroke or tumor, no indication of cardiovascular disease."

Jack grumbled. "I could have told you that."

Elias ignored his comment. "I believe you're suffering from a vitamin deficiency—vitamin B12. An insufficient intake of one B vitamin can create imbalances and deficiencies in others."

Jack looked confused. "How could that be? I've always been careful about having a good diet." Lucky waited, confused herself, but sure that Elias would explain his diagnosis.

Elias had pushed hard for Jack's lab and MRI results to be expedited. The written reports hadn't arrived, but Elias had talked to the laboratory supervisor and radiologist to get the results quickly from Woodside.

"There are different causes for this. There are disease processes that interfere with vitamin absorption. The B vitamins are absorbed by the body in the small intestine. In your case, part of your intestine was removed years ago because of the shrapnel wound, and that particular part of the small intestine is the one place in the body where absorption takes place. Most people go for years before any signs or symptoms present themselves. And you've been suffering from these symptoms for a while—fatigue, heart palpitations, confusion, memory loss, which can eventually lead to dementia. All your scans were normal, all your other blood work was normal. So, I'm going to start you on a regimen of intramuscular shots right away. Every day for now, and then tapering off to once a month, taking blood samples along the way to make sure we're clearing up the problem. Eventually you'll only need oral supplements. Trust me, you'll feel like a new man. I'm only sorry you didn't come to the Clinic sooner."

Lucky breathed a huge sigh of relief, so grateful for the positive diagnosis she could have cried.

"I'll have the receptionist set up your appointments, and I'll see you very soon." Elias smiled. "Any questions?"

Jack shook his head slowly. "No. I just hope you're right, doc."

"Give the treatment time, but I suspect you'll feel better with your first shot."

Elias stood and moved toward the door of his office, holding it open for Lucky and Jack. Jack shrugged into his jacket in the corridor.

"Jack," Lucky said, "you go ahead. I'll catch up with you at the Spoonful."

Jack waved and exited to the front. Lucky turned back to Elias. She cleared her throat. She felt as if she were about to cry from relief, and she would hate to embarrass herself like that. "I can't thank you enough."

"It's not magic. We ruled out every other possibility— aneurysm, tumor—actually many people suffer from the deficiency for years and it isn't properly identified. Jack will have to have regular shots and then we'll test again and make sure it's working. Eventually, these can be reduced and then finally oral supplements with lab tests every so often. I'm quite certain his symptoms will disappear."

Elias returned to his desk and sat, straightening out a

stack of patient charts. He avoided looking at her. "I have some other patients waiting if there's nothing else."

Lucky felt her face grow hot. She had to somehow find a way to explain why she had broken the date and refused to talk to him. "I . . . I am so sorry that I couldn't talk to you the other day . . ." Lucky trailed off.

"That's quite all right. I understand you were upset." He looked up, his eyes boring into her. "I would like to know, however, why you were grilling my receptionist about my whereabouts on the night of the murder."

Lucky was paralyzed, unable to respond. Rosemary had told Elias that she was asking questions. Should she give Elias the same excuse she had given Rosemary for her questions? Obviously she hadn't fooled Rosemary one bit. How could she hope that Elias would swallow the lie? He was maintaining his distance and was undoubtedly hurt by the fact that she had suspected him.

Suddenly her embarrassment flared into anger. The fact remained that a light-colored sedan with a parking permit was seen at Honeywell's house—twice if you count the time Hank was almost hit by a silver sedan flying out of the driveway.

"Were you Patricia Honeywell's lover?" The words came out of her mouth before she could censor them.

"What?" Elias almost shouted. "Why would you ask me something like that?" His face was suffused with anger. "Certainly not."

"Your car was seen at her house on two occasions." Lucky couldn't guarantee that it was Elias's car, but she tossed it out to see his reaction.

"My car?" He looked genuinely perplexed. "That couldn't be. I wouldn't even know where that house is. I have never been there. And I never even met the woman—alive, that is." His voice had become louder. He glared at Lucky. Now he really was angry. "If you had only talked to me first, instead of going behind my back . . ."

"How do you explain the car?" she shot back.

He shook his head in confusion. "I can't. I keep my car

here most of the time, in case I have to run over to Woodside. The keys are on a hook at the nurse's desk. If it *was* my car, which I seriously doubt, then anyone could have taken it when I wasn't around." He took a deep breath to calm himself. "Any other questions?"

His response was straightforward, but there was no mistaking the anger lurking under the surface. He had good reason to be angry with her. First she had questioned him about his partner. He was upset her questions would cast a shadow on Jon Starkfield's reputation. Then she suspected he had been Patricia Honeywell's lover and perhaps her murderer. To add insult to injury, she hadn't gone straight to him and confronted him. If it hadn't been for the nurse at the hospital in Lincoln Falls, she might still have doubts about Elias. It was too much for him to forgive. She realized she had blown any possibility of a relationship with him. She only wished she could break through the wall that Elias had thrown up around himself. Her heart sank. There was no way now to bridge the gap.

"No, I guess not."

"Perhaps if I had been in your place I might have thought the same." He rose from his chair and moved to the door, holding it open for her. "Good-bye."

Lucky stepped into the corridor. Elias closed the door firmly behind her. *Dismissed, you idiot,* she thought. It was probably exactly what she deserved—suspecting him, breaking a date, refusing to talk, shutting him out of her life. What else should she expect?

Her heart was racing, and she thought she would burst into tears, torn between embarrassment and anger. She was right to suspect Jon Starkfield. If it was common knowledge that Elias's car was often parked at the Clinic, and the keys readily available, Jon Starkfield was more than ever a likely suspect.

A flash of something from the window to the back parking lot caught her eye. She turned and walked slowly down the corridor to the rear door and peered through the glass. Jon Starkfield was placing a heavy briefcase in the trunk of a black Volvo. He walked slowly around the car toward the driver's door. This was her chance. There wouldn't be a better one. After her confrontation with Elias, she didn't think she'd ever be able to come here again.

Lucky pushed through the door and approached him. She called out, "Dr. Starkfield." He turned and, was it her imagination? Something shifted in his face, although on the surface his expression was pleasant.

"Lucky, isn't it?"

Lucky nodded. "Yes. I just wanted a moment to speak with you."

"What can I do for you?"

"You may already know that an earring was found in your parking lot and turned in to the receptionist. But you may not know that a witness has claimed the murder victim was involved with a doctor." His jaw tightened ever so slightly. If she hadn't been watching his reaction so carefully, she might have missed it.

"I wasn't aware of a lost earring, nor was I privy to that woman's private life."

Lucky felt her heart racing. But what other choice did she have? Sage had already been arraigned with no hope of bail. Soon the whole matter would be ancient history and the jail cell door would clang shut for good. It was urgent to push hard and see if anything broke loose. She had to dive in with both feet. "Dr. Starkfield—were you involved with Patricia Honeywell?"

Starkfield's face turned a shade of gray. He took two steps away from her, his keys dangling in his hand. "Certainly not. How dare you accuse me of having anything to do with that woman? And I certainly hope you're not accusing me of being involved in her murder!"

"Where were you that night? The night of the storm?"

"Young lady, this is highly insulting. In fact, it's ridiculous. Be careful what you say, because this is nothing less than slanderous. In fact, it would be ludicrous if it weren't so horrifying. Abigail and I were at home all evening—

snowbound—as was everyone else in town. Now, I'm late for an appointment. If you'll please step away from the car."

Lucky thought if her questions were so ludicrous, he certainly didn't look like laughing. She backed up several steps and watched him climb into his car. He shot her one last angry look and started his engine, peeling out of the parking lot at too fast a speed to be safe.

Lucky felt she'd collapse like a spent balloon. She sat down on the back steps of the Clinic and rested her head on her knees. She shivered from the cold. The warming trend was over, and increasingly heavier clouds had gathered, blotting out the weak winter sun. She had been so sure she was on the right track. Now what did she have? Sage was still in jail, the restaurant was failing, Honeywell's murderer was still on the loose and Elias, and now Jon Starkfield, wasn't speaking to her. She sighed and stood up. She should head for the Spoonful and get to work. What she really wanted to do was to go home and crawl under the covers. In the distance, she heard the bells of St. Genesius carried by the wind. What was it Starkfield had said? *Abigail and I were at home all evening.* Why did he mention Abigail? Lucky gasped. St. Genesius—that's where Starkfield was heading in such a hurry, and now she knew why.

She rushed back into the Clinic and flew down the corridor, pushing through the door to the waiting area. Elias was nowhere to be seen, but Rosemary was at the front desk.

"Rosemary, call Nate at the police station. Tell him to meet me at St. Genesius. It's urgent."

Rosemary looked at her blankly, trying to understand why an emergency would involve a call to the police and not the hospital.

"Please. Just do it right away. Tell him to meet me at the church."

Rosemary nodded and picked up the telephone. Lucky didn't wait to listen. Instead she ran out the front door and took off for the church. She turned the corner, past the Spoonful and then Marjorie and Cecily's shop. Four more blocks to go. If she ran and didn't slip on any ice, she could make it in a few minutes. She couldn't have explained it, but somehow she knew in her heart it was urgent to get to the church as quickly as possible. Starkfield had had a head start.

Her car was behind the Spoonful, but she could get to St. Genesius quicker on foot. She raced down sidewalks cleared of the last snow and across two intersections. She reached the end of a cleared path and ran into the street. A driver leaned on his horn, coming quickly to a stop. She didn't slow down. Several people stared after her, her scarf flying behind her. By the time she reached the front gates of the church she was out of breath. She leaned over, her hands on her knees, to give her muscles a chance to relax. She took a deep breath and pushed open the creaking wrought iron gate. Hurrying to the front door, she stepped inside the entryway. She stood still for a moment, straining her ears. Low murmurings came from inside the nave. She took a deep breath to stay calm and slow her heart rate. Then she pulled open the door and stepped quickly into the aisle. Two heads turned to stare at her. Jon Starkfield placed his arm protectively around Abigail's shoulder.

"What do you want?" he demanded, his voice echoing off the rafters.

A chill ran down her spine. Her legs were shaking but her voice was firm. She glared at Jon Starkfield. "You knew. You knew all along."

Abigail's face crumpled. She tried to take a step toward Lucky, but Jon's arm held her back. "I didn't . . ." Her voice broke on a sob. "I never meant it. I only wanted to talk to her. To tell her to stay away . . ."

Jon's face was flushed with anger. "Leave us alone. You have no right!"

"She can't live with this. It's no good." She held out her hands toward Abigail. "Come with me." Lucky felt tears fill her eyes.

Abigail looked up at her husband and said softly, "I'm so sorry."

Jon grasped Abigail's hands. "Shhhh." He looked at her

tenderly. "Don't say another word. We'll fix everything, darling."

Abigail's body shook with sobs. "It's too late. I'm so sorry, Jon." She pulled away from him and ran toward a small wooden door inside the archway of the side chapel.

"Abigail!" Jon cried out.

The door from the front entry swung open. Nate stood in the doorway, his gaze moving from Lucky to Jon Starkfield. "What's going on here?"

"Nate. Stay with him. Please. I can talk to her." Lucky ran past Starkfield, who stood helpless, a dazed look on his face. She pulled open the small wooden door and climbed the narrow twisting stairs, steps worn from years of bell ringers traversing them.

She heard Abigail's sobs above her. The stairway was completely dark, with just a small hint of light filtering down from above. Lucky hurried up the stairs, holding on to the narrow railing. "Abigail, wait!" Lucky continued to climb, then halted, listening. The footsteps had stopped. She continued up as quietly as possible. As the narrow stairway turned, she looked up and saw Abigail.

"Don't come any closer."

"Come back, Abigail. We can talk about this," Lucky pleaded. "Please don't do this. Think about Jon."

"Jon . . ." Abigail spoke the name devoid of emotion, as though recalling someone she once knew from long ago. "He swore it was over—years ago, when we were in Boston. But she would never leave him alone. Phone calls, notes in the mail. She didn't care if I knew. She *wanted* me to know. She didn't care about the wreckage in her wake. She didn't care who she hurt. That's why we came here—to get away from the past. Jon swore it was a new beginning and then . . ." Abigail sobbed. "The nightmare started all over again. I found out she was here in Snowflake and then I discovered Jon was seeing her again. His meetings on Tuesdays at the hospital . . . I was such a fool! I found out he was never there. There were no meetings. He was with her.

Maybe he was with her every chance he could get. I couldn't live with that humiliation anymore. I thought I could talk to her . . . crazy, it was crazy to think that, but I was desperate." Abigail's voice dropped to a whisper. "You can't imagine . . . believe me or not, I never meant to kill her. Something . . . something else took over."

Lucky spoke softly. "People will understand."

Abigail shook her head. She turned quickly and began to run up the staircase. Lucky followed as fast as she could. She counted three curves in the spiral stairway and finally reached the top, entering a small chamber where heavy ropes hung from openings in the wooden ceiling. The room was empty. Where was Abigail? She scanned the chamber and spotted the wooden ladder, fastened to the wall. It led to a hatch in the ceiling. She grasped a rung of the ladder and started to climb. Near the top, she pushed up against the small wooden hatch. It gave with a creak. She continued up the ladder through the sound chamber, cold air blowing against her face as she rose higher. She reached the top and climbed out into the belfry. Wind whipped through the openings, caressing the surfaces of the ominous bells. She felt rather than heard their low vibration in the wind as though they spoke a language too deep for the human ear. Abigail stood in an arch just large enough to contain her. Several louvers were missing, and the few that remained were pitted with rot. Her face was twisted and stained with tears, her dress scored with black dirt. "Go back. There's nothing you can do."

"That's not true. We can turn around and go down. It will be very easy. Take my hand."

"It's too late," Abigail cried. The wind pulled her words away. "I only wanted to talk to her. I never meant to hurt her."

"I believe you. You'll have a chance to explain."

"She laughed at me. Can you believe that? She laughed at me. And then she told me . . ." Abigail's eyes took on a faraway look. Lucky could barely hear her words. ". . . she was carrying Jon's baby. You see, I couldn't ever . . ." Abigail took a deep breath and held her hands out toward Lucky plaintively. "I couldn't have a child."

"Please. Give me your hands." Lucky took a few tentative steps toward Abigail, trying not to look down. She reached out one hand, stepping carefully around the ledge toward Abigail. Footsteps sounded from below. Nate had followed them. She heard the creaking of the ladder as he climbed to the belfry. Lucky prayed he would stay below and give her time to reason with Abigail.

She crept sideways and finally reached Abigail. She gently grasped Abigail's hands, careful not to frighten her. At the same moment the hatch flew up and Nate heaved himself through the opening, Abigail wrenched her hands away. Terrified, Lucky caught her breath and struggled to maintain her balance. Abigail tumbled backward through the opening, the wooden slats cracking from the weight of her body.

Lucky felt as if her heart had stopped. She heard a soft thud from below and then only the wind through the open belfry. She gripped the edge of the arch, too frightened to look down.

IT WAS A long time before she could stop shaking. With a hand from Nate she managed to climb down to the ringing chamber and descend the spiral staircase. Jon sat in a pew at the front, his head in his hands, moaning. Outside, a distant siren wailed. Lucky walked down the aisle past Jon Starkfield and outside to the freezing air. Nate had covered Abigail's broken body with a blanket from the trunk of the cruiser.

Nate turned to her, his expression unreadable. "Are you all right?"

Lucky nodded, wiping tears from her face. "She fooled me. She let me take her hands and then she just . . ."

Nate nodded. "Why don't you wait inside?"

"I can't go back in there."

An ambulance pulled up and turned off its siren. "They made good time—for all the good it will do." He turned to her. "How did you know?"

"I didn't . . . at first. Starkfield told me that he and Abigail were home all that evening, but the choral group had been rehearsing here that night. They cut short their rehearsal because of the storm. He said, 'Abigail and I were *both* home.' He didn't say, 'I was home all evening. My wife can vouch for me.' It was odd—the first name he mentioned was Abigail. Why? Then it hit me like a thunderbolt. He wasn't concerned about covering for himself, it was Abigail he needed to protect."

Lucky watched as two men in uniforms climbed out of the ambulance. Bradley had arrived and was on the sidewalk directing the onlookers to stay back.

"If you can wait a bit, I'll drive you home or back to the Spoonful." This was probably the closest Nate would ever come to saying he should have listened sooner.

Lucky shook her head. "You have enough to deal with. I'll walk."

Nate reached out and grasped her arm. "I hope you know—it wasn't your fault. Nothing you could have done."

She nodded. "You know where to find me."

Lucky walked down the path and pushed through the iron gate, avoiding the stares of the curious. A few people called out to her, but she continued walking with her head down, refusing to meet anyone's eyes or answer questions. She wrapped her scarf tighter around her neck. Another cold front was coming in. She could smell the dampness in the air. Snow would soon cover the town again.

Chapter 38

"OKAY EVERYONE, ARMS around one another and big
smiles." Jerold Flagg from the pharmacy had offered to take
a group picture of everyone at the Spoonful for a full-page
ad in the *Snowflake Gazette* announcing the grand revival
of the By the Spoonful Soup Shop. Sage stood in the center,
surrounded by Jack, Lucky, Janie and Meg and even Remy.
The restaurant was overflowing with well-wishers, all of
their regulars and most of the town.

Jerold called out. "That's great. Let's do a few more just
to be sure." They waited quietly and smiled on cue.

"Perfect." Jerold checked the view on his camera and
gave them a thumbs-up. Everyone in the restaurant broke out
in cheers. Sage smiled shyly, and Sophie jumped up and ran
to his side, giving him an enormous hug.

"Lucky, I'll e-mail this over to the *Gazette* to run with
your ad."

"Great. And send one to me too. I'm having some flyers
printed up to pass around at the Resort." Now she was
sure their business would be back on track—perhaps even
busier.

"And I'll put some music on to get this party started," Jack shouted to her above the noise. "That's what we always needed, my girl. Gives our little place some atmosphere."

Lucky smiled back at him. "We always had atmosphere, Jack. This just makes it official."

When word got around that Sage had been released and a party was planned, their neighbors arrived with casseroles, cakes, breads and all kinds of goodies to stage an impromptu welcome home for Sage. Janie and Meg along with Lucky were busy lining up plates and silverware, creating a buffet at the long counter.

Sage kept attempting to help out, but everyone pushed him away, telling him this party was in his honor and he wasn't allowed to work. Somehow he managed to slip behind the counter and approached Lucky.

She turned to him, laughing. "Hey, go away, you're not allowed back here. You're supposed to be enjoying yourself."

"Boss . . . Lucky, I can't ever repay you . . . If it hadn't been for you . . ." Tears flooded his eyes.

"Sage—we knew you weren't guilty and we just wanted you back."

"It's okay about . . . my past? That doesn't bother you?"

"Not at all. You got a bad break that you didn't deserve."

Sage reached out awkwardly and grabbed her in a bear hug. He whispered in her ear, "Thank you." Then he turned, his face flushed, and went back to sit next to Sophie. Lucky looked at them and smiled. They seemed so happy. Sophie's face lit up and she blew a kiss in Lucky's direction. She envied them their happiness. If only . . . if only she hadn't managed to drive Elias away.

The tables and chairs had been pushed against the walls, and an elderly couple was dancing in the center of the room. Flo Sullivan was there, her flaming orange head bobbing through the crowd. She was scouting the room looking for Jack, who kept moving from group to group in hopes of avoiding her flirtations.

The noise level had reached the point where Lucky couldn't hear the conversations around her. The door opened and Eleanor stepped in followed by a portly gentleman with an unruly mane of white hair. She stood on her tiptoes and waved at Lucky. Then she took the gentleman's hand and led him to the counter.

"Lucky," she shouted, "I'd like you to meet . . ."

Lucky laughed. "Wait," she shouted back. "Come down to the office." She waved them over to the swinging door while Eleanor and her companion maneuvered through the crowd to reach her.

"Come down here. We can at least hear ourselves think." Lucky opened the door to her office and indicated the two chairs by the desk.

"Whew! This is quite a party." Eleanor collapsed into one of the chairs. "Lucky, I'd like you to meet Professor Horace Winthorpe."

Lucky was momentarily confused, not sure who this man was or why Eleanor would bring him to the Spoonful to introduce him.

"*Retired* professor, my dear. A pleasure to meet you." He reached across the desk to shake her hand.

"Horace has absolutely fallen in love with your house and would like to rent it long-term, if you approve."

"Approve? I'm thrilled." Lucky felt an instant liking for this elderly man. "You're retired?"

"Yes. And I love this town. I need a quiet place to work for a few years. I'm writing a book, you see. I taught history my whole life. My field is the Revolutionary War years in New England. I hope you approve of me as a tenant, and I hope you haven't changed your mind about your home— your parents' home, I understand from Eleanor."

"Not at all. I think it will be a perfect fit. Welcome to Snowflake." Lucky smiled.

"Thank you, my dear. And I know I'll be a regular customer here as well. Delightful restaurant, and I understand your chef is back in the kitchen now?"

"He certainly is."

"Lucky, would it be all right if we stayed for a while?" Eleanor asked. "I'd like to introduce Horace to people, so he'll get to feel at home."

"Absolutely. Please do. Everyone's welcome."

"We'll just rejoin the party then. Horace plans to move in next month."

"I hope you'll be very happy here, Horace."

"Thank you. I'm excited about living here. So close to Bennington and that famous battle."

BY TEN O'CLOCK the crowd had thinned. Lucky was scraping casserole dishes and stacking them on the kitchen hatch. Remy, on the other side, was rinsing and loading the dishwasher.

Lucky saw Nate sitting at a corner table with Jack sipping a beer. She called to Remy that she was taking a break and joined them.

Nate smiled at her as she pulled up a chair. "I was just telling Jack that I wish I had listened to the two of you sooner." He shook his head. "I just hope that poor guy"—Nate indicated Sage with a nod of his head—"doesn't hold a grudge."

"I think Sage is over the moon, and no, I don't think he will."

"I'm still having a hard time getting my head around it—of all people. She was a real nice lady."

Lucky felt a wave of sadness wash over her, remembering Abigail's song at the concert, the notes echoing from the rafters.

Nate shot her a look. "Starkfield's completely fallen apart. He's told me everything. How he pushed you down the stairs at the house . . ."

"Oh." Lucky blushed. "I was hoping you never found out I was there."

Nate's lips tightened. "He was in a panic that something in the house would point to his involvement with Honeywell.

He was desperate not to have it known he was seeing her. He's admitted to taking Elias's car to go up to the house. He was afraid to use his own car—afraid someone might recognize it. I really don't think he had any suspicion about Abigail at first—just afraid he'd be a suspect in a murder investigation."

"I'm sure that's true. My guess is Abigail used Jon's phone to text Honeywell to meet at the Clinic. Honeywell thought she was meeting Starkfield, but Abigail was waiting for her."

"That's what Starkfield's told me," Nate replied. "It was only later that he saw there was a text sent the night of the murder. That's when he started to put it together."

"You think Abigail planned to kill her?" Jack asked.

"No. Not at all. I'm sure Abigail only wanted to tell her to stay away from her husband. She told me . . . that day in the belfry . . ." Lucky closed her eyes for a moment to shut out the memory. "She said Honeywell laughed at her and told her she was pregnant with Jon's child. It must have been devastating for Abigail. When Honeywell's body was discovered the next day, I'm sure Starkfield never suspected Abigail. Once he figured it out, he was only concerned with protecting her."

"You could press charges against him—for assault—if you wanted."

Lucky shook her head. "To tell you the truth, I'd rather never see the man again, if that's possible."

"And then again, I could charge him with obstructing my investigation. But he might have to kiss his license to practice medicine good-bye." Nate raised his eyebrows and watched Lucky. "What do you think?"

"It's up to you, but I think we should let the whole thing go. He'll have to live with the consequences. I can't imagine anything worse."

"Yeah, I agree." Nate shook his head. "We just don't know how she did it. And Starkfield swears he doesn't either. He never confronted his wife about what he knew. We searched the house, both cars, even the Clinic—we still don't have the murder weapon."

Lucky had a clear image of Abigail in the church preparing for a baptism. She sighed. "You need to have a good look at the candelabra on the altar. I think you'll find your murder weapon."

Chapter 39

IT WAS AFTER midnight by the time the last guest had gone. Jack had stretched out his legs and was sipping his beer at one of the tables. "I'll swab the deck in the morning, my girl, if that's all right with you."

"That's fine, Jack. We should all go home and get to bed. It's looking like we'll be busy tomorrow."

With Janie, Meg and Remy helping, they loaded all the trash and napkins into garbage bags, started the dishwasher and put away their leftover food. Jack finished his beer and slipped on his jacket. Lucky gave him a hug and walked him to the front door.

"Go home and get some rest. I know you're feeling better, but don't push it."

"I will, my girl. It's just past eight bells. Midnight's not late when you're young at heart." He leaned over and gave her a kiss on the forehead. "You'll be okay on your own?"

"Sure will. No worries."

"You've gotta learn to take your own advice." He smiled and walked out to the sidewalk. Lucky locked the door after him.

"We're done here, Lucky. Okay if we take off?" Janie called.

"Go ahead. I'll be fine. Just leave the trash bags by the back door. I'll dump them."

Remy and the girls called good night from the corridor. Lucky heard the door to the alleyway slam behind them.

She was relieved the night was over. It had been a lot of fun, but she was very, very tired. She walked around the room, turning out the lamps and finally the neon sign in the front window. She thought she heard the laughter of her parents, but when she turned around there were only shadows. She sighed and slipped on her jacket. Opening the back door, she lugged four large trash bags down the stairs to the Dumpster. She tossed them all in and dropped the lid. She shivered, suddenly realizing she was standing on the very spot where Patricia Honeywell had been found. She shook the feeling off and locked the back door, shoving the keys in her pocket. She followed the narrow alley out to Broadway and looked up and down the street. Not a soul in sight. The night was so cold the air crackled. A wolf cried in the distance.

A week before, she wouldn't have thought a night like tonight possible, but now Jack was in good health and spirits, Sage was back to his job and their customers and neighbors would no longer be afraid. She didn't notice the shadow on the steps of her apartment building. She jumped when she realized someone was sitting on the top step.

"I didn't mean to scare you." He stood.

"Elias!" She was still for a moment, not sure what to say. He had been invited tonight. She had looked out for him all evening but knew he hadn't been there in the crush of people.

"I was waiting for you. I just wanted to say I'm sorry."

"No, I'm sorry. I handled everything badly. I was just so frightened . . ." she trailed off.

Elias loped down the stairs to envelop her in a hug. "I was wrong. I was pigheaded and stubborn and I should have listened to you the first time. Can you forgive me?"

Lucky's heart leaped. "Of course." Elias leaned down and, holding her chin, kissed her long and passionately. There was no doubt of his intentions any longer.

"There's just one thing I want to know."

Lucky waited. "What's that?"

"What does Lucky stand for?" She couldn't see his smile in the dark but she was sure it was there.

"You're very persistent."

"It's my middle name."

"It's short for Letitia," she mumbled.

"That's a beautiful name." Elias pulled away and studied her face. "But why not Lettie?"

"I told you, Jack named me. Someday maybe I'll tell you why—if you're lucky."

Recipes

POTATO-YAM SOUP

(Serves 4)

1 red pepper
4 carrots
2 large potatoes
1 yam
4 cups chicken stock or chicken bouillon
½ teaspoon white pepper
½ cup cream
Dash of paprika

Remove seeds from red pepper and chop into cubes. Place pepper cubes in soup pot, cover with water and simmer for 10 minutes. Slice carrots and add to pot. Peel potatoes and yam, cut into cubes and add to pot. Add 4 cups of chicken stock to cover vegetables. Bring to a boil and reduce heat. Let simmer for 20 minutes. Add white pepper and stir. Potatoes should be quite soft. Continue stirring until potatoes have softened completely and soup is thickened. Add cream and stir again. Serve with a dash of paprika in each bowl.

WILD MUSHROOM SOUP

(Serves 4)

    2 cups dried porcini mushrooms
    1 cup warm water
    2 tablespoons olive oil
    2 leeks, finely sliced
    2 shallots, chopped
    1 garlic clove, chopped
    8 ounces fresh wild mushrooms
    5 cups vegetable stock
    ½ teaspoon dried sage
    Salt and ground black pepper
    ½ cup light cream
    Fresh thyme to garnish

Add dried porcini to bowl of warm water and soak for half an hour.

Remove from the liquid and finely chop, reserving the liquid for later.

Heat oil in large pot. Add leeks, shallots and garlic, cooking slowly for 5 minutes, stirring until softened. Chop fresh mushrooms and add to pan. Stir mixture over medium heat for 5 more minutes. Add vegetable stock and bring to boil.

Add the porcini mushrooms, sage and reserved liquid. Season with salt and pepper to taste.

Simmer gently for 20 minutes, stirring occasionally.

Puree soup in food processor or with a wand. Stir in cream and reheat gently. Garnish with a sprig of thyme.

TOMATO SPINACH SOUP

(Serves 4)

2 cups of jumbo pasta shells
1 tablespoon olive oil
½ medium onion, coarsely chopped
1 clove garlic, chopped
1½ pounds of tomatoes (or substitute a 16-ounce can of crushed tomatoes)
6 carrots, peeled and chopped
3 cups frozen or fresh spinach
2 tablespoons of dried oregano
2 tablespoons of dried basil (fresh basil leaves are even tastier)
6 cups of vegetable broth
Salt and pepper to taste
½ cup grated Parmesan cheese

Bring salted water to boil in a large pot. Add 2 cups of jumbo pasta shells to the boiling water with a few drops of olive oil. Stir and lower heat slightly. When pasta is only slightly al dente, drain and set aside.

Sauté the onion and garlic with olive oil in the pot for 5 minutes, then add the tomatoes, carrots, spinach, oregano and basil. Add vegetable broth to the mixture. Bring to a boil, lower heat and simmer for 20 minutes. Ladle soup over the pasta shells and serve with grated Parmesan cheese for garnish.

GOAT CHEESE AND PANCETTA SANDWICH

    2 slices of crusty bread
    1 tablespoon of olive oil
    1 tablespoon of balsamic vinegar
    ⅓ cup goat cheese
    3 slices of pancetta
    3 figs, chopped

Brush olive oil and balsamic vinegar on two slices of crusty bakery bread.

Spread goat cheese, then a layer of pancetta and a layer of chopped figs.

FRENCH TOAST SANDWICH

    1 egg
    ⅓ cup milk
    2 slices of white or whole wheat bread
    Sliced mushrooms
    1 slice Swiss cheese
    Worcestershire sauce

Whisk one egg in a shallow dish, adding milk to the egg mixture. Dip each slice of bread in the mixture, coating both sides. Using cooking spray or a small amount of butter, place bread slices in a pan, cooking until both sides of the bread slices are browned.

Layer mushrooms on one slice, add a layer of cheese, cover with other slice of bread and, flipping over, heat both sides until the cheese has melted. Drizzle Worcestershire sauce over the top.

Turn the page for Connie Archer's next book
in the Soup Lover's Mysteries . . .

A Broth of Betrayal

Coming soon from Berkley Prime Crime!

Chapter 1

Neigeville 1777

NATHANAEL COOPER CREPT slowly, staying as close as possible to the trunks of the larger trees. He moved silently, fearful of giving his presence away. His heart beat so heavily he thought his chest would burst. Fragrant pine needles and dead leaves, dry and crumbled from the summer heat, carpeted the forest floor. A small twig crackled beneath his feet. He uttered a curse under his breath and froze, terrified the sharp sound would give him away. There were watchers now—watchers everywhere—on both sides. The town of Neigeville had formed a committee of volunteers to monitor the roads and report all movement, particularly British, immediately. At the slightest alarm, the church bells would be rung to wake the countryside.

He had lain awake that night until he was certain everyone in the house was asleep—his mother, father and sisters. He hoped they'd sleep deeply and not wake to find him gone. He did not want to explain to anyone what he was about. Once certain it was safe, he crept softly down the stairs and out into the fragrant humid night. No one must know. He would never be forgiven. He would be killed, no doubt about that, and most likely his entire family as well. At the very least, their home and all their goods would be confiscated by the militia.

His feet were encased in gray homespun socks and soft leather boots that made little noise but even so, a chorus of cricket song quieted at each step he took. A small animal scurried away through the underbrush. It was the dark of the moon, just a day or two to the new moon. Hard to see anything at all, much less among the trees. He edged closer to the clearing where only thin saplings would offer him protection, careful not to step out of the shelter of the dark. A single lantern burned in the window of the tavern below where the British officer had approached him that very afternoon. Somehow the man knew about his brother, knew that Jonathan was missing. Nathanael had last seen his brother driving away in the family's horse drawn cart to deliver ale to a neighboring town. The family had asked everyone in town if they had seen Jonathan or heard any news of him. They had searched for him but had learned nothing. His mother was consumed with worry, sure her missing son had been shot by the British. At best, his brother had been taken prisoner. At the very worst, he was dead.

His family was terrified by the events unfolding around them, as were many others. Angry at the arrogance of the British regulars, the townspeople wanted to drive them out. Yet many believed that as British citizens they still owed allegiance to the king. Feelings had reached a boiling point and now there was no more time to debate. Everyone must choose a side. Nathanael's father was eager to fight, held in check only by his mother's fears. It was his father's hesitation that had caused the town to turn a suspicious eye in their direction. Against his mother's wishes Nathanael himself had joined the militia, more in an effort to protect his family than for any other reason. He had no desire to fight, to kill other men, even if they were British. Like his brother, he had little interest in politics and wished only to live the quiet life of a farmer. He hoped he'd never be forced to kill anyone, British or Yankee.

The strange man had worn the clothing of a local, short trousers and a coat of homespun cloth, in shades of brown, but there was no mistaking him for a colonial. His manner was high-handed and arrogant, used to giving orders. He hadn't fooled anyone in the tavern, not even the young boy who swept the floor. Another man followed in his footsteps and took orders from him—a servant. Only a British officer would keep a servant. Perhaps the pastor was correct—if the town did not take up arms, if the rebellion were quashed, they'd be slaves to the crown forever. Nathanael was torn—stay loyal to the king and hope for peace, or join the rebels in their hatred of the king's authority? An iron fist was closing over all their land. The loyalists were called traitors and the rebels were at risk of their lives. To be hesitant to take a side might mean death at the hands of a neighbor.

The man had accosted him that afternoon outside the tavern. He had news. His brother Jonathan had been taken prisoner on the road to Bournmouth, his cart, ale and horses confiscated. The officer swore to Nathanael that Jonathan was still alive and promised to reveal where his brother was being held. In exchange, he wanted information. Young as he was, Nathanael was no fool. He knew there'd be a price to pay, but gasped when he learned what the man wanted. He demanded to know where the gunpowder and arms were hidden in the town, and how many might march toward Bennington. Even more, he wanted details of the stores at Bennington.

The Committee of Safety formed in Neigeville were certain the British, approaching from the north, planned to confiscate all the guns and ammunition that had been so carefully stockpiled, and ultimately gain control of the armory at Bennington. At meetings, townspeople had learned that the ranks of Burgoyne, the hated British general, were swelled with Hessians, loyalist Canadians, Indians and French. They knew their horses and cattle would be confiscated to feed the soldiers on their march. A fierce

battle was coming, if not here in Neigeville, then closer to
Bennington.

Nathanael knew that, with the blessing of their minister,
guns and powder were hidden under the pulpit of the white
steepled church on the Village Green, but he was not privy
to any information about the armory at Bennington.
Nathanael would happily give the lobsterback all the details
he wanted, if only he could free his brother and bring him
home. He shivered in spite of the warm night. *Where was
the man?* He was terrified of the officer, but far more terrified of discovery by his fellow townsmen. He hated to think
what would happen to him if it were known he had provided
information to the enemy. A branch crackled and Nathanael
jumped in terror. The man had come through the woods
behind him and now had stepped out into the clearing.
Nathanael watched and waited. His heart finally slowed its
rhythm. He took a deep breath and stepped out of the trees.
He recognized the linen shirt and brown vest, the wide-
brimmed hat, but when the shadow turned toward him, his
blood ran cold. This was a different man, shorter and stock-
ier, not the officer he had promised to meet. The man raised
his gun. A shot rang out. Nathanael reeled back, falling
against a tree. More surprised than in pain, he looked down
at his chest to see his life's blood flowing from a wound. The
last word he heard was "Traitor."

Chapter 2

"HOW DID YOU ever manage it?"

Lucky stopped in her tracks, almost losing control of the dolly loaded with bottled and canned drinks. "Manage what?"

Sophie smiled. "Getting Pastor Wilson to host the demonstration. Unbelievable."

"Well, I don't know about hosting, but he's volunteered the meeting hall."

Sophie shook her head. "Amazing. I mean he's so stuck in another century, and you've virtually talked him into rabble-rousing."

Lucky smiled. "He's not a bad sort at all. I really like him."

Sophie wrinkled her nose. "He smells of mothballs."

Lucky laughed. "Maybe that's why I like him. I love the smell of mothballs."

"Nobody loves that smell. You must be kidding."

"I do. Really. Always makes me think of summertime . . . you know, when everyone puts away their wool clothes and stuffs mothballs into drawers and closets."

Sophie guffawed. "Maybe you do. I sure never did. Just the same, you charmed him."

Lucky smiled, shrugged her shoulders and grasped the handle of the dolly more firmly. She was thrilled that her friendship with Sophie had been renewed. Several years before when she had left their small Vermont hometown to attend college, Sophie had taken it very badly, reacting with coldness and cutting remarks. A serious rift had formed between them. Now, all that was past and Lucky couldn't have been happier. Months before, Sage DuBois, the chef at Lucky's restaurant, and the love of Sophie's life, had been arrested for the murder of a winter tourist. Lucky had uncovered the real murderer and Sage was freed. She and Sophie had mended their bridges and Lucky could count her a close friend once again.

"Pastor Wilson's just providing a space at the church for the demonstrators to take breaks. We'll bring over half sandwiches tomorrow and part of the profits will go to the church. But that's not why he agreed. He believes in the demonstration—no one wants to see a car wash built in the middle of town."

Sophie shook her head. "I'd like to see all those town council people recalled. How they ever . . . *why* they ever voted for that disgusting thing, I'll never understand. It'd make much more sense to build it up at the Resort."

In winter months Sophie was a top ski instructor at the Snowflake Resort perched halfway up the mountain from the town. During the summer, her schedule was much lighter—giving occasional swimming lessons to summer tourists. That left plenty of time for Sophie to visit the Spoonful, help Sage with his chores and spend more time with Lucky. Right now she was wheeling a dolly of her own, identical to Lucky's, loaded with drinks for the start of the demonstration the next day.

"I really appreciate your help with this." Lucky paused to wipe her brow with the back of her hand. Temperatures had soared on the first day of August and the heat had shown no signs of abating. The morning had the stillness that comes when summer heat is at its peak, no crickets, no birds, the heat rising off the asphalt in waves. "Can you believe this weather? And it's still early in the day too." She checked her bare arms quickly. She'd have to remember her sunblock when she was out running errands.

They had managed to maneuver their carts to the edge of the Village Green and now, single file, navigated the path to the Congregational Church, a white-steepled building erected in 1749 that sat at the head of the Green. Lucky took a deep breath, relishing the smell of freshly mown grass. "That's my other favorite summer smell."

"What's that?" Sophie didn't look up, she was focused on making sure none of her crates slid to the ground.

"Grass—the way it smells when it's just been cut."

"Hmmm. Okay. I'll buy that. I like that smell. So . . . cut grass and mothballs . . . anything else remind you of summer?"

"Remember that white cream we used to put all over us when we were kids whenever we got sunburned?"

Sophie laughed. "Oh, I remember. We'd always peel after we had worked so hard to get a tan. Don't tell me you *liked* the way that stuff smelled? It stunk. We used it 'cause it was all we could find in our parents' medicine cabinets." Sophie stopped and looked toward the other end of the path. "And speaking of stinky . . ."

Lucky spotted a woman with bright strawberry blonde hair leaving the church. Rowena Nash—her hair was unmistakable.

"What's she doing here?" Sophie whispered. "I can't stand her."

"Shush . . . she'll hear you." Rowena looked in their direction and waved energetically. Changing course, she walked straight toward them. "We're about to find out."

Lucky and Sophie had both attended school with Rowena who now worked for the *Snowflake Gazette*. Rowena's zeal in chasing down a story made it clear her sights were set far beyond the *Gazette*.

"Hey Lucky, hi Sophie. You setting up for tomorrow?"

Rowena bestowed a large smile on Lucky while her gaze slid over Sophie.

"What are *you* doing here?" Sophie asked.

"Oh, I just came over to talk to Pastor Wilson but he's busy right now. I saw Harry Hodges go into his office. I was thinking of writing something about the demonstration and hopefully getting an interview with Richard Rowland too—you know, the developer of the car wash—kind of airing both sides of the dispute."

"That sounds interesting," Lucky offered, sure that no one in town had one ounce of interest in hearing Richard Rowland's point of view.

"Since you're here Rowena, you want to give us a hand with this stuff?" Sophie smiled sweetly.

"Oh, sorry. Love to. But I can't right now. I have a meeting with my editor. I'll catch you later." Rowena flounced off with a last beaming smile and continued across the Village Green.

Lucky turned to Sophie. "You're incorrigible, you know that, don't you?"

Sophie smiled impishly. "I thought the prospect of actual work might send her scurrying." Sophie shook her head. "She hasn't changed a bit since we were in school. She was a self-important little snob then and she's worse now."

"Come on. Let's get this stuff inside. I have to get back to the Spoonful before the lunch crowd hits." They reached the church and navigated the pathway to the side door that led to the meeting hall. Lucky pushed open the heavy wooden door and held it while Sophie bumped her dolly over the threshold. The smell of polished floors and chalk-covered erasers hovered in the air. Sophie held the door for Lucky in turn. They wheeled their carts through the meeting hall and into the large kitchen.

"Where should we put this stuff?"

"Hang on. There are some long tables in the storage room we can set up." With Sophie's help, she hauled out two long folding tables. Sophie lifted one end and together they pulled the retractable legs open, setting both tables up by the entry to the kitchen. Lucky rummaged through drawers and found long paper tablecloths in plastic wrappers. Ripping them open, she shook out the paper cloths and spread them over the long tables, placing stacks of paper napkins at one end. She opened the large refrigerator. "Let's cram as many drinks as we can in here, and I'll bring a couple of big plastic bins tomorrow for the ice. Can you dig out the coffee urn?"

"Sure. I'll find it," Sophie replied, opening and closing cupboard doors in her search.

Lucky unloaded canned and bottled drinks from the carts until the refrigerator would hold no more. "That should do it for now. The rest can go on ice tomorrow. I should let Pastor Wilson know the drinks are here and the ice will be delivered early tomorrow."

"I'll rummage around and see what other supplies are on hand."

"Be right back." Lucky pushed through the door leading to the main part of the church. She followed the corridor to the end hoping to find the Pastor in his office. As she approached the door, she caught the unmistakable sound of sobbing. Then silence. Someone was having a very emotional conversation with the Pastor. Was it Harry? She tiptoed back a few steps, but before she could retreat from the corridor, the office door opened. It was Harry Hodges, the town's auto mechanic and one of the major forces behind the demonstration. Harry's voice carried clearly through the partially open door. "I had to talk to someone."

The Pastor's voice was closer now. "You did the right thing. Be calm. We can talk again . . . whenever you're ready."

It was too late to retreat. Harry stepped into the corridor. He started visibly when he saw her standing nearby. His face darkened. Pastor Wilson peeked around the doorjamb. "Lucky! Hello. I didn't know you were here."

"I didn't mean to interrupt. We just came over to unload drinks. I wanted to alert you that an ice delivery would be coming tomorrow."

"Oh, good, good. That's wonderful. Harry and I . . . well, we were just discussing the plans . . ." Lucky suspected the Pastor was making an effort to cover for Harry, who seemed embarrassed she might have overheard his conversation.

Harry turned to the Pastor and said, "I'll call you very soon." Without a backward glance, he turned away and left by the door leading into the church.

Pastor Wilson cleared his throat and opened the office door wider. "I can't thank you enough. This is truly wonderful what the Spoonful is doing. It'll really help keep everyone's spirits up tomorrow."

"I am sorry if I interrupted anything."

"That's quite all right, dear. Harry and I were just finishing our little chat. Anything I can help you with?"

"No. I have a helper today. But you might want to lock that side door now that the drinks are there."

"Good idea. I'll just get my keys." Lucky stood in the doorway and watched the Pastor as he rummaged through his desk, littered with papers, books, a Bible and remnants of a piece of toast. Pastor Wilson was tall and thin with a prominent Adam's apple. His face was pale, his hair a shade between sand and gray. His movements were disjointed, as though confused by the objects around him—as if the furniture of his life belonged to someone else. She detected a faint whiff of naphthalene. She smiled to herself. Sophie was right about the mothballs.

"Now what did I do with those keys?" Pastor Wilson brushed a few wisps of hair from his forehead and replastered them over a bald spot on the top of his head.

Realizing this search could take quite a while, Lucky said, "I'll be on my way then."

"Oh, yes, yes, my dear . . . you go on. I'll find them eventually."

Lucky headed back down the corridor to the meeting hall and pushed through the swinging doors. Sophie was leaning against one of the dollies, waiting for her. "Ready?" Lucky nodded, grabbed her dolly and followed Sophie out the door.

She was silent as they headed across the Village Green to Broadway.

"Something wrong?" Sophie watched her critically.

"Oh, no. Nothing." Sophie waited, aware that something was on her friend's mind.

"Well, actually, I think I overheard something I wasn't supposed to hear." Lucky repeated the exchange between Harry Hodges and the Pastor as they walked.

Sophie shrugged. "Probably nothing at all. Maybe Harry wanted to confess he had dipped into the collection box."

Lucky didn't respond to Sophie's jibe. "It was more than that. There seemed to be a . . ." She hesitated. ". . . an emotional charge to the words I guess. I could have sworn Harry was crying. More than that—Harry almost jumped out of his skin when he saw me standing in the corridor."

"Hard to imagine him being emotional. The most excited I've ever seen him was when he was staring under the hood of my car."

Lucky chewed her lip. Sophie was right of course. Harry definitely took more interest in the workings of internal combustion engines than in people. She pictured his shocked look when he saw her in the corridor—as if afraid she might have overheard something. Harry was a man of few words, not rude but taciturn, definitely not forthcoming. All the same, Harry's tone hinted at a very painful subject—something deeply buried.

FROM THE NATIONAL BESTSELLING SERIES BY

B. B. HAYWOOD

TOWN IN A
Lobster Stew

A Candy Holliday Murder Mystery

In the quaint seaside village of Cape Willington, Maine, Candy Holliday has a mostly idyllic life, tending to the Blueberry Acres farm she runs with her father, and occasionally stepping in to solve a murder or two . . .

Includes delicious lobster-based recipes!

penguin.com

facebook.com/TheCrimeSceneBooks

M941T0811

Someone's out to make a killing . . .

FROM NATIONAL BESTSELLING AUTHOR
PAIGE SHELTON

Crops and Robbers

• **A Farmers' Market Mystery** •

Thanks to her delicious farm-made jams and pre-
serves, Becca Robins's business has been booming.
But when an unhappy customer turns up dead in
Becca's kitchen, she's afraid it will really sour her
reputation . . .

penguin.com
PaigeShelton.com
facebook.com/TheCrimeSceneBooks

M945T0811